BURNING HEAT

Burning Heat

David Burnsworth

FIVE STAR
A part of Gale, Cengage Learning

Farmington Hills, Mich • San Francisco • New York • Waterville, Maine
Meriden, Conn • Mason, Ohio • Chicago

LIBRARY OF CONGRESS CATALOGING-IN-PUBLICATION DATA

Burnsworth, David.
Burning heat / David Burnsworth. — First edition.
pages ; cm
ISBN 978-1-4328-3111-0 (hardcover) — ISBN 1-4328-3111-9 (hardcover) — ISBN 978-1-4328-3107-3 (ebook) — ISBN 1-4328-3107-0 (ebook)
1. Veterans—Fiction. 2. Charleston (S.C.)—Fiction. I. Title.
PS3602.U76755B87 2015
813'.6—dc23 2015013111

First Edition. First Printing: January 2016
Find us on Facebook– https://www.facebook.com/FiveStarCengage
Visit our website– http://www.gale.cengage.com/fivestar/
Contact Five Star™ Publishing at FiveStar@cengage.com

Printed in the United States of America
1 2 3 4 5 6 7 20 19 18 17 16

For Patty, with all my love

ACKNOWLEDGMENTS

Writers do not write in a vacuum. At least I don't—more like I can't. There are many people who have offered a helping hand along this journey, some of whom I'm bound to forget here thanks to my ever-limited memory. However, I will play it safe and begin with my wife so as not to have to spend any more time in the dog house than I usually do. Patty, you are the love of my life. I am so thankful for your support. Without your nudging, I would never have written the first word, much less a second book.

I'd like to thank my mother and stepfather for so many things that I don't have room to mention them here. I'd also like to thank my Uncle Al and Aunt Treva. They've traveled many miles to be my favorite groupies at signings.

Every author should have someone who works behind the scenes, helping to organize and remove obstacles. I have that in Rowe Copeland, the Book Concierge. At almost any time of the day, I can send her an email request and have a response within minutes. She is responsible for taking me from having no Social Media presence to where I am today. And just about every signing I've been able to book is thanks to her.

Five Star/Gale is wonderful to work with. Thanks so much to Gordon Aalborg, Erin Bealmear, Deni Dietz, Nivette Jackaway, Tracey Matthews, and Tiffany Schofield. You all have had way more patience with me than I had any right to expect.

Jill Marr from the Sandra Dijkstra Literary Agency holds a special place here. I am blessed to have such a savvy agent.

Chris Roerden is an amazing editor. She turns my sometimes gibberish into prose.

The South Carolina Writers Workshop will always be near and dear to me. I could not ask for a better critique group than the Greenville Chapter. Y'all rock!

Killer Nashville was where my dream of publication became reality. Clay Stafford and Jaden Terrell are the best.

And, thanks to all you readers. The emails I receive from you are highlights of my day. You are the reason I want to keep going. God bless!

Chapter One

"Man can't afford to lose his own soul while he is trying to do right."

Brother Thomas

Charleston, S.C.

My head buzzed from a second-hand high as I stepped out of Mutt's Bar and onto the cracked sidewalk of one of the worst streets in the city. The night had not brought relief from the summer heat, but outside was cooler than inside. A plume of reefer smoke escaped the open door behind me, promising to stone the rest of the neighborhood.

As if they needed help.

The wail from Blind Man Jake's Fender Stratocaster pierced the walls of the ramshackle watering-hole and tried to lure me back in. Termite dust and decay of the structure could not restrain the howl from the way-over-maximum-occupancy crowd within. The purple haze in the air was a small price to pay to hear the best blues man no one from the white side of the tracks but me ever heard of. Mutt had said the twenty I put in the tip jar would go right up Blind Man's arm. The blues master looked a hundred years old, but he played a mean guitar.

It was way past my bedtime and I'd been on this street enough times to know not to stop—for anything. So I didn't—for two blocks. Even in the bad part of town, it could be hard to find convenient parking.

With my Ram pickup in sight, I dug keys from the front pocket of my cargo shorts. Two figures ran toward me, one following the other. I regretted not packing anything tougher than a pocket knife.

One of the runners, a man, growled, "Get in the car!"

"I won't!" The other, a woman, huffed and did not turn around.

The man caught the woman on the stretch of sidewalk between me and my ride. He grabbed her, spun her around, and slapped her across the face. The sound cracked like a whip.

Through gritted teeth, he repeated, "Get in the car."

I opened my mouth to intervene and a third figure, a little girl, darted out of the shadows ten feet from me. She screamed, "Willa Mae!" and rushed toward the woman.

The man backhanded the child. I sprinted and caught her before she hit the ground. She grabbed onto me, crying.

I said, "Pick on someone your own size."

"Beat it, cracker," the man snarled. "This ain't yo bidness."

The little girl tightened her grip around my shoulders.

I said, "I was talking to the kid."

The woman called Willa Mae said, "Please help us."

The man closed the distance between me and him. "You a smart mouth. Gonna be a dead smart mouth."

I lowered the girl and sat her down behind me, and the man punched me in the mouth—a good enough hit that I saw stars for a half second. Experience told me to be ready for the next swing and I was. He went for another head shot. I blocked it, grabbed his arm, and wrenched it behind his back. Then I shoved his face into the roof of a parked car. Hard. His knees buckled and I let him drop to the ground.

Willa Mae said, "You better get outta here, Mister. He wakes up and we in trouble."

The little girl hugged her. In the moonlight, I got a good look at the two females.

To Willa Mae, I said, "I know you."

"Lots of men know me," she said.

"I can give you a ride if you want. I know a preacher who lives nearby."

She said, "We'll be all right. You should leave."

Motioning to the little girl, who couldn't have been more than six, I asked, "Is she yours?"

Willa Mae wrapped her thin arms around the child. "She's my sister."

The man behind her groaned, raised himself, and stretched out his arm. My eyes focused on the object in his hand. Before I could react, the click-click sound of a revolver hammer being cocked echoed in my ears.

Willa Mae shoved the child to me and spun around to face the man. "No!"

The weapon exploded and Willa Mae collapsed.

The little girl screamed, "Willa!"

I picked up the little girl, turned, and ran for cover. The pistol boomed again. Only my back shielded the girl as splinters of wood flew off the siding of a house we ducked around. Running full-out, I cut the next corner to the back of the house.

A V-8 engine roared to life close by and tires screeched, the noise quickly receding in the distance. No house lights turned on that hadn't already been lit.

Something in the backyard tripped me and we fell. My elbows kept me from crushing the girl when we hit the ground.

"Willa," she mumbled again.

A grim thought came to mind. Willa Mae was gone.

The shooter, whoever he was, ought to be thankful I didn't still have the M4 rifle and night-vision glasses the Marines had taught me to use. He deserved a Bin Laden special—two shots and a splash.

There were no other sounds.

In the darkness, I got to my knees. We were alone.

I asked, "You okay?"

Sniffling, she let me help her up.

With both of us standing, I pulled out my iPhone, scrolled, and tapped on a number. My eyes scanned the backyard.

Brother Thomas, the local pastor and a good friend of mine, answered on the second ring. "Mm-hmm," came his sleepy voice.

Ever since he'd helped me solve my uncle's murder last year, we'd become good friends. I knew enough to know I was going to need him for this.

"It's Brack," I said. "I've got a situation here."

The girl raised her arms and I scooped her up with my free hand. She hugged my neck and buried her head in my shoulder.

"Brother Brack?" He cleared his throat. "What kind of situation?"

"You know a woman named Willa Mae?"

"Yes."

"She just got murdered."

"Murdered? What you talking about? By who?"

"Someone with a death wish. He also slapped a little girl and took a shot at me."

Brother Thomas sounded very alert when he asked, "Little girl? What little girl?"

"The one with me right now." I took the phone away from my ear and asked her, "What's your name?"

Between sniffles, she said, "Aphisha."

With the phone back to my ear, I heard Brother Thomas say, "Oh, Lord. Where you all at?"

"Two blocks from Mutt's. You better get out here. I'm going to need you when I talk to the police. You know I'm not one of their favorites." I read him the street names off the closest sign.

Chapter Two

Brother Thomas stopped the Volvo a widow had donated to him by the curb where Aphisha and I stood. He wore his usual black suit with minister's collar. Two inches taller than my six feet, and a hundred pounds over my two-ten, he was a force to be reckoned with in any situation.

And he wasn't alone. With him was an elderly black woman who walked with a cane. She embraced Aphisha.

"Brother Brack," Brother Thomas said, "this is Mrs. Jasper. She Aphisha's grandmother."

The old woman nodded at me. "Thank you for hepping Aphisha, here. I don't know what I'da done if somethin' happen to her."

"I'm sorry I couldn't have done more," I said.

A police cruiser arrived. Two uniforms got out, introduced themselves, and took my statement. Aphisha was too scared to say anything, even while being held in her grandmother's arms. The officers must have realized they weren't going to get anything else from her any time soon. They radioed in what I told them and went to find Willa Mae's body.

While we waited for them to return, Brother Thomas said in a low voice, "You leave anything out?"

"No."

"Mm-hmm."

I felt his eyes on me. "I didn't."

"You know I love you as if you was my own, Brother Brack.

And I know you pretty good, too. So tell me what you didn't tell the po-lice."

I pulled a cigar out of my pocket, took off the cellophane, clipped the end, and lit it with my late uncle's Vietnam Zippo. My friend didn't partake so I didn't bother to offer him one. The smoke from the ten-dollar stogie filled my mouth and I exhaled, my body beginning to unwind.

Brother Thomas was right—I'd held something back.

Quietly, I said, "Willa took the bullet for the kid. She took it for me, too. Just turned around and faced it." I took another pull on the cigar and blew out the smoke. "Last time I saw something that courageous was Afghanistan." And I made sure the ones who killed my fellow Marine paid for it.

The cruiser returned, pulling to the curb beside me. The officer riding shotgun lowered his window and said, "You're gonna have to show us where the shooting occurred. The victim's body isn't where you allege."

"Okay," I said. "Do you mind if Brother Thomas takes the girl and her grandmother home?"

The officers collected contact information before dismissing them. Brother Thomas drove away with the woman and child and I couldn't help but think this was business as usual for them. Except for the kid. She was jacked up for life.

After they left I said, "It happened near my Ram pickup. Did you find it?"

The officer driving the cruiser said, "Yeah. But like we said, no body."

I folded myself into the backseat of the patrol car behind the steel kick panel, like I'd done enough times before to know how to make myself feel a little less cramped, since comfort was out of the question. We drove to where I directed them.

The scene was dark and quiet. No one strolled along the sidewalk. The cruiser pulled next to a fire hydrant.

The rear doors of the patrol car didn't have handles on the inside, for obvious reasons, so I said, "If you let me out, I'll show you where it happened,"

The two officers and I got out and walked to where I was sure Willa Mae went down but the ground was clear of both the body and any blood. I pointed out the dent in the roof of the parked car I'd smashed the man's face into as well as the bullet holes in the side of the house. One of the officers shined a light into the bed of my truck and I watched the beam reflect off something metallic that didn't belong there.

"Is that your handgun?" he asked me.

I closed my eyes. This was about to get uglier. "No, sir."

The officers called for a technician and I spent the next two hours waiting for detectives to show. My never-sunny disposition lost some of its luster with each tick of the clock. From a seat on the ground twenty feet from my truck, I watched the detectives, a man and a woman, approach. The last time I'd been in a similar situation things didn't end well.

"Mr. Pelton," the woman said, "I'm Detective Warrez." She looked fit in black suit pants and a white shirt, with a holstered Glock clipped to her belt. If I had to guess, I'd say she was mid- to late thirties, about my age. She continued, "This is my partner, Detective Crawford. We need to ask you a few questions."

I stood and shook their hands. "Sorry to get you called out so late on this fine May evening."

Detective Warrez said, "It's our job." She tucked dark, chin-length hair behind her ears and pulled a notepad from her back pocket. "You want to tell us what we're doing here?"

I wanted to say, "Your job." Instead, I said, "I was walking to my truck when I heard a man and a woman arguing in front of me."

"That would be the man with the gun and the alleged

deceased?" asked Detective Crawford.

"Yes. The man chased and struck the woman. The little girl ran to the woman and the man struck her, too. That's when I intervened."

The female detective asked, "What do you mean by 'intervened'?"

"I put myself between the little girl and the man. He punched me and I shoved his face into the roof of that car over there. I thought I'd knocked him out but he pulled a gun and shot the woman. I grabbed Aphisha and ran."

Detective Warrez asked, "Aphisha?"

"The little girl."

Crawford asked, "Is that the last time you saw either the man or the woman?"

"Yes."

"What about the man?" he asked. "Can you describe him?"

"African-American, I'm pretty sure. Aside from that, it was too dark for me to really see him."

Detective Warrez said, "And the gun the officers found in your truck, a Beretta nine millimeter, isn't yours and you don't know how it got there." It wasn't a question.

Too many discussions with police detectives had taught me to not take the bait. So I didn't.

She turned to her partner. "Can you check and see if the technicians are done with Mr. Pelton's pickup?"

Crawford nodded and walked away.

I pulled out another cigar and lit up. Something told me it might be rude, but I really didn't care. The clock had passed midnight, Cinderella was nowhere to be found, and my four-cigar limit had reset with the new day.

I asked, "You want to tell me what you're thinking?"

The crime scene lighting showed Detective Warrez's skin to

be a natural shade of tan. She said, "That would go against protocol."

"Humor me."

She closed her notepad. "I've got an alleged murder with no body. I've got a recently fired pistol found in the bed of your truck with no fingerprints. And since the officers let the only other witness leave the scene, I've got you."

Exhaling a cloud of smoke, I said, "And you're not smiling."

"Mr. Pelton—"

"Call me Brack."

"Mr. Pelton, we checked you out on our way here."

I said, "I'll bet that was enlightening."

"To say the least," she said. "You have a history of gunfights and meddling in police investigations. What I can't understand is what's going on here."

"What do you think is going on here?"

"I'm not sure, but if I find out this is a ploy to drum up business for your bar, I will personally nail your coffin shut."

Detective Warrez was a few inches shorter than me and had to look up when I stepped in close. "You said it yourself—I have a history of gunfights."

She didn't back off and didn't flinch.

I locked my eyes on hers. "That alone should tell you I know what someone getting shot looks like. A woman was murdered here tonight in cold blood. If you choose to chalk it up to some bogus accusation and slander me, then you're not going to like it when I find the shooter and nail *his* coffin shut."

She held my gaze. "Mr. Pelton, I'd recommend you exercise your right to remain silent before I decide to read the rest of them to you."

Crawford returned. "Everything all right here?"

Straightening up, I took another pull on my cigar.

Warrez said, "Mr. Pelton wants to be a good citizen and help us any way he can." To me, she said, "Give your contact information to Detective Crawford. We'll be in touch." With that, she turned and walked away.

It occurred to me as I watched her leave that I'd just dived into a big pile of sewage and forgot to shut up before I swallowed a mouthful.

CHAPTER THREE

The next morning, Sunday, I awoke early from a night of not much shuteye. Close-range gunshots did that to me sometimes. While I contemplated falling back to sleep versus getting up, Shelby, my rescue mixed-breed dog, cast his vote by giving an excited bark from the doorway. So I forced myself out of bed, let Shelby out to make sure the yard was still his turf, and gulped a large glass of orange juice before putting on jogging shorts and running shoes.

"Ready to go?" A needless question.

Shelby spun around, grabbed the leash that I kept coiled by the door, and ran to me. I clipped it to his collar and we went for our morning jog. The Isle of Palms, where Shelby and I reside in the single-story shack I'd inherited from my uncle, was a barrier island a few miles north of Charleston and a favorite tourist vacation spot. The sun barely peeked over the water. Outlined in white trim, the beach-front homes that went for two million, even in a down market, bloomed in pastel shades of yellow and pink and blue, and were elevated thanks to new codes after hurricane Hugo hit the lowcountry in '89.

Willa Mae had haunted my dreams—not only because of the shooting but also because I'd met her before. Following my return from Afghanistan, where I'd been deployed after my wife, Jo, died of cancer, I spent a couple months trolling the bars and nightclubs of downtown Charleston. Loneliness and heartache plagued me and I'd tried to placate them with booze and one-night stands.

It had been during one of these escapes that I'd run across Willa Mae. At a crowded bar, she stood next to me while we waited for one of the busy bartenders to take our orders. I noticed her tight dress, straight black hair, and dark eyes and asked how she was doing. After I paid for our drinks, we sat at a corner table and talked. Her laugh was full of life and her smile showed perfect white teeth. Too soon, a tearful friend pulled her away from the table and they made a quick exit. I went home alone that night, but unhappy only because I hadn't gotten her phone number.

I didn't see her again until last night. My telling Brother Thomas how she'd faced the gun did not do adequate justice to her act of bravery.

In the early afternoon, I sat sipping an iced tea at my bar, the Pirate's Cove, located on the ocean side of the Isle of Palms. Like the shack Shelby and I called home, I'd inherited the place from my late uncle and had decided to keep it going instead of selling out. Its elevated structure was covered with green planks, the whole thing in the shape of an old Spanish frigate. She flew her flags proudly in defiance to the high-end hotels and beach shops surrounding her.

Satellite radio's beach station filled the place with a tropical-drink-sales-pitch of a song courtesy of Kenny Chesney. The surf charged up the sand like platoons of soldiers in an ever-repeating siege.

Bonny, the bar's macaw mascot, landed on my shoulder, gave my ear a gentle nip, and squawked, "I love you, Brack."

I stroked her head. "I love you too, girl."

Seemingly satisfied, she flew up to her perch and pruned her red and blue feathers.

Too late for the lunch crowd and not quite happy hour, for

once the bar had no customers. Just me, Bonny, and the infinite beach assault. Pure solitude. Shelby had elected to stay home and sleep and I felt his absence. To my right rested today's edition of the *Palmetto Pulse,* folded to expose a headline:

BURNED BODY FOUND AT
CONSTRUCTION SITE

A confidential source identified the victim as a middle-aged Latino man, so it wasn't Willa Mae. Her story was buried on page four in a short paragraph describing the "alleged" shooting. Even if I hadn't read the five sentences minimizing the loss of a life, I would have known my name wasn't mentioned. The lack of customers told me that much. The last time I made the paper for a shooting, it packed my bar for weeks. Detective Warrez knew what she was talking about when she suspected my "escapades" as publicity seeking. She just didn't know me.

I felt a tap on my lower back. A lifetime ago, that would have sent me reaching for a gun. Today, I eased around and found myself looking at a little black girl wearing a pink dress, her pigtails held by pink clips. She seemed about six and with brown eyes that looked, to me, curious and amazed at the same time.

"Aphisha?"

She nodded.

"Brother Thomas with you?"

Aphisha shook her head no, pigtails wagging, her fingers clutched tightly to a small pink purse. I waited for her to speak, but no words came directly.

"No, Mr. Pelton," said a voice I'd heard before, "I brought her." Aphisha's grandmother stood at the entrance to my bar, stooped over her cane.

Out of respect, I climbed off my stool and walked to her. "Yes, ma'am."

She smiled.

Seeing her support herself with the cane bothered my sense of being a good host. "Would you like to have a seat?"

"Thank you," she said. "I'd appreciate that."

I guided her to the closest chair at a table across from the bar. "You all want something to drink?"

Both ladies nodded.

Aphisha hoisted herself up on a barstool.

Not sure what they preferred, I asked, "Iced tea?"

The younger lady shook her head no.

"How about cherry Cokes?"

That drew smiles and nods from both.

I scooped ice into two glasses, poured in cherry syrup and Coke, and added maraschino cherries. In honor of my good friend Detective Wilson, currently residing in Myrtle Beach, who asked for them with every drink order, I dropped in small cocktail umbrellas. Aphisha took her drink at the bar with a coaster. I carried Mrs. Jasper's glass to her, then sat on a chair next to her. "Did someone give you all a ride over here?"

The old woman took a sip of her drink and wiped her mouth with a napkin. "I borrowed my nephew's car. He don't need it 'cause he in jail. People sure is crazy drivers these days."

"Yes, ma'am." The spectacles Mrs. Jasper wore were almost as thick as the decorative glass blocks of a fifties diner.

"Reason we here, Mr. Pelton, is—"

"Please call me Brack."

"And my name's Clara. Clara Jasper."

Aphisha said, "I want my sister back."

I didn't know what to say to that. The child had been with me when her sister was shot. There was no issue of mistaken identity. All I could think of was Aphisha's suspension of disbelief must've been better than mine.

Clara Jasper said, "What my granddaughter is trying to say is the police ain't telling us nothing."

"I'm really sorry," I said. "They can be difficult at times." Even my good friend Detective Wilson had been a real jerk in the beginning.

Aphisha's grandmother cleared her throat. "Brother Thomas said you was good at finding things . . . investigatin'."

"I'm not so sure about that."

"He said you found and shot the man who killed your uncle. Said the po-lice weren't doin' nothing about it, and you solved the case yourself."

She was right. About most of it, anyway. Except that I had help. A lot of help. From my Uncle Reggie's ex-wife who owned the *Palmetto Pulse* paper and one of the local news stations. From Darcy Wells, the paper's star reporter. From Mutt, a good friend and the owner of Mutt's Bar, where I'd been last night, and Brother Thomas. And from Detective Wilson, who lost his job with the Charleston Police Department because of it.

"Mrs. Jasper," I said, "I appreciate the need to know what happened. As Brother Thomas told you, during my nightmare I was kept in the dark just as you are now. And it almost killed me, and a few others."

The old woman teared up and sniffled. "If Willa Mae gone, I'm all Aphisha got. And I won't be around forevah."

"Yes, ma'am." What I really thought was that my friend Brother Thomas had set me up real good. And the old lady thought Willa Mae might be alive, too. Like her granddaughter.

Aphisha asked, "What are you crying for, Gramms?"

Mrs. Jasper took a handkerchief out of a worn pocketbook and dabbed at her eyes. "I just love you so much, child."

The double doors to the kitchen swung open and Paige, my bar manager, came through them. Her thin, aerobic instructor-like build sported a modified version of the bar's official T-shirt: the Pirate's Cove insignia of a cigar-smoking Jolly Roger wearing aviator sunglasses and a bandanna with the South Carolina state flag on it. Today's version, a size too small, had no sleeves and was tied tight above her belly button. Not that she'd listen if I suggested a wardrobe change. I motioned her over.

"Mrs. Jasper and Aphisha, this is Paige. She's going to fix you all some cheeseburgers on the house and I'll be right back, okay?"

Aphisha's eyes opened wide. "Cheeseburger!"

Before Paige could ask me what was going on, I stepped outside onto the back deck of the bar overlooking the Atlantic Ocean. A slight breeze of clean, ocean air reminded me once again why I'd chosen to spend the rest of my life in this paradise. I dialed Brother Thomas and was startled by his voicemail's electronic voice booming his name. At the beep I said, "Brother, this is Brack. If you happen to be missing a pint-size parishioner by the name of Aphisha as well as her grandmother, they're at the Pirate's Cove with me and Paige."

I hung up and made another call. This time a live person answered. Through a lot of background noise, the voice said, "Shut up, Willie, and let me see who dis is." A slight pause, and then, "Mutt's Bar. What can I do you outta?"

"Mutt," I said, "this is your competition calling."

"My what? Competition? Yeah right, like I wanna compete for the bidness of all them fat soda crackers from New Jersey. How you doing, Opie?"

"Same ol' same ol'," I said. "Only different."

"How! You pretty quick for a white boy. Word here is you almost caught the bus last night. I told them you got more lives than all them stray cats in animal control. What's up?"

"At this very moment, I'm looking at a little girl named Aphisha and her lovely grandmother."

"They at your place?"

"Yep. And I can't find Brother Thomas."

Mutt said, "You want me to tell him to call you?"

"Sure, if you can find him. I got his voicemail."

"Consider it done." He hung up.

The communication system in the poor section of Charleston, where Brother Thomas's Church of Redemption and Mutt's Bar were two sides of the same coin, would baffle Verizon Wireless. Three minutes later, I received a call.

"Brother Brack," Brother Thomas said, "I heard you have Aphisha and Clara Jasper."

"Yes, sir," I said. "I was just wondering how Mrs. Jasper came up with the idea that I was in the dead missing persons business."

"Mm . . ." Brother Thomas paused. He never paused. He never closed his mouth except to chew his food.

"While you think about that," I said, "Mrs. Jasper needs some help getting back across the river. I don't think she should really drive."

"She drove?"

"See you when you get here, Brother." I hung up and walked back inside the bar.

It didn't take long for both of my visitors to clear their plates of burgers and fries. Afterwards, Aphisha helped Paige roll silverware sets into napkins. Mrs. Jasper moved to the back deck and sipped her second cherry Coke while watching the ocean from underneath the awning that shaded the bar.

Brother Thomas stepped through the doorway wearing his usual tight-fitting 3XL black suit and minister's collar. "Well, there you are, young lady."

Aphisha beamed. She set the silverware and a napkin on a table and ran to him.

My friend and pastor hugged her tightly, then held her at arm's length. "Did you talk your grandmother into coming out here?"

The little girl's eyes opened wide. "I didn't. I swear!"

"Now, Aphisha," Brother Thomas said, "what did we learn in bible study about swearing?"

She lowered her head. "We shouldn't swear."

"That's right. Now go tell your grandmother I'm here to drive you all back home."

"Okay." She walked out onto the back deck.

"Paige," I said, "why don't you help Aphisha and Mrs. Jasper? I need to talk to Brother Thomas in my office."

Paige nodded and followed Aphisha.

The large pastor trailed me across the bar to the office. Stopping at the doorway, I let him go in first, and entered, shutting the door behind me so the other wait staff couldn't hear. I turned on my friend. "Why did you tell them I could find Willa Mae? She was shot. Or don't you believe me, either?"

The poor man, all six-foot-two, three-hundred-plus pounds of him, stood there looking into my eyes. "She wasn't found. And ain't no one else gonna look."

"She's dead."

"Probably," he said.

"Why, then?"

"Because I known Willa Mae since she was a baby. Because I don't like anyone attacking one of my flock. And because I'm asking you to, mm-hmm."

I wiped sweat off my forehead with the back of my hand. With the door closed and the AC on the blink, the office warmed up quickly. "I'm not a private investigator."

The heat didn't seem to bother Brother Thomas. "I know that, Brother Brack. The po-lice aren't going to do anything. Aphisha's grandmother is taking care of her. She can't afford to pay no one no how."

The chair my uncle used to sit in when he'd run the bar squeaked when I took a seat. Like a lot of things in the place, it was old and worn out. "What do you think is going to happen when I show up in your neighborhood and start asking questions?"

Brother Thomas eased into the sagging couch that my dog and I took turns sleeping on now and then. "People know you, Brother Brack. Most of 'em, anyways. I'll tell 'em it's okay to talk, mm-hmm."

"Why not just ask them yourself?"

He pulled out a white cotton handkerchief and dabbed at his forehead. "Sometimes, people tell me what they think I want to hear. You got a way about you. Got a lot of light around you, too. They're not sure what they're dealing with and might open up."

"But she's gone."

His voice got loud. "We don't know that!"

I swiveled back and forth in the chair, shifting the force from one foot to the other, considering what the best plan was. "Okay, setting logic aside, what if she is alive but doesn't want to be found?"

"Find her anyway. I'll take care of it from there."

"What are you going to do? Drag her back, kicking and screaming?"

Brother Thomas said, "If I have to."

His posture was rigid as he waited for some kind of acknowledgment from me. I looked away and thought about his request. What did I know about finding someone? Maybe this Man of God was only acting from desperation. I remembered how I was when my own life fell apart. My desperation sent me to war. At the time it was the best way I could think of to kill myself. Maybe I should be looking at this situation differently. Maybe the poor pastor simply wasn't thinking clearly.

I stood. "I'll see what I can find out."

Maybe I wasn't thinking clearly, either.

Brother Thomas bounded off the couch and wrapped me in a crushing bear hug.

Through wheezes for breaths, I said, "Easy, there, Brother."

He gave me a final squeeze and let go. "Sorry, Brother Brack. I had nowhere else to go. I'm just happy you gonna do this, mm-hmm."

I wasn't sure why I agreed. There were many good reasons not to. First and foremost being that Willa Mae was surely dead. But Brother Thomas had become my friend and I couldn't let him down.

"Come by the church tomorrow morning," he said. "I got someone you should talk to."

We collected Aphisha and her grandmother from Paige and left out the front door, convincing Mrs. Jasper that we'd return her nephew's car later. In the crushed shell parking lot of my bar, Brother Thomas tried to use the remote unlock button on his car.

"Blasted things," he said, pressing the button harder and harder. "Lord, tell me who designed such a contraption."

"Now Brother," I said. "What did we learn in bible study?"

Aphisha giggled.

Brother Thomas straightened up. "Very funny. It would be even funnier if you showed up to bible study once in a while, mm-hmm."

Mrs. Jasper said, "Lord, I hope you two know what you doin'."

Chapter Four

At half past ten in the evening, Jonathan Langston Gardner, Junior, strolled into the Pirate's Cove with three of his buddies. His father was running for South Carolina Treasurer in the upcoming primary election and had been trying to push the Isle of Palms Town Council to close us down or sell out for the past six months.

From my perch at a table in the corner, I watched Paige's eyes taper into slits when she recognized the junior Gardner, nicknamed Jon-Jon by those of us who were less than fond of him. Not any better than his father, the punk wasn't on our favorite customer list. In fact, I wasn't sure he was on anybody's favorite list.

Jon-Jon and his entourage, all of them twenty-somethings, approached the bar, where Paige and Regina, one of my waitresses, were restocking the shelves. The men had sunburned faces, golf hats rimmed by collar-length shaggy hair, and sunglasses hanging down their backs from straps. And all of them well on their way to drunk.

Paige helped Regina serve them beers, each woman smiling professionally despite the comments and leers from the group. Seated at a table nearby, I went back to reviewing inventory counts and invoices. The beer vendor was hosing me, and I was determined to find out by how much. As I came across another discrepancy, Jon-Jon pulled out the chair in front of me and sat down.

I smelled the beer on his breath. "How's it going, sport?"

"Great." He chuckled.

When I sat back in my chair my eyes met his dilated pupils, and I plastered on my best fake smile, the one I reserved for annoying drunks I was about to escort out.

Paige came over before I could say another word.

"Hey, Jon-athan," she said, careful not to call him by his nickname to his face, "you want a menu?"

Jon-Jon grinned big. "Naw. We're just gonna drink. If you bring me a beer, you might get a good tip. I know you single moms need the money."

"Come back to the bar," she said. "Regina's got a new shot for y'all."

Too drunk to take the hint, he turned back to me. "I'll be there in a minute. I got some business to discuss here."

Paige stared at me. I smiled bigger to assure her everything was okay. Her slow return to the bar told me she didn't buy it.

To Jon-Jon, I said, "What can I help you with, sport?"

"Why you calling me sport? I look like a sport to you?"

Stretching my arms above my head, I tried to ease a growing pain in my neck. "You want me to have the kitchen make you guys something?"

With a laugh, he said, "Kitchen. Yeah, right. Like I'd eat here."

I felt the smile reappear on my face. "Okay."

"I was wondering something."

"What's that?"

"How much longer you think you're going to own this dump?"

It had taken a lot of personal growth for me to stop overreacting to stupid people. But Jon-Jon was pushing his luck. "Why do you care? I thought you hung out at that transgender bar downtown. What's it called, The Pacifier? The Stroller?

Something like that."

"Don't worry," he said. "When I get this place, I'll let you come back and wash dishes. Maybe get that piece at the bar to give me the same extracurricular activities she gives you. With a kid, she oughta be desperate enough for a job."

I wanted to saw Jon-Jon in half, eat his liver with a spoon, and dance around his carcass like a cannibal.

Before I could lay eyes on the closest utensil, Paige yelled, "Shots up! Jonathan, your friends are waiting."

The jerk ignored her. "There's just one thing I can't figure out."

As I pondered how to handle the baited hook in front of me, a sermon I'd heard Brother Thomas give came to mind. The one that talked about what happened when people succumbed to their anger. An assault and battery charge tonight and both junior and senior Gardners would own me.

So I stayed quiet.

Jon-Jon said, "Why you helping out that coon bar downtown? From what I hear, the place needs a bulldozer. Or a good fire." He tapped the table. "When you lose this place, I might just see about that."

His gaze lingered on me in triumph. After a few seconds he stood and walked back to his buddies, who were laughing and having a good time. He raised his shot glass to me from the bar and downed it.

I took a breath, rubbed my two-day shadow and got up, grabbing my cell phone as if I'd gotten a call. The music was usually loud enough in the bar that everyone stepped outside to talk. On the front deck, I looked down at the street. Below me sat Jon-Jon's Porsche Cayenne Turbo parked in front of a fire hydrant. I dialed a number.

A female voice answered. "Dispatch."

"Hey, Marlene. This is—"

"Hey, sexy. You finally calling to make an honest woman out of me?"

All of the bar owners on the Isle of Palms knew Marlene, the graveyard shift dispatcher at the police station on the island. I said, "If Fred didn't when he married you, I'm not sure I'd be much help."

"Shh!" she said. "Not so loud. I haven't told him the kids aren't his."

"You adopted them from China," I said. "I think he probably already knows."

"Oh, all right. Be that way, Brack. I suppose you got another fight brewing or something *important* like that."

"Not yet, but it's early. What I do have is a Porsche SUV in front of a hydrant. I know how you guys like to tow cars parked in red zones and then fleece the owner to get his car back. I figured I'd do my good citizen deed for the day."

She said, "Earl does love impound duty."

"Tell him to bring the flatbed. Don't want you guys to tear anything up and then have to pay for it."

"Hold on." In the background, I heard her page Earl on the radio and notify him of the tow. After she finished with Earl, she said, "Next time, Mr. Pelton, call me with a legitimate proposal. I'll have your babies any day."

"Marlene," I said, "your husband would shove my head in a blender and drink it for his morning protein shake. I think next time you'll be hearing from Paige."

"Typical," she said. "Send in a woman to do a man's job."

Marlene liked getting the last word so I laughed and hung up. Her husband, my personal trainer, was an ex–University of South Carolina linebacker. At sixty-three, Fred benched four hundred pounds.

I returned to the bar, went into the kitchen, and had the cooks make a large plate of loaded nachos. Using a hot pad, I carried the plate to the pool table where Jon-Jon and his friends were having a game.

Setting the plate and hot pad on a nearby table, I said, "Here you go, guys. On the house. Thanks for coming in."

"All right!" one of them said.

"Thanks!" said another.

Jon-Jon smirked at me as he chalked his cue.

I nodded and went to the bar, slapping the polished oak surface. "I'm gonna take off, Paige. Call if you need anything."

With the two twenty-five-year-old male cooks in the kitchen, and Paige's black belt in karate, I wasn't too concerned about leaving the women with Jon-Jon and his buddies.

Paige smiled and I saw relief in her face, and I think a little respect, as if I had actually done something noble. Pulling out of the parking lot and feeling all noble, I waved at Earl as he hooked chains to Jon-Jon's Cayenne. Earl waved back. Brother Thomas was right—sometimes taking the high road was better.

I picked up Shelby at my cottage and we headed to my home away from home. Six months ago and flush with some extra inheritance cash, I bought an old vacant factory twenty minutes from the Pirate's Cove in Mount Pleasant. Its big roll-up door, hidden from the street at the rear of the building, led to a large open area. I pulled to a stop beside a post that concealed a keypad, and entered a code into the security system. The door raised automatically and the interior lights came on. I drove in and parked. Shelby dashed out and watered the bushes lining the outside of the building. Once he'd finished and trotted back inside, I closed the door using a button on the wall.

In the open space and sitting on jacks was Uncle Reggie's '76 Eldorado convertible. Its overhauled five-hundred-cubic-inch V-8 was mounted on a stand and gleaming in fresh blue paint. Once back together, the Caddy would serve as my next promotional tool for the bar. Under a cover in the corner of the shop was my uncle's other car, a recently restored '68 Shelby GT500 Mustang convertible. Because salt spray from the ocean was not a preservative for vintage steel, I had to wash it every time I drove it. And thanks to all the televised car auctions, it was now worth six figures.

My dog, named after the man whose name was on the car, circled his mat several times, came to a just-right position, and plopped down. I turned on the Wurlitzer jukebox pirated from the Cove and listened to Tom Petty sing about American girls.

Using an overhead hoist, I lifted the Eldorado's rebuilt transmission from the bed of my truck. I'd picked it up before going into work at the bar earlier today. My phone vibrated in my pocket and I checked the number and answered. "Hey Darcy."

"I'm pulling up to the door," she said. "Hit the button."

Last year, Channel Nine News reporter and *Palmetto Pulse* columnist Darcy Wells helped me find who killed my uncle. My aunt, Patricia Voyels, owned the local news empire that employed Darcy and had sent her best and brightest correspondent on the trail.

I didn't bother to ask Darcy how she knew I was in my secret garage and not at the bar or my house, merely pressed the button to open the roll-up door. When it rose far enough, she drove in and I pressed the button to close it back. As she got out of her convertible Infiniti, Shelby ran up to her. Stooping to scratch his back, she looked at the Caddy on jacks. "You were serious about fixing that thing?"

"Yeah. Why?"

"I thought you were joking." In addition to being relentless, Darcy was beautiful, with blue-green eyes identical to my late wife's and perfect blond curls. She also had something not many twenty-seven-year-old women had—scars from a gunshot wound. Plastic surgeons had done miracles in making the entry and exit holes in her shoulder from the bullet of a nine millimeter Sig all but disappear, not that I could see them now. I knew they were there because I was with her when she got shot.

I said, "You come here to laugh at my project or what?"

"Touchy, touchy," she said. "I just heard Jon-Jon had his car towed. From in front of your bar, no less."

"It's not my fault he parked in front of the hydrant like he always does. I was only being a good citizen. Probably did the brat a favor. He was a DUI in the making."

"His daddy would have gotten him out."

"He ought to be thankful it wasn't his Ferrari. Earl would have pulled the front end right off it." I grabbed metal shears from a nearby workbench and knelt down over the skid. "So, to what do I owe this visit? Or are you just being neighborly?"

"How about you and me and Mr. Shelby here go for a boat ride tomorrow?"

"Maybe. Tell me what's going on."

She smiled, brushed off imaginary dust from a stool, and sat, khaki shorts showing off nicely tanned legs. An aqua V-neck shirt hid the bullet wound. "I can't get near the crime scene where they found that burned body. We may be able to by water."

"In other words, your cop sources aren't giving you enough mouth to mouth."

"Disgusting analogy," she said, "but yes. All I got was that the victim was a man about five-foot-four, of Latin descent, as they put it. Probably an illegal."

"Rules out Willa Mae," I said, testing to see if she knew about it.

"The woman the cops couldn't find?"

"Yeah."

"The police don't trust you, you know."

"I know."

The next day, Monday, when the clock hit nine A.M., I drove downtown in Mrs. Jasper's nephew's car, an old Chevy Caprice that smoked, and met Brother Thomas at the Church of Redemption. The gleam from the white steeple stood majestically above the decay of the surrounding homes.

Brother Thomas greeted me when I walked in the unlocked front doors.

"Have a seat," he said. "I'll be right back."

I did as he asked and sat at the end of one of the rows of chairs. The usual smell of strong soap permeated the air. Someone took great care in cleaning the place. Bibles were lined up, evenly spaced along each chair. A grand piano that Darcy and I had found at an estate sale for a thousand bucks looked as if its regal wooden surfaces had been given a fresh coat of wax.

Hard-soled shoes echoed on the worn but polished linoleum floor. I watched a skinny girl walk toward me with Brother Thomas.

"Brother Brack, this is Mary Ellen. She a friend of Willa Mae and a sister with us in Christ."

Mary Ellen had dark skin and her eyes held a vacant look. Her ripped jeans and Carolina Panthers hoodie were several sizes too big. I guessed she might be early twenties, but her empty stare suggested to me a hard life.

"Please call me Brack."

She grasped my hand lightly and then backed away.

"Mary Ellen," Brother said, "why don't we sit down."

She took a seat across the aisle. I moved close to the poor girl, but not so near as to make her uncomfortable. Brother

Thomas put an arm around her shoulder. Her bottom lip quivered.

I asked, "Do you mind if I take some notes, Mary?"

She shrugged. I pulled out a small notebook and pen.

Brother Thomas said, "If you're up for it, Mary El', you wanna tell Brother Brack what you told me?"

Mary Ellen fixed her eyes on a spot on the floor. "Um, Willa Mae gone."

"Yes," Brother said.

"She tol' me she pregnant. Say she gonna talk to the man done it. Ax him fo' some money."

"Do you know who the father was?" I kept my voice as gentle as I could.

"She didn't say, 'cept that he white. And rich."

I wrote that down. "Anything else? Tall? Skinny? Fat?"

She shook her head.

"Old? Young?"

The poor girl's head half-disappeared into her sweatshirt like a turtle's. "She din't say."

"She say how he dressed?"

"Just dat he was good lookin'."

Brother Thomas asked, "How'd they meet, Mary?"

"At the club. She was there dancin' and havin' a good time."

I asked, "Which club?"

"The Cradle."

That was the name of the club I couldn't remember last night when I challenged Jon-Jon. I'd called it the Pacifier.

Brother Thomas stared at me. I knew someone rich who hung out at the Cradle. Someone I'd love to get busted for this. Except Jon-Jon was a different douche-bag from the one who shot Willa Mae, and his father had powerful friends. And there were probably a lot of other rich guys that hung out there.

Brother Thomas said, "Thanks, Mary. Brack here will do his

best to find out what happened. Why don't you go into the kitchen? Sister Paula is back there cooking something that smell real good."

Mary nodded, stood, and left the sanctuary.

"How old is she?" I asked.

"Twenty-one," he said. "She grow up fast, mm-hmm. What you think about what she said?"

"I'm going to need more to go on."

"The next person I want you to talk to is Willa's aunt," Brother Thomas said. "She lives in Orangeburg. I'll set it up."

He gave me a ride home.

Chapter Five

My motorboat really liked the choppy harbor water and was one of the smoothest rides around, thanks to its twin-hull structure. With Darcy at the helm, I leaned forward and switched on the radio to the classic rock station. Credence Clearwater Revival's *Green River* belted from the speakers. Shelby licked my face as I fed him ice cubes. Darcy took us down the Intracoastal Waterway, past Sullivan's Island and million-dollar homes, and then up a cove toward Mt. Pleasant, dipping into the hundred-and-fifteen-horse Suzuki. High tide meant we got deep into the marshland. She cut the motor and reached for her bag.

I lifted the prop out of the water. "What are we doing here? You aren't going to take advantage of me, are you?"

"Like I'm that desperate."

The mosquitoes homed in on us and I dug through the boat's compartments for the repellant I kept there. "Well, I still haven't met your fiancé so I figured—"

"Figured what?" she asked, a little sharper than usual.

"Um—"

"Let's just keep our opinions to ourselves, 'kay?" She finished me off with a smirk.

Wrapping up a master's on top of a law degree at Emory University in Atlanta, Darcy's fiancé had professional student written all over him. The peckerwood never came to see her in the hospital when she got shot. Yet she had committed to moving in with him in Atlanta at the end of summer in an attempt to become a big-city reporter. Something told me she didn't want it anymore. Part of me hoped that was the case. I didn't want to think about her leaving. Or marrying the peckerwood.

I drenched myself with the repellant. "You want any of this?"

"Some of us plan ahead."

Ignoring her sarcasm, I asked, "So what are we supposed to be looking at?"

From inside a bag she pulled out a pair of binoculars. Like her credit cards, she never left home without them. "Fiddler's Marsh."

The area of interest was located a couple hundred yards away. It was named for its fiddler crabs, the male of which possessed one greatly enlarged anterior claw that made the crab look as if he carried the musical instrument. The land that met the marsh had been subdivided into lots, and houses were being constructed.

"What's all that yellow tape . . . ?" My voice trailed off. I knew exactly what all that yellow tape roping off the area was—crime-scene tape. I'd seen enough of it.

Darcy pulled the caps off her binoculars and scanned the area. "That's where the burned body was found. The police shut down the whole site and won't let me or anyone else, including the building crew, come anywhere near it. Right now, this is the closest we can get." She handed me the binoculars, got out a camera with a big zoom, and snapped pictures. "My source tells me the police don't have a clue what's going on."

"They could be just playing stupid," I said.

"One of the construction workers told me they found the remains in a barrel like people used to burn trash in."

"That's terrible."

From our vantage point, and with the optical help, we could see men and women in Sheriff's Department shirts working the scene. After a while, it got boring to watch.

Darcy took a lot of pictures, then put the camera away.

"All done?" I asked, ready to get out of there and away from the death.

She nodded. "You can lower the prop."

The tide was on its way out so I was glad to exit the cove. Darcy didn't say much else as she piloted into open water.

I took my shirt off, lathered on sunscreen, and stretched out. "Where are we headed now?"

"You'll see."

Twenty minutes later she slowed as we approached Capers Island, an uninhabited barrier island, and shut down the motor. I raised the prop so it wouldn't drag, jumped into shallow water, and walked the boat onto the sand. Three other boats were beached there, so we didn't have the place to ourselves. After tying off the anchor and shoving it into the sand, I lifted a cooler Darcy had brought along. Then I held her hand as she climbed over the edge, carrying a canvas bag.

Shelby jumped out and worked the area with his nose, and Darcy and I grabbed the handles of the cooler and lugged it across one of the few beaches around still covered with shells. We found a level spot and set the cooler down. Darcy withdrew a worn blanket from her bag, spread it out, and then unloaded the cooler. Over the past year of getting to know her, I had learned to overlook Darcy's quirky diets. We sat on the blanket and ate hummus on pita bread, olives, and cucumber salad.

She offered some to Shelby but he wouldn't touch it. Instead, he circled at our feet twice and then lay down. Within ten seconds he was snoring.

I asked, "So you wanna tell me what angle you're working for the Fiddler's Marsh case?"

Darcy took a sip of her drink. "The work crews building the new homes found the body. So far, the police have no leads.

They haven't made a real I.D. yet, either. I think there's a connection to the building site."

"What kind of connection?" The herbal tea concoction she served me was not southern sweet tea, so I tried not to wince when I took a drink.

She said, "I don't know, but why would someone burn the body there, of all places?"

Following the lead Brother Thomas gave me earlier after my visit with Mary Ellen, I parked my pickup in front of the Coat-of-Arms apartment complex. The name made it sound like a place where royalty hung out. The only royalties here came once a month from the U.S. government in the form of welfare. Faded brown wooden siding on the buildings showed signs of rot and maybe half of the ten cars in the lot appeared capable of mobility.

The drive up I-26 to Orangeburg had taken about an hour. Shelby stayed at home sleeping off his busy afternoon boat ride and I missed his company. I grabbed a box of groceries from the backseat and pressed the lock button twice on the key fob. The truck's alarm system responded with a blow of the horn. The brick tenement building with faded shutters that couldn't shutter did have several doors along its length. I located the unit number Brother Thomas had given me and knocked on the door. "Miss Pervis?"

"Hol' on," called a raggedy female voice from inside.

While waiting I checked out the area. A few feet away, a stray cat licked a discarded frozen dinner tray. The thump of bass from a passing car throbbed under my feet.

A security chain scratched against the inside of the door and at least two more locks released before the door opened. A woman about five feet tall stared up at me as if I were the jolly green giant.

Ho ho ho.

Her lined face defined her age. "You mus' be the man Brother Thomas tol' me was comin'." Dentures clicked in her mouth when she spoke.

"Yes ma'am," I said. "My name's Brack."

She looked at the box I was holding.

I said, "Brother Thomas told me you liked ravioli and mac and cheese."

Her whole face turned into a smile. "Well now, that was sure nice of you, young man. Come in, come in."

She held the door open and I entered, catching a whiff of cat urine and moth balls. I watched as she closed the door, turned both locks, and latched the chain. We stood in her small, dim living room. The old TV had knobs and a digital converter box, the couch was covered with worn plastic, and over it hung a picture of Jesus.

"Where would you like me to set the groceries, ma'am?"

"Right this way." She led me from the living room to a kitchen area. About five paces. A small table and two chairs stood against the wall to my right. I set the box on the table because the microwave took up all the counter space.

I said, "Can I help you put this away?"

"Naw." She picked up a can of Chef Boyardee. "What you want, anyway? Brother Thomas jus' said you wanted to ax me some questions."

The unpleasant odors and confined quarters closed in on me. I placed a hand on the back of one of the chairs. "Yes, ma'am. I am looking for your niece, Willa Mae. She's, um, missing."

Her eyes pierced me. "What a good-looking man like you wanna get mix't up wit' Willa Mae for? I heard she dead. And if she ain't, she still nothin' but trouble."

"Her sister wants to know for sure."

"Hmm." She clicked her dentures again. "That chile is better off never seeing Willa again." The woman shook her head. "Nothin' but trouble, yessir."

"So you haven't seen her?"

"Son," she said, "let me tell you something. You ain't the first white boy been by here lookin'. Willa had lotsa callers. And I'm being polite in calling 'em that."

I pulled out a notepad and pen from the pocket of my cargo shorts. "These men, any of them give you their names?"

"Yeah, they got names. John. Every one of them."

"You saying she was tricking?" Brother Thomas had not mentioned that detail.

The old woman mumbled something and shook her head again. "I prayed every day for that girl. I told her she get Jesus, she don't need nothing else. Look at me. I ain't got much. But I'm happy. No troubles of my own. Only from men knocking on my door looking for my lost relations." She put her hand on the box as if she anticipated I might take it back. "You go looking for snakes, you gonna find 'em. The one you looking for gonna steal more than your heart, yessir."

She grabbed two cans and set them in a cupboard.

I said, "Willa Mae take something from you?"

"That girl had so much promise. She so pretty. That what got her in trouble. Men come looking and give her nice things and money. Willa Mae see she got a way to get what she want. Then she got hooked on them drugs and that was that. Now she no good. I wiped my hands clean of her when she started dancing at one of those strip clubs." Miss Pervis slapped her hands together.

"Do you know which one she worked at?"

She thought about it. "Treasure Island or something like that."

I jotted down a few notes. "You said I'm not the first white boy coming here to ask you questions. How many of us were there?"

She closed the cupboard. "One other."

"Can you tell me about him?"

"What you mean?" she asked.

"Like tall, skinny, fat, big nose . . . anything?"

"He was rich."

I felt my eyebrows raise. "Rich?" Exactly what Mary Ellen had said.

"He give me a hundred dollars and ax me if I know where she was. I don't know nothin'."

"Can you tell me what he looked like?"

"Good lookin' white boy, like you." She pointed at me. "But younger."

"You see what kind of car he drove?"

"Naw," she rasped. "He let himself out when I tole him I didn't know nothin' and was gone. Same with Trevor."

"Trevor? Who's that?"

"Willa Mae's old boyfriend." She grunted again. "When they was growing up. He got to where he thought he owned Willa. She spent a lot of time running from him."

"What about Willa Mae's sister, Aphisha?"

"She a half-sister. They got different daddies. Poor chile. Who watching over her?"

"Brother Thomas said Aphisha lives with her grandmother."

She said, "Clara a good woman. She on Aphisha's daddy's side. If that don't work out, the girl is welcome to come live with me."

I drove home and spent a quiet evening with Shelby, thinking about what I'd learned. Willa Mae had not been the person I thought she was. Stripping. Prostitution. Drug use. But, none of that really mattered. She'd shown me who she could be when she took the bullet. Afghanistan illustrated to me that the true test of a person occurred during the heat of battle. Everything else was just window dressing.

My iPhone buzzed and vibrated on the nightstand, waking Shelby and me. I felt my dog's wet nose on my hand and scratched his ears. The phone vibrated again and I snatched it up to check who was calling at—what the—?

"It's five A.M.," I said into the phone.

Paige said, "I'm glad you can tell time, boss. We got a problem."

"Can't it wait until, oh, I don't know, daylight?"

"I got a call from the security company since you made me the point of contact. Someone broke into the bar, but I guess I'm the only one who cares about your business."

I sat up in bed, blinked a few times. "What did they take?"

"The police are already there," she said. "I'm on my way. Thought maybe you might want to tag along since, oh, I don't know, you own the place and all."

"On my way," I said.

It took me five minutes to pull on a pair of shorts and find a clean T-shirt. Shelby and I were out the door and at the bar in five more.

Two cruisers were parked on the street in front of the bar, blocking the fire hydrant where Jon-Jon's SUV got towed from. Flashing blue lights bounced off all the buildings.

Paige stood by the new Jeep Wrangler I'd bought her as a bonus for turning the bar around. Its white paint twinkled violet from the illumination coming off the police-issue Chargers. Her six-year old, Simon, slept in the front seat. I noted he was the same age as Aphisha.

Ron Bates, the police chief, wore his usual khakis and a polo shirt with an Isle of Palms police department monogram over the left breast. Even without the monogram, his six-foot-four frame telegraphed an air of authority.

Shelby and I got out.

"Chief," I said. "Thanks for coming."

Shelby, in violation of the city's leash law, sniffed the Chief's hand.

He gave Shelby a pat on the head. "It's not everyday we have a B and E here, you know. But don't worry, it's good practice for us."

Paige said, "They broke in through the door in the back."

The Chief said, "You wouldn't happen to have security cameras, would you?"

"Didn't think we needed them," I said.

My bar manager said, "We do now."

The four of us, Paige, the Chief, Shelby, and I, walked up the back steps and assessed the damage. Someone had thrown a brick through the window. Shards of glass littered the inside of the doorway. We walked around the mess on the floor, me carrying Shelby so he wouldn't cut his paws on the glass.

Paige walked into the back office and after a moment shouted, "The safe hasn't been opened."

The cash registers, empty as the staff had been instructed to leave them, had also not been tampered with. As far as I could tell, all the liquor was still present. We searched for thirty minutes and found nothing out of place. The Chief leaned against the bar.

I said, "Can I get you something to drink?"

"Coffee if you got it."

Paige apologized for not thinking of it herself and brewed two pots for the men.

"You think someone was just playing a game?" I asked.

"Who knows," the Chief said. "I recommend getting a camera system just in case."

After finishing off both pots of coffee plus a third, the police left. Any other day, I might have wisecracked about needing to get them doughnuts, but they were doing their jobs. The fact that they stayed and helped us clean up the mess showed a level of class that their chief was known and respected for.

In the back office, Paige sat at the desk. I stretched out on the couch. Shelby slept on the floor between us.

Paige said, "Something's not right."

"We went over the place three times and didn't find anything wrong. Someone's playing with us."

She got up and left the office. I closed my eyes and drifted off.

"Ah-ha!" she yelled, waking me up.

"Ah-ha, what?"

"Come here."

Rising, I put my feet on the floor, and eased up. With a roll of the neck, I made my way to the front.

Pointing to a blank spot on the wall by the bar, she said, "What's missing?"

I shrugged.

"Typical man," she said. "It's our liquor license."

"Why would someone take that?"

"Not sure," she said, "but I'll report it missing and apply for another one as soon as the government opens up."

Later that morning, the city of Charleston closed Broad and East Bay Streets for a parade to kick off the summer. Citizens cheered their favorite floats sponsored by local businesses while high-school bands played their best marching music. The Pirate's Cove waitresses had worked hard on our float, a four-wheeled, ten-foot by twenty-foot platform I pulled with my pickup. They turned it into a pirate ship to resemble the bar. Three twelve-foot masts were spaced evenly along the centerline of the platform, complete with sails displaying the bar's logo and a fairly decent attempt at rigging. The top of the center mast featured the traditional Jolly Roger.

For the coup de grâce, the girls wore eye patches in honor of my late Uncle Reggie and tight Pirate's Cove T-shirts and shorts. The parade's rules prohibited anything flashy or revealing. We had the "not flashy" nailed down but probably pushed the other stricture a few degrees starboard.

A parade official signaled our position in the middle of the line. Ahead was a float from another beach bar, this one decked out with surfboards, a fake palm tree, tiki bar, and staffers waving at the crowds. But because of the rules, none of the females on that float could wear bikinis, which made the whole scene unnatural.

One of the women on that float, Mora, was a regular customer at my bar. Paige would have hired her, but she wasn't a single mom and so didn't make the cut. Fifteen minutes into the route, the convoy stopped. Mora looked back and recognized me. I waved. She turned her petite figure my way and waved back.

I was enjoying myself communing with Mora when someone rapped on the door of my truck. The knock startled me and I turned to see a smiling Darcy.

When I lowered my window, she said, "Having fun?"

"I was."

"Too bad." She walked around the front of the truck and got in the passenger seat.

I glanced at Mora and saw her busily throwing candy to the crowd.

"Romeo lives," Darcy said.

The float ahead inched forward and I eased my foot off the brake.

I said, "Covering the parade . . . or are you here only to give me a hard time?"

She slipped her sandals off, rested her feet on the dash—ten perfectly-painted, violet toenails attached to the prettiest woman this side of my late wife—and said, "Heard something you might be interested in."

"I'll bet."

"Has to do with that burned body I've been looking into."

Forcing my eyes to maintain the distance to the float in front of me, I said, "I'm listening."

"Guess who owns the construction company?"

"Who?"

The parade stopped again. I looked at her.

My favorite reporter leaned back against the door. "I think he's motioning you to move."

I looked through the windshield. A police officer was waving me on. The float with Mora had pulled away. I took my foot off the brake too quick, forgetting about the float with five women on it behind me. We lurched forward. In the rearview mirror, I saw that two had lost their footing and fallen to their knees. The others had found something to hold onto. All of them gave me nasty looks that promised I'd pay later. I waved my hand in apology and we were slowly on our way.

Once we crept at a steady pace, she said, "Jonathan Langston Gardner, Senior. He's the sole owner."

"You're not just saying that because I dislike him and his peckerwood son, are you?"

"No," she answered. "I'm saying it because *I* don't like either of them very much. It also happens to be true."

"I guess Senior won't be getting our votes," I said.

Chapter Six

An internet search didn't find a Treasure Island, which Willa Mae's aunt, Mrs. Pervis, had mentioned, but I did locate a Treasure Chest. While I could think of a few people who'd want to back me up in a strip club, the only one I trusted was Mutt, my six-foot-three friend and fellow Marine. At dusk I pulled into an open parking spot, this one close to Mutt's Bar for a change, and noticed Brother Thomas sitting on a porch across the street with an elderly couple.

He called when I got out of my vintage GT500 Mustang. "Brother Brack! You got a minute to meet some folks?"

I walked over and stood at the edge of the porch, not daring to add my weight to the rotted boards under their feet.

Brother Thomas said, "This is Alfonse Jameson and his wife, Nelia."

Mr. Jameson's face held a pleasant smile but his thick glasses couldn't hide the reality that his eyes were sunken in. So was his mouth, although I suspected that was due to the absence of any teeth. When he shook my hand, I felt heavily callused skin.

"Brother Brack here is Reggie's nephew," Brother Thomas told the Jamesons. "Remember? The man come by and ask about the children getting sick?"

"I do," Nelia Jameson said. "He got that old chemical plant cleaned up, didn't he?"

Like her husband, Nelia also had no teeth. But her eyes were clear and unassisted.

"Yes, ma'am," I said.

"We was just talkin' about Willa Mae," Brother said. "Alfonse and Nelia's grandson went to school with her. Maybe he know something."

"Trevor is such a good boy," she said, getting up from her seat. "I got a picture around here somewhere."

Trevor was the name Mrs. Pervis had supplied for Willa Mae's ex-boyfriend. Mrs. Johnson opened an ancient screen door and went inside. It sprang shut behind her. I watched it bounce twice before she caught it and came out carrying a few photographs in her shaking hands.

She handed me a picture. "Here's one at his high school graduation."

"He the first one in the family," Mr. Jameson said.

Looking at the photo, I asked, "Any idea where he might be?"

"Nossir," Mrs. Jameson said. "That boy come for supper every now and then, though."

After viewing a few more pictures, Brother Thomas and I excused ourselves.

On the sidewalk out of earshot of the Jamesons, Brother Thomas said, "What do you think?"

The burden of my friend's grief weighed heavily on my shoulders. I didn't want to let him down.

"That's the second time Trevor's name has come up." I stood there looking at a street with few working streetlights. "Something doesn't feel right."

"Keep doin' what you're doin'," my friend said. "I'll see what I can do from my end."

I nodded.

He put a hand on my shoulder. "I really appreciate this, Brother Brack. Ain't too many others woulda taken this on."

Brother Thomas was probably the best person I knew. Unlike

the ones I went to war for, he had what born-again Christians called "righteousness." And I would gladly go to the grave for him. Looking into what happened to one of his flock seemed like small potatoes in the grand scheme of things.

I headed across the street to Mutt's Bar. One thing Brother Thomas did not need to know about was where I planned to take Mutt. I grabbed the handle of the bar's rusty screen door and opened it. The smell never changed—tobacco smoke and bar wash. Across the small room, I could see Mutt use a towel to mop sweat off his black face as he told Willie a story.

"An' you know what she said to the man?" Mutt added from behind the bar, a big grin highlighting his missing front teeth.

Willie's drunken smile showed his own weathered and cracked teeth. "Naw, man. What she say?"

"She say that wouldn't even get her started." Mutt slapped his hand on the bar. "How!"

Willie swayed back and howled with him and almost fell off the barstool, but caught himself in time to prevent something else from cracking.

Mutt's eyes met mine.

I said, "I can come back if you're busy."

He scratched the side of his boxed afro. "Naw. We out of good jokes. You always give us something to laugh at, Opie."

I pulled out three cigars and a cutter from the pocket of my linen trousers and sat on the barstool to Willie's left. Mutt and Willie watched as I clipped the end off each cigar and handed them out.

Mutt read the label. "Ma-can-u-do."

Willie had the cigar in his mouth, ready for someone to light it.

I flicked open the Zippo lighter my uncle brought back from Vietnam and lit their stogies before catching my own. The ten-dollar special was probably wasted on Willie, but Mutt seemed to enjoy the smoke.

"You want a soda or something, Opie?" He knew I was on the wagon.

I nodded and he went to the rusty cooler at the corner of the bar, opened the lid, and pulled a can from the ice water. We puffed on the stogies and took in the captivating aroma that pushed the baked-in smell of bar wash to the outer edges of the room.

Mutt leaned against the back counter and took the Macanudo out of his mouth, curling his index finger around the stogie to brace it against his middle finger. "Every time you come in here with a cigar, you got somethin' up your sleeve."

I tilted my head back and blew a stream of smoke to the exposed rafters. "Now, what would give you that idea?"

"Tell him, Willie," Mutt said.

"Aw, ma-an," Willie grunted. "Mr. Brack is good people."

Anyone else calling a white man Mr. anything in this bar would have received a stiff backhand from any of the patrons. But I knew Mutt well enough to know that he loved Willie too much as his friend to disrespect him.

"I wouldn't go that far, Willie," I said.

Mutt cackled. "You got that right."

"Besides," I continued, smiling at Mutt, "I do need a favor."

He smiled back, showing me gums flanked by two fangs. "I knew it."

"Yeah, but I think you're gonna like this," I said.

Mutt leaned forward to listen. "Uh-huh."

"Ever hear of a place called the Treasure Chest?"

By the way Mutt's face lit up when I mentioned the name, I sensed we were heading into dangerous waters.

Mutt rode shotgun in my uncle's Shelby Mustang. "This is one nice ride. It never looked like this when Reggie had it."

I tried real hard not to think about my having parked the six-figure car on the darkening street in front of Mutt's Bar.

The parking lot for the Treasure Chest was at least partly lit. We found a spot close to the door and pulled in. The rundown building could have been a nice place twenty years ago. Now, two of the neon letters that spelled its name flickered on and off, and not on purpose. The place seemed the right type for a new girl on her way up or a worn-out one on her way down.

The doorman nodded when we walked up. Short but stocky, he wore a leather vest but no shirt and looked like Martin Lawrence in the first *Bad Boys* movie.

He said, "How you doin', Mutt?"

"Not bad, Robbie. Not bad."

One of the Pirate's Cove regulars who used to work the door to a gentlemen's club once told me he got kickbacks from the strippers for pointing out to them the big spenders. I'd asked him how he identified them.

He said, "When they flipped open their wallets to pay I made a special point to look for cash and plastic. The real players had fat money clips and peeled off twenties like Kleenex."

So tonight I made sure this doorman saw the thick fold of bills I had, held together by a shiny, silver clip I'd bought for the occasion from Big Al's Pawn. After handing him two twenties for Mutt's and my cover, he personally walked us inside. As my eyes adjusted to the darkness, the smell of cheap perfume and stale smoke accompanied a bass thumping hard. On stage, a plump black girl dangled from a hopefully well-anchored pole. The doorman led us to a half-booth just off to the right of the performance. I scanned the room and noticed a dozen other men, most of them sitting on chairs at the base of the stage.

The girl slid down the pole, faced away from the crowd, and bent over. A young patron wearing a Tarheels basketball jersey and matching ball cap stood and stroked the back of her thigh.

She squealed and jumped away. The doorman went over to the kid, grabbed a handful of Carolina blue, and yanked him back in his seat.

"Must not be his team," I yelled to Mutt over the thumping.

"That's Wanda up there," Mutt said.

I sat back in the worn vinyl-covered seat and tried to relax, which was kind of difficult at the moment with the music so loud and half-naked women everywhere.

A tall, solid black woman in a white bra, dark hot pants, and spike heels came up to our table. "It's a two-drink minimum. What can I get you?"

"You can get me a hello, Kali," Mutt said.

The woman looked up from her order pad. "Sorry, Clarence." She smiled at me. Her mouth was big and full. "And who'd you bring with you?"

"This here's Opie," Mutt said. "He wants a root beer. Who workin' the bar tonight?"

"Cherise," she said. "You want one of her specials."

"You got that right, mamma."

Kali left to get our order.

I said, "I don't get it."

Mutt said, "Don't get what?"

"The name Treasure Chest," I said. "I expected the minimum to be double D's, not two drinks."

Mutt put his hand on my shoulder. "It's where they keep all the booty, my man."

"I should have known."

"Maybe you could hook your place up wit this one. They both got that pirate thing goin' for them."

Kali came back with our drinks as the D.J. announced that Glitter would be the next act.

I looked at the stage. The young woman Brother Thomas had introduced as Mary Ellen strutted on. She wore a bad imitation of a nurse's outfit complete with mini skirt, tight blouse, and white cap, and looked a little different up there dancing around than when she was crying in the church.

I handed Kali an extra twenty. "When the nurse gets done with her routine on stage, we'd like a private session."

She nodded and walked away.

Mutt said, "You gettin' into this, ain't you?"

"That's Willa Mae's friend up there."

After a few minutes of watching Mary Ellen work the pole, a man in a suit came to our table and asked us to follow him. We grabbed our drinks and were led behind a curtain into a twelve by twelve room with a couch and table.

The man in the suit said, "Would you gentlemen like a bottle of champagne?"

It kind of cracked me up, this man acting suave in this dump. But it was his world.

"Naw, man," Mutt said. "Just get us our second round."

"No, problem," the man said. "I'll have Glitter bring them to you. We do ask for this room to be paid in advance, though."

I said, "How much?"

He opened his mouth to say something, stopped, then said, "Two hundred."

Mutt and I looked at each other, and I realized the price had probably just doubled. I winked at my friend and handed the man the money.

He folded the bills and placed them in his front pants pocket. "Thank you, gentlemen," he said. "Make yourselves comfortable. Glitter'll be right up."

After the man in the suit left, Mutt lit a cigarette. "What you wanna ax the girl?"

"Why she lied."

"Well, can you do it after she give me a lap dance? I'd hate for yo' money to go to waste."

Before I could reply, the curtains parted. The woman Brother Thomas had referred to as my sister-in-Christ, now a.k.a. Glitter, walked in, carrying our drinks on a tray. The nurse's outfit had found its way back onto her small, young body, and she swayed on four-inch stilettos, giving me a smile, oblivious to our having met before. Her eyes were solid black pupils. It wasn't the heels causing her to be off balance.

She set the tray of drinks on the table and went to a stand with a small stereo system and CDs stacked on it. "What kind of music you like? We got Jay Z, Snoop, um—"

"Got anything *good* up in here?" Mutt asked.

Mary Ellen steadied herself as she looked through the disks. I walked over, studied the titles, and pointed to one. She put it in the player, hit the start button, and turned to me.

The wail of harmonica came out of the speakers as Mannish Boy began.

She said, "Who first?"

Bom bom bom bom bom, dum dum dum . . .

"How!" Mutt dropped backwards onto the couch and snapped his fingers. "You know it's me."

The girl concentrated on Mutt. "I know you."

Mutt opened his mouth to say something, but I beat him to it.

"Do we call you Glitter, or Mary Ellen?"

She gave me a lazy smile, her sway a little more exaggerated now, and rested a hand on the stereo stand. "What you talkin' about, sugar?"

"Aw, come on Opie," Mutt said. "This can wait, can't it?" He looked at Mary Ellen and patted his leg. "Come on over here, baby."

"Look, little girl," I said, "you better watch your back. I was there when Willa Mae got shot."

"She gone," Glitter said, her voice trying to get an edge that might have worked sober, "and so am I."

I watched her leave, deciding that her soul was not mine to rescue today. "Remember what I said, Mary, or it might happen to you, too."

She managed a half-hearted effort of storming out, stumbling only a few times, as if a new focus had come into her life. The black curtains parted and swung back in a whoosh after her exit.

"We better get out of here before they throw us out," I said.

"This the last time I come out wit you, Opie. You all business and no party."

We went through the curtains and ran into the manager and two tall bodybuilders on bulk juice.

The manager said, "It's time for you gentlemen to leave."

"Leave?" I asked. "I'm not waiting half the night for you to send a girl up. I want my money back."

The manager grabbed my shirt and moved me to the door. I popped his ears with my palms and he let go. When he did, I decked him. He went down.

The other two rushed us. Mutt sidestepped and shoved them. I swung hard and hit the closest with a solid uppercut. The second meathead caught me in a headlock and squeezed. It felt like my head was in a vise.

Mutt threw a wild punch and busted the guy's nose. He released his grip on my head and Mutt finished him off with a solid blow to the jaw. The guy crumpled to the ground next to the manager and his buddy.

My sidekick and I walked out the door.

Chapter Seven

Outside the Treasure Chest, Kali, the tall one who'd taken our drink order, leaned against my Mustang smoking a cigarette. She said, "I knew you wasn't right."

"Whaddaya mean?" Mutt asked. "You know me."

She had changed out of the hot pants and into shorts and added a blue polo to cover her white bra.

"Clarence, you never come here unless Willie win the double," Kali said. "This white boy put everybody on edge."

I checked the entrance to the Treasure Chest. "This is nice and friendly and all, but if they come out that door, it will get ugly."

"You right about that," Mutt said.

"You off the clock?" I asked Kali.

"I am for you, baby."

"Then if you got something to say," I said, "hop in and we'll give you a ride."

We piled in the Mustang and I laid two black streaks of burnt rubber while exiting the parking lot. A mile down the road, the tension in my shoulders loosened. Kali sat in the middle of the backseat, leaning forward and holding the factory-installed roll bar above our heads for support.

"My house is the other way," Kali said. "You ain't gonna try nothin' are you?"

"No, honey," I said. "I think Mutt and I are already outnumbered here."

"How!" Mutt yelled.

She touched my cheek. "Why not, baby? Buy me a drink and let's see what happens."

Taking Kali to Mutt's Bar was out of the question. Any time a female set foot in that place, every able-bodied man in the neighborhood showed up. I drove to Calhoun Street and got lucky again with a parking spot.

The rooftop bar overlooking Marion Square seemed like a good place to go this time of night. On the elevator ride up, I reappraised Kali. In flats she stood eye to eye with me. Even if she hadn't been so solidly built, her height would have been enough to intimidate me.

The exotic-club waitress caught me looking, smiled, and said, "That's right, baby."

On the rooftop, we sat at a table. Kali and Mutt lit cigarettes in one of the few bars in the tourist district that allowed smoking. I excused myself and went to the restroom. On my way back, I pulled out my cell and made a call.

"Hello," boomed Brother Thomas.

"Hey, brother," I said. "Sorry to bother you so late."

"Brother Brack? Is that you?"

"Yessir," I said.

"Everything okay?"

"Not really. We're fine. It's—"

"Oh, Lord," he said. "What happened now?"

I told him Mutt and I found Mary Ellen at the Treasure Chest, tried to talk to her, and almost didn't make it out.

"Mm-hmm."

"Anyway, she might be in trouble now is all I'm trying to say. Can you check on her?"

I felt Brother Thomas's sigh through the phone. He said, "You really know how to keep the pot boiling, don't you,

Brother Brack?"

I didn't say anything.

"Okay," he said. "I'll see what I can do."

"Good. By the way, you know a girl by the name of Kali? I'm not sure if it's her real name."

"Yeah, her son comes to Bible school most Sundays. She's another lost one needs found. Too smart for her own good."

I asked, "Can I trust her?"

There was a pause.

"Brother Brack, most people around here don't trust white folk. It's a fact of life. If she talkin', she got a reason. May be a whole bunch of things. Be careful. I'm on my way to get Sister Mary Ellen."

With that, my phone chirped off. I had been standing with my back to the hallway leading to our table. When I turned around, I found Kali staring at me, arms folded across her chest.

She asked, "You think I'm gonna set you up?"

"I'm not sure," I said. "I'm looking for a lost woman named Willa Mae."

"Well, I was lookin' for you," she said. "Mutt tried to grab my leg."

I couldn't take that mutt anywhere.

"If you want," I said, "I'll sit between you and him. He probably won't grab my leg."

"I wouldn't be too sure about that," she said. "He so wound up from the club, no one's safe." She brushed my cheek again. "But you can grab anything you want, baby."

Ignoring the proposition, I led Kali to the table and sat next to Mutt. Kali sat next to me, leaving a chair between her and Mutt at the four-top table.

"The floor is yours," I said to Kali.

She said, "Why you care about some junkie ho? Willa Mae wasn't nothing but trouble."

"I'm doing this for her six-year-old sister," I said.

"Yeah, well Willa Mae burned a lot of people," Kali said. "It might've caught up to her."

"If that's the case," I said, "then at least her sister will know. One way or another."

Kali picked up her drink, a gin and ginger. "One way or another."

"Spill it, girl," Mutt said. "We ain't got all night."

"I do." She looked at me. "And all day tomorrow, too. I got all the time you want, baby."

"Cool it," I said to the both of them.

She put the short, red straw of her drink to her lips and pulled in the liquid, smiling at both of us with her eyes.

"How much?" I said.

Her smile focused on me and she lowered her drink. "How much for what?"

Mutt lit another cigarette. "To tell us what you know, girl."

She ran her fingers through my hair. "I like you."

"That's great," I said, "but I'm interested in the junkie ho."

Kali pulled her hand away and sat back in her chair. "She ain't the only black girl around needs a rich white boy."

Mutt said, "Who you foolin'?"

She sighed. "Willa too good for her friends. She stop comin' around. I hear she tryin' to get clean, too."

I asked, "How do you know?"

"I was her friend."

"What I mean," I said, "is did she tell you or did you stop seeing her?"

"Both. Heidi at the Chest say she stop using."

Mutt and I looked at each other.

"Stopped using what?" I asked.

"Coke."

"That all?" Mutt asked.

She said, "Far as I know. That and weed, but I ain't sure why she stopped."

Shelby's bark echoed through the thin walls of my inherited Isle of Palms domicile. I turned over to look at the digital clock on my nightstand. It said seven A.M.

A rap at my door sent me sitting straight up. Shelby ran to the living room, barking away. I swung my legs onto the floor, grabbed the baseball bat I kept behind the bedroom door, and followed my dog.

Another rap, harder, rattled the front window.

"Brack?" said a familiar female voice through the dried-out wood.

I leaned the bat in the corner and opened the door. Shelby stopped barking and greeted my visitor with a lick of the hand.

I said, "Couldn't this have waited a couple more hours?"

Darcy walked past me into the living room. "Nope. I tried to call but your phone was off."

"That might have been because I was sleeping." I closed the door and turned around. "Burning the early morning oil, I see."

She held up a thick manila folder. "Since you're up, go ahead and put on a pot of coffee."

I rubbed my eyes, trying to decide if I wanted to give her the boot and get more sleep. "What's in the folder?"

"A copy of Willa Mae's diary."

Her answer made the decision for me. I lowered my hands from my face.

She smiled. "I thought you might be interested."

Shelby sat on his back legs and raised a paw in front of her. Darcy obeyed his request and knelt to pet him.

I walked past two of my best friends and turned on the automatic coffee pot. It had been loaded and set to run anyway—in two more hours.

She looked at the design on my boxers. "Pigs riding tractors. Real cute."

With the coffee brewing, I sat on the couch and put a foot on the coffee table. "If I'd known I was getting company, I'd have dressed for the occasion."

She tossed me the file and continued to stroke Shelby's fur.

The manila folder was about an inch thick and held together by a rubber band, which I slipped off. "How did you get this?"

"I'd love to say I'm that good," she said, "even though we know I really am."

I gave her a smirk.

"Someone sent it to me at the paper. I found it yesterday while going through a stack of mail."

Yellow sticky notes marked several pages. I flipped through a dozen sheets. The handwriting was almost illegible. "You read any of it yet?"

"All of it," she said. "I marked the good parts."

Shelby stretched out on the floor and Darcy scratched around his collar and ears.

I turned to one of the marked pages and read aloud, *"Made it with Jon-Jon again. He said he gonna hook me up. Get me out of here."*

Apparently, even the prostitutes he paid didn't have enough respect for him to call him by his birth name. I looked at the date. "March eighteenth. Four months ago?"

Darcy smiled. "See where this is going?"

"Yeah," I said, "right into the toilet."

"For Jon-Jon and his daddy," she replied.

"I think you're enjoying this a little too much."

"Keep going."

I moved to another marked page. *"Camilla and me got some good weed and got hi. Spent the afternoon at her crib talking about Jon-Jon. How he say he love being with me. He got a lot of money."*

I looked at Darcy. "I met a friend of Willa's by the name of Mary Ellen. Who is this Camilla?"

"Not sure," she said. "Keep reading."

I turned the sheet over. *"Got a plan to get Jon-Jon. I'm gonna say I got pregnant and he need to pay."* I shook my head. "You know what this is?"

Darcy nodded. "Motive."

She was right, of course. If Willa Mae was dead, one or both of the Gardners were in trouble. Deep trouble.

Kali had given Mutt and me the address of an apartment in West Ashley to check out. Later that morning, Mutt, Brother Thomas, and I drove there in my Uncle Reggie's vintage convertible Mustang—with the top down.

Mutt said, "Tell me why I gotta ride back here."

" 'Cause Brother Thomas won't fit there," I said.

"How!" yelled Mutt.

Brother Thomas shook his head. "Jesus must be exposing a little more of my pride is all I can think of."

The landscaping at the entrance to the apartment complex was tastefully designed with flowers and trimmed bushes, all banked in fresh mulch. The buildings faced each other with the door to each unit opening from inside an atrium. Wooden decks faced the parking lot. I pulled into a vacant spot by the rental office and killed the motor.

Brother Thomas got out first. "I'll be right back, gentlemen." He went in a door marked "Property Manager."

I stuck a piece of gum in my mouth to stave off the want for a fat Dominican.

A few minutes later, Brother Thomas exited the office holding up a key so we could see it. "The super is a friend."

I said, "I hope Willa doesn't have an alarm system."

Brother Thomas and Mutt turned to face me at the same time.

"What?" I asked. "Don't tell me you didn't think of that."

Mutt asked me, "You an expert on breaking and entering?"

"It's not breaking and entering if we have a key," I said.

"You and I of the same mind, Brother Brack, mm-hmm."

I didn't know how to react. This was the first time Brother Thomas had agreed with me and not countered with a biblical perspective on how I was about to screw up. If I contemplated what that meant, I'd probably decide we were both wrong.

Mutt said, "I'm sure the po-lice would love to listen to you two explain why three of us be in some girl's apartment with no invitation."

"Brother Clarence," Brother Thomas said, "sometimes you got to have a little faith."

To get to the second-floor apartment was up a set of outdoor stairs. Brother Thomas approached the door and knocked. "Willa Mae? It's Brother Thomas."

We listened for a response. All I heard were sounds of traffic from the nearby four-lane.

"She ain't home," Mutt said, speaking the obvious.

"Willa?" Brother said. "We comin' in."

He put the key in the lock and opened the door. When we stepped inside, a musty, sour smell assaulted my nose. The apartment was dark and the AC was off. Sweat dripped down my back from the heat.

"Gawd, it stinks," Mutt said.

Brother Thomas called out again. "Willa Mae?"

I felt the wall beside the door for a switch and flipped on a light. The place was simple with bare white walls and minimal furniture. An empty orange-juice container and a bag from a fast-food restaurant littered the kitchen counter to our left. The living room lay to our right. An old couch faced a new flatscreen

TV and a single-unit stereo system with a smartphone jack.

I walked past the front rooms and stopped at a door that led to the bathroom, the sour smell floating more strongly in the air. I found the light switch and turned it on.

"I think I found what stinks," I said.

It looked like Willa had tried to get to the commode to throw up but hadn't made it. Flies buzzed around the dried puddle on the floor.

Brother Thomas approached. "Whew! What in heavens . . ."

Once recognition came into his eyes, I nodded.

"She been sick," he said.

"Maybe trying to get clean," I said.

Mutt said, "Kali tol' us something changed in her."

I said, "I wonder when she rented this place."

"My friend said three weeks ago." Brother Thomas wiped his forehead with a handkerchief. "She paid first three months in advance."

I said, "So where does a junkie go when she's trying to detox?"

"If it got too bad, back to her dealer," Mutt said.

Brother Thomas thumped the counter hard with his fist, pushed past us, and stormed out of the apartment.

After turning off the lights, Mutt and I met Brother Thomas by my car.

A black man with a blue work uniform and a thick head of hair walked up. "You find anything, Brother?"

"Not enough." Brother Thomas handed the man the key and got in the car.

"I hope nothing happened to that girl," the man said. "She sure is pretty."

It'd been four days since she was shot. I had a feeling she was no longer with us.

Chapter Eight

Mutt and Brother Thomas knew all the dealers in the projects downtown and what each one specialized in. Our plan was simple—kidnapping. For the second time today, breaking the law did not seem to bother Brother Thomas.

I pulled up to the curb in front of a boarded-up house where a douche-bag dealer named Tucan sold cocaine. He controlled the money while his partner, a runner, handled the merchandise. At least three others hung around who I deemed part of the business.

This kid hadn't seen twenty yet. He put his hands in his pockets. "Nice ride! What you want?"

Brother Thomas got out of the car, stepped to the curb, and clocked Tucan with an uppercut to the jaw. In one motion, he caught the falling kid and threw him into the backseat with Mutt, the lowered convertible top giving the preacher a clear shot. It was the fastest I had ever seen Brother Thomas move.

Another kid I took to be Tucan's partner said, "What the—"

Brother Thomas hopped back in the car. Before his door closed, I floored the gas and dumped the clutch. The big-block motor got us out of there in a hurry. Loud pops erupted behind us. A bullet hit the back of the car with a thump. I gritted my teeth and aimed for the first side street. Another shot went through the windshield as I cut the wheel to round the corner. After that, the deep moan from the engine's open-element air intake and the roar from the custom exhaust overwhelmed everything else in the world.

We merged onto the new bridge and I slowed our pace to match the afternoon traffic around us. Once across the Cooper River and into Mount Pleasant, I pulled into a vacant parking lot behind an empty strip mall and stopped the car. In the rearview mirror I saw Mutt with Tucan in a headlock. The dealer's white tennis shoes stuck out over the side of the car.

I said, "You mean we drove the whole way like that?"

Mutt held up a hand. In it was a nine millimeter. "He had this on him. We need to find out what else he got."

"Let him up," Brother Thomas said.

Mutt stood in the backseat, lifted a still knocked-out Tucan to me, and got out. We propped the kid against the side of the car. A more thorough search of his pockets yielded another nine millimeter, a switchblade, and a large amount of cash.

Brother Thomas took off his jacket and minister's collar and rolled up his sleeves.

I walked to the back of my car and examined the bullet hole.

"Tucan," Brother said in an authoritative voice.

Tucan's head did a slight roll. "Huh?"

Brother Thomas said, "Which one of you all supply Willa Mae?"

"Huh?"

"Willa Mae," Brother repeated. "Who her dealer?"

"Ma-an," Tucan said slowly. "Why you hit me?"

I came around my car and stood beside Brother Thomas. "Answer the question."

Tucan looked from the preacher to me. "I don't know what you talkin' 'bout, mother—"

Brother Thomas slapped him across the face.

Tucan winced.

"I'm not going to ask you again," Brother Thomas said, spittle dripping out of his mouth, "so you best answer me, boy."

I jacked a round in the chamber of one of the kid's nines.

Tucan's eyes opened real wide. "Wi-wi-willa Mae? I-I ain't seen that ho in weeks."

"How many?" I asked.

"Huh?" Tucan's favorite word.

Brother Thomas slapped him across the face again.

The poor kid cowered. Tears ran down his cheeks.

"I didn't hear you answer, boy," Brother Thomas said.

"Couple," Tucan mumbled. "Two or three."

I said, "Which is it? Two or three."

"I don't know, man," Tucan said. "I ain't got no calendar."

"Who's her dealer?" I asked.

Tucan took a deep breath. "I ain't no rat."

Brother Thomas raised his hand a third time.

Mutt put up an arm, stopping the preacher. "Enough, Brother. You too, Opie."

For a second, I saw something in Brother Thomas's eyes. Something I had seen in my own mirror. A combination of anger, vengeance, and blood.

Two uniformed officers stood in front of the main building of the Charleston Police Department and watched us pull to the curb fifteen feet away.

Brother Thomas opened his door and got out. He grabbed two fistfuls of Tucan's shirt and lifted the drug dealer from the backseat, setting him on the sidewalk. "This where you get out. I see you on the corner again, we go another round. I find out you know where Willa Mae is and don't tell me, you'll meet God. You hear me, boy?"

The officers stepped toward us.

Tucan nodded like a jackhammer. I wasn't sure if it was because of Brother Thomas's threat or where we dropped him off. Inside his pockets the cops would now find two unloaded and print-free pistols and the switchblade—more than enough for jail time, especially if he had any priors. And I'd bet he had at least one.

Brother Thomas got back in and I eased away from the curb, granny shifting through the gears, and wondering if the cops had spotted the bullet holes in my hundred-thousand-dollar ride. In the rearview mirror, I saw Tucan turn and run.

After taking Mutt back to his bar, I drove Brother Thomas to the Pirate's Cove. Pam, one of the bartenders, poured two iced teas which I carried to the back deck, handing one to Brother Thomas. He leaned against the far railing, looking out at the ocean. Dusk had not yet taken the edge off the day's heat. Reeds washed up on the beach marked where high tide had reached.

I asked, "You want to talk about it?"

Brother Thomas drank half his tea and set the glass on the railing. He hunched forward, putting a hand on each side of the glass, and lowered his head. I patted his shoulder. He took a handkerchief out of his pocket and wiped his face. I watched the ocean and gave him time to collect himself.

After a moment he spoke. "Every day I see those kids on the corner selling that death, and every day I pray for God to give me the strength to have the faith I preach about every Sunday morning. The faith I need to be there for the people of the community." He blew his nose and wadded up the white cotton fabric. "I threw everything away today. I let my anger get hold of me. As sure as I'm standin' here, I'da killed that boy."

I took another pull from my tea and said, "I know you can't see it this way, but that kid is nineteen years old and had two guns on him. He sells drugs because he wants to." What I didn't say was that I would have drilled him with his own nine millimeter to get answers if Mutt hadn't intervened.

Brother Thomas said, "It's all he knows."

"Has he been to any of your services?" I asked.

"His mother used to bring him when he was a boy."

"And you preached that it was okay to sell drugs?"

He cleared his throat. "Course not."

"Then that isn't all he knows. It's all he chooses to know."

Brother Thomas looked at me. "You wouldn't understand."

"Let me tell you something, my friend. My wife died, and it was the hardest thing I ever had to live through. You want to talk about anger? I went to war with the sole purpose of killing or being killed. I wanted people to die because my wife died. It was my choice, and I have to live with the things I did. Just like Tucan has to live with the choices he makes."

"God did not put me on this earth to beat up sinners."

I said, "You think God wants you to allow them to stand on the street corner and sell drugs?"

He finished his iced tea and set the glass down.

"All I'm saying," I said, "is that I haven't met any perfect people who had their lives together. You know what's right and wrong. We needed information on Willa Mae. He would have talked sooner or later."

"Brother Brack," he said, "man can't afford to lose his own soul while he trying to do right."

Darcy gave me Jon-Jon's city address, an apartment downtown on King Street overlooking the historic shop-lined lane. I had no other leads at the moment, and I wanted to see what the jerk-off did with his time. A quick search revealed the building was owned by Jon-Jon's father, the senior jerk-off. After dropping off Brother Thomas, I found a parking spot close by and did a reconnaissance of the area.

Across the street from Jon-Jon's apartment stood a line of shops. I chose a store specializing in soap and body lotion that had a big front window—a good place to position myself and watch. I'd been standing inside for all of five minutes when someone cleared their throat behind me.

I turned to see a very clean-cut kid about fifteen years my junior with spiked up hair in front wearing a really white polo.

He asked, "May I help you?"

I resumed scoping out the entrance to Jon-Jon's place. "I'm just using your window to watch the building across the street."

"Wow," the kid said, a little too excited, and a little too effeminate. "What are you? Some sort of private eye?"

"No," I said. "How much for you to leave me alone and let me stay here for a while?"

"We'll have to ask the manager. Hey, Elizabeth?"

No one else had been in the store. I'd checked that before I walked in. My attention veered off target to the back of the shop as a pin-up beauty stepped from the rear office. Long, blond hair. Perky lips. Blue eyes. Everything. A slender aqua summer dress fit an hourglass figure. She strolled up to me like a runway model and stopped inches away. Her first words were, "You can breathe now."

"Thanks," I said, and did, inhaling the fragrance of apricots.

Her underling, the kid with the spiky hair, said, "This man, who looks so much like that guy from *Mad Men* that I call dibs, wants to use our window to spy. Should we let him?"

Elizabeth asked, "Who are you spying on?"

The kid said, "The building across the street."

The supermodel looked out the window at the residence of my mark. "Jonathan Langston Gardner lives there."

Apparently I wasn't very good at this whole investigation thing. Either that, or I just seemed to walk headfirst into brick walls.

"The biggest mistake of my life was dating Jon-Jon," she said. "I hope you give him everything he deserves." She spun on her heels and returned to the back room. If Elizabeth was twenty, she'd just had that birthday.

Her coworker put his hands on his cheeks and said, "Oh. My. God." He twirled around and ran after Elizabeth.

I took their actions as indications that I could stay a little while longer.

Ten more minutes passed. No customers came in. The staff stayed in the back room. And there'd been no sign of Jon-Jon.

My back was stiff from standing in one place, but it stiffened even more when I smelled apricots again.

Elizabeth spoke from behind me. "I made fresh coffee. Would you like a cup?"

"It's a hundred degrees outside," I said.

"I know," she said. "Can't help it. I drink it all day long."

I turned to face her. "It's gonna stunt your growth."

She did a slow spin, holding her arms out, saying, "Does it look to you like it's affected me?" Her dress accentuated more shapes than an engineer's French curve.

I watched her finish the pirouette and then focused on Jon-Jon's place again. "Got me there. I take mine black, hold the ballet. It's a little too distracting."

"Just a little?"

Still looking out the window, I said, "Okay. A little more than a little. You into older guys? Or just those who are after your ex-boyfriend?"

I sensed her move close.

She whispered, "All of the above."

Her breath touched my ear and I felt a shockwave run through me. As if on queue, Jon-Jon and a dark-haired girl about Elizabeth's age exited his building, turned to their left, and walked up the sidewalk.

"Gotta go," I said.

"Wait!" Elizabeth grabbed my arm and handed me a business card. "Call me."

I stuffed the card in the front pocket of my shorts and bolted out the door. Jon-Jon was twenty feet ahead. The female, a slender brunette in pumps, did her best to keep up with him. I followed at a distance. They turned into the stairwell of a parking garage and I immediately knew my tail was over. Jon-Jon was going for his car.

Lucky for me, there was only one exit. I jogged to where it was and positioned myself across the street. When Jon-Jon pulled out in his Cayenne, I used my iPhone to snap as many pictures as I could of his passenger.

Ten minutes later I sat in my Mustang checking out the photos. The girl looked familiar, but I couldn't place her. So I did the usual thing when stumped and sent the best of the photos to Darcy along with a note asking if she could I.D. the girl.

She called thirty seconds later. "That's Eve White."

"And?"

"And, what?" she asked. "I'm in the middle of something here. Look her up."

With that, she was gone.

At least I had a name. Since I hated using my phone to do internet searches, I walked the four blocks to the library, entered through the big glass doors, and signed up for a computer. A few keystrokes on a real keyboard later and Ms. White stared back at me from the flatscreen monitor. The differences between her professional picture and the ones I sent Darcy were many. Whereas mine were side shots into a moving vehicle, the photo I was looking at showed Ms. Folly Beach—as she had been crowned—sporting a bikini and a smile.

The guy using the computer next to me said, "Whoa. What site is that?"

Ignoring him, I clicked off the newspaper's site and found her own website. Apparently Eve White was an aspiring actress and model, no surprise there, with a string of local commercials to her credit. Since I didn't have a TV in my house and kept the bar's bigscreen on ESPN, I'd missed the privilege of seeing her in action. The bikini shot alone would have been enough of an audition for me.

Not sure what help this information would be, I logged off and prepared to leave the library.

I felt the figure behind me before I saw him and wondered how long he had been watching me. In hunting insurgents in Afghanistan, I had developed a keen sense of trouble. Via his reflection in the big glass doors, I sized up this new threat. A black male wearing shorts and a T-shirt, trouble appeared to carry a backpack over one shoulder.

I exited the main branch of the Charleston County Public Library and walked down the sidewalk along Calhoun Street toward King. At a crosswalk, I stooped down to resecure a buckle on my sandal and glanced behind. In my periphery, I saw him focused on me. I stood and continued walking, trying to decide how to learn who he was without spooking him. At a coffee shop on the corner I opened the door and went inside. Four people stood in line at the register, and I joined them which gave me a chance to make sure my tail hadn't vanished. He stood outside the doors pretending to watch the people walking by.

When my turn came, an adolescent girl working the register said, "May I help you?"

"I'd like a large regular and a mocha, please."

She totaled it up.

Handing her money, I said, "Can you do me a favor?"

The girl raised her eyebrows as if expecting me to turn into a pervert in front of her very eyes.

I pointed to the guy standing out front who'd been tailing me. "I'll give you twenty bucks if you'll deliver the mocha to that guy out there."

"You've got to be kidding."

I handed her the twenty. "Tell him I'd like to have a chat."

She looked at the Jackson in her hand and said, "Deal!"

I picked up my coffee from the counter when it was ready, grabbed a local paper from a free stack, and took a seat at a table facing the front window. From my vantage point I also watched the cashier get someone to cover the register for her, take the mocha outside, and hand it to the guy who was doing a bad job of imitating a tourist.

He gave her a look like she was crazy. She pointed me out to him through the window and walked back inside. I motioned for the stranger to come in and join me in the other chair at my table. First, he stared at me for a few seconds, then at the coffee in his hands, before coming inside and sitting down.

He was early twenties, maybe my height. Familiar looking.

As he settled in I said, "So you want to tell me why you followed me from the library?"

His eyes avoided mine. "I wasn't following you."

I slouched in my seat and hung an arm over the back of my chair. It took me a moment to figure out where I'd seen this guy—in the photos I'd been shown on the Jameson's porch together with Brother Thomas. Mrs. Jameson had called her grandson Trevor. I said, "I've seen you before in some pictures."

He glared at me. "Blacks must all look alike to whites."

"Not me. I'm usually pretty good at facial recognition."

"Gee," he said, "that makes me feel so much better."

"Back to what I said earlier, I've been looking for what happened to a woman named Willa Mae. You know her?"

His glare seemed to hold a lot of anger. "What about it?"

"Well, if you know her I'd appreciate anything you can tell me."

He stood up and yelled, "You best stay away!"

Everyone in the coffee shop looked at us.

I rested my hands on the table. "I would if I knew where she was. Is she still alive?"

He shoved his chair forward, knocking the table toward me a couple inches, almost spilling the coffees, and stormed to the exit.

I called to him. "Trevor!"

He turned around at the door.

Gotcha!

In the silence of the crowd, I said, "Her six-year-old sister hasn't seen her in a week. If you don't want to talk to me, have Willa call her. Okay?"

He pushed through the door and walked away. Soon, the sound of clatter and conversation filled the room again. I finished my coffee and had the untouched mocha for dessert, wondering if I'd ever find Willa Mae, dead or alive.

Before I could plan my next step, my phone rang.

Paige, my bar manager, said that a State Liquor Commission Representative happened to show up at our doorstep. Our missing license to sell alcohol, the one that had been put in a frame and hung behind the bar for all to see until it had been stolen, had caused a problem. Not being able to produce it was a violation.

And now we were looking at a nice fine. Of course, the fine would be dropped when we received our replacement license, but it was still not a good situation.

Chapter Nine

The next morning, Thursday, Brother Thomas called and asked me to meet him at his church. He said he'd gotten another tip that might help us locate Willa Mae. After he and I piled in my truck because I didn't feel like exposing my vintage Mustang to any more bullet holes, he guided me to a part of the city I'd never been in before.

"People live here?" I asked.

"Mm-hmm."

The shotgun homes lining the street were different shades of a single color—crumbling. A roof had caved in on the house closest to me. Everywhere I looked weeds broke through the asphalt and sidewalk and stood straight up as if reaching out to God for rescue.

A frail black man in tattered clothes stumbled along the sidewalk in a daze, mumbling to himself as he passed us.

Brother Thomas waited until the man was a safe distance away before he said, "Okay, let's check it out."

I scanned the area once more, took a deep breath, and opened my door.

The thick air held a musty, mildewy smell from the rotting structures. In the lowcountry heat, beads of sweat appeared on Brother Thomas's forehead. As always—religiously, I might say—he wore his black pants and black shirt with his minister's collar. It was not exactly summer wear in the Deep South.

I asked, "Don't you own a pair of shorts?"

He laughed. "People knew Jesus because of who He was. These same people look at me, all they see is a old, fat, black man. My clothes try to give them a little hint."

A loud crash made us turn around. A man had dropped a large plastic bag filled with empty cans. He snickered. "Made you all jump, I did."

Brother Thomas raised his hand to his forehead to shade his eyes from the sun. "That you, Scooter?"

The man called Scooter watched us intently. He wore a tattered red T-shirt that didn't quite cover solid-looking shoulders and arms. His brown pants were grease stained, along with his torn and dirty tennis shoes. A wheeled dolly beside him had three milk crates strapped to it with a bedding roll. "What you doin' out this way, Brother? You lookin' for more folk come to service Sunday?"

"I'm always lookin' for souls to save," the minister said. "Today, I'm lookin' for a girl might live out here named Willa Mae. You know her?"

Scooter pressed a finger to his right nostril and blew out the other. "Naw. But I don't hang around here, much. No good cans."

"He's more right than he knows," I said. "No good cans and no rich johns. She won't be here. She's already moved up the food chain."

Scooter picked up his cans and moved towards us close enough so we could smell him. "Can you help a man down on his luck?"

I reached for my wallet but Brother Thomas put a hand on my arm.

"I can do better than that," he said, handing Scooter a business card. "Come by Saturday mornings. We got good food and a lot of clothes. Fix you right up."

Scooter looked at the card, then at Brother Thomas.

"We also got a bunch of cans," Brother said.

With that, the poor man's face lit up. "Really? Okay, Brother. I'll make it." And he turned away.

For the rest of our time in this part of town, we didn't find anything or anyone that would help us. In the silence of the drive back, I asked, "Everything all right, Brother?"

"That girl done lied to me," he said, "and I'm gonna find out why."

He didn't have to tell me who he was calling a liar. Sister Mary Ellen would have some explaining to do if we caught up with her. Brother Thomas guided me up another side street and into another rough part of town. More run-down homes and beat-up cars. Black teen-agers played basketball at a cracked asphalt court. The hoops had no nets.

"Where do we happen to be?" I asked.

"Sorry, Brother Brack. This place ain't one I'd normally bring you to."

"I don't have a gun, you know." After all the gunfights last year, I'd vowed not to want another. But lately, I'd begun to change my mind.

"I know." He had me double-park beside a ten-year-old Lexus with big rims. "You can come with me or stay here if you want. Not sure which would be safer."

Six young black men, all wearing the same red bandanas, stood beside a doorway like pillars of the community.

"I guess I'm your wingman," I said.

I could compare any situation I found myself confronting to my time in Afghanistan. I'd seen women fully covered except for their beautiful eyes strap C4 explosives to their bodies and kill hundreds of people along with ending their own lives. I'd seen young boys eager to prove themselves machine-gun into crowds because they believed in a deity that rewarded them for hating others. Compared to that, visiting the poor section of

North Charleston was like a day at the spa. Or would be if I'd had a firearm.

We got out of the truck and I followed Brother Thomas. The pillars watched us approach and stop a few feet away from them.

"Afternoon, gentlemen," Brother Thomas said.

A kid about seventeen took a drag from his cigarette and said, "Brother." He had an air of confidence about him that indicated leadership. His piercing stare suggested having seen a lot in not so many years. The others with him glared at me. I made no eye contact, focusing on an ear or a forehead.

"What you want?" the spokesman asked.

"Raymond," Brother Thomas said. "If Mary Ellen is here, I'd like to speak with her."

"She ain't here, and my name's Pain."

Brother Thomas asked, "Where might we find her?"

Pain looked at me. "I know you?"

Brother Thomas put his hand on my shoulder. "This here's a friend of mine. He's helping me around the church."

A kid about my height came up to me, invading my space. His eyes locked on mine. "Looks scared to me."

I smiled.

Sneering, he asked, "What you smiling at?"

In a calm voice I said, "Why don't you tell me?"

The kid pulled out a knockoff Beretta automatic and stuck it under my chin. "You laughing at me?"

Brother Thomas said to Raymond, "Call him off before someone gets hurt."

The kid pushed the muzzle into my skin. I kept my eyes on his, not giving him anything.

Raymond said, "D-Go's just playing, Brother. He don't wanna hurt nobody. Specially no scared white boy. Do ya, D-Go?"

In my periphery, I saw the other kids look at Brother. Then, one by one, they laughed. D-Go lowered the pistol. I felt a familiar burning sensation start in my stomach and begin to make its way through my bloodstream, like caged fire looking for an exit.

Brother Thomas squeezed my shoulder to stop me from doing anything that might provoke someone to start shooting at us. "We're just looking for Mary," he said. "We talk to her, then we gone."

D-Go said, "I'll tell you. But white bread has to kneel first."

I tasted violence in my mouth.

Brother Thomas got in D-Go's face. "You tell me where she is and I'll try to forget that parole violation you're carrying around."

"You a rat now, Brother?" Raymond asked.

"What I am is irritated," Brother said. "I come here, show respect, and you spit in my face and insult my friend. You tell me what I am and what I'm going to turn into in about thirty seconds if'n I don't get some answers around here."

D-Go racked the slide and aimed two inches from my face. The blood in my eyes boiled. Six armed hoods against Brother Thomas and me. This might have been one of those bad situations that ended in another short story on page five of the paper. One that read TWO MEN SHOT DEAD. NO WITNESSES.

"You wanna shoot, D-Go?" Brother Thomas asked. "That make you feel like a man?"

"I don't like the way he lookin' at me," D-Go said. "All bad, like he got the yard stare."

" 'Cause he been arrested before," Brother Thomas said.

"That true, white man?" D-Go lowered the gun, the muzzle aimed almost to my right. "You been inside?"

"I been in the box," I said.

"How come you still walking around?" D-Go asked.

"I got a good lawyer."

D-Go laughed and looked at his buddies. "Hear that? He got a good lawyer. Thinks he's bad 'cause he been in the box. I been in the box too. Five-oh ain't got nothing outta me."

I said, "My advice is get out while you still can. Otherwise get either a good lawyer or a butt plug."

A few snickers followed and D-Go's eyes squinted. He raised the gun and pointed it in my face again.

Something snapped inside of me. In one motion, I grabbed the gun with my left hand and popped D-Go in the nose with my right. Within a second I felt a muzzle against the back of my head. I held up D-Go's gun, palm open, and it was taken from my hand.

"It didn't have to go down like this," Brother Thomas said.

D-Go squealed. "My nose, man!"

I heard the hammer being cocked on the gun against my head and thought this might be it. Jo's face flashed in front of my eyes, followed by Uncle Reggie's. And then my dog's and Darcy's.

"But here we are," Raymond said. "What we gonna do now?"

"I say shoot the cracker." D-Go grabbed for his gun, which was in Raymond's hand.

Raymond said, "I got this."

"We're leaving." Brother Thomas grabbed my arm and pulled me away from the man holding the pistol on me.

"Not if I don't say you can," Raymond said.

Brother Thomas turned and faced him. "It was you disrespecting me. I say we leaving. You wanna shoot an unarmed man in the back, go ahead."

"You better watch out, whitey."

I didn't have to turn around to know it was D-Go.

We walked to my pickup and climbed into the front seats.

As I started the truck and drove us out of there, my friend

said, “You really gotta do something about that anger you carry, Brother Brack.”

We passed a young black boy who looked to me to be a few years older than Aphisha. He held a cell phone to his ear with one hand. In his other was a leash incapable of controlling the pit bull it was connected to if the dog decided to act up. I thought about Shelby.

“D-Go will wanna square things up,” he said.

“Yeah,” I said, “and I’m sure it won’t be man to man.”

“No matter,” he said. “I don’t want you to give him a chance.”

“Don’t tell me you think those kids are outstanding citizens.”

“I know they ain’t, mm-hmm,” he said. “In fact, I got a girl in my congregation who got gang raped by D-Go and his friends but she won’t tell the po-lice ’cause she scared for her baby.”

“Jesus.”

Brother Thomas said, “That name got power. Be careful how you use it. Those kids think they tough. When they ain’t rapin’ innocent girls and shootin’ people, they hang out in a old garage behind D-Go’s grandmother’s house. She a good woman ain’t got a sense what her grandson doing. If she ever found out . . . Oh, Lord.”

If Brother Thomas was trying to discourage me from finishing with D-Go, he had a funny way of showing it.

Chapter Ten

We pulled into the parking lot of the Church of Redemption and I turned off the ignition.

"Well, here we are," I said, "back where we started."

"Sometimes when you find yourself heading in the wrong direction, all you gotta do is go back to where you last knew where you was and try a different path."

He led me to the rear of the church and into a storage room full of file cabinets.

I looked around. "Who are you, the J. Edgar Hoover of Charleston?"

Brother Thomas gave me a serious look that made me think I'd offended him. Then his face broke into a smile. "Um, Brother Brack? Most black folk who know about the man wouldn't appreciate being associated with him, mm-hmm."

"What's all this, then?"

"At the risk of proving you right, these here are everything I got on the people of my community. Where they come from and where they are now. For some, it's where they were last seen. Them's the sad ones."

"You got anything on Willa Mae?"

"I do and already checked. Nothing recent." He found the file with her name, pulled it from a drawer, and opened it. "See, I date the inside of the folders when I add something."

I saw three dates written on the folder, the most recent was four years ago. "What do you have on her?"

"Well, let's see," he said. "I got a picture of her baptism, a letter I sent her, and a copy of her release from Juvenile Detention."

"How did you get that?"

He looked at me. "Her mother was too drunk to pick up her daughter, so I got the privilege." He reflected a moment, then said, "For Willa's sixteenth birthday I gave her a locket I bought off a vendor in the Market. She still had it on the last time I'd seen her."

"You put up with a lot, don't you?" I asked.

"Brother Brack, it's what the Lord put me here to do. I take care of the people in this community. They give what they can. We manage." He put his hand on my shoulder. "We been managing a whole lot better since that anonymous donation we got."

"You keep talking about it."

"Well," Brother Thomas said, "one of these days someone will tell me where it come from."

Around the time last year when my uncle's murderer had been arrested the Church of Redemption received two hundred fifty thousand dollars in cash, exactly the sum I'd found in a crab pot my uncle had stashed off the coast of one of the barrier islands. As his executor, the money as far as I could tell had been unreported income in his estate.

"Anything else on Willa Mae?" I asked.

"No." He closed the file and put it back in the cabinet. "We're not here for that, anyway." He pulled a different drawer out and selected another file, flipping it open. "Here we go."

"Whattaya got?"

"Mary Ellen's latest address."

I looked at him. "Well why didn't we go there first? I'd have rather not met Pain or D-Go."

"Because I got a thousand people to keep track of, Brother

Brack, and I forgot she moved into her cousin's house."

We left the church and walked two blocks. From the sidewalk in front of her cousin's address, we heard moaning. Brother Thomas made a move like he was going to charge the door to the small house but I tugged at his arm.

I put my index finger to my lips. "Shh."

The curtains to the front room were only partially drawn and the window was open. From where we stood, we could see a big white back moving up and down. Bed springs creaked.

Brother Thomas shook his head, went to the door, and gave it a few good raps. "Mary? You in there, girl?"

The creaking stopped.

A man's voice said, "She's busy right now."

"And I'm her mother," Brother Thomas said. "I count to three and then I'm calling the po-lice."

I went around to the back of the house, picking up a broken broom handle that had been tossed on the ground with other litter. After a few seconds, a half-dressed, fat, white guy, beads of sweat dripping from his forehead, came out the back door.

I spun him face first into the side of the house and put the stick in his back. "Gotcha."

"I-I didn't do anything." The man shook and acted scared. "What-what's this about?"

"We saw it all," I said. "The payoff. The saddle ride. All I know is the wife won't be happy when she hears about this. No, sir."

"Let him go," said Brother Thomas from the back door, his voice low but nevertheless booming.

"You sure?" I asked.

My friend nodded.

I kicked the fat john in the rear end. "Git."

Behind Brother Thomas, Mary Ellen giggled as the man took off running. "That was funny." The T-shirt she wore did a poor job of covering her breasts and bare thighs. Her eyes were dilated. "You boys wan' a turn? Fifty dollars a piece."

Brother Thomas, still looking at me, said, "Get some clothes on, girl."

Mary Ellen frowned and went inside.

"She won't be much help the shape she's in," I said.

"I'll put her under a cold shower." Brother Thomas pulled out his cell phone and hit speed dial. A few seconds later, he said "Trudy?" then asked her to bring another lady with her to Mary Ellen's address.

A bang came from the front of the house, like a door slamming. I sprinted around to the street and saw Mary Ellen, still in her T-shirt, duck around another house across the street. At the same moment, a Lexus with big chrome rims approached. D-Go hung out the back door aiming a submachine gun. I dove to the ground seconds before bullets flew, peppering the house. Something burned across my right shoulder. The bullets stopped. The V-8 engine roared as the Lexus sped away.

A moment later Brother Thomas stood over me. "Brother Brack! You all right?"

I rolled onto my back and sat up, putting pressure on my arm. Blood seeped through my fingers. I looked up at him. "Tops," I said.

Inside the Church of Redemption, I sat shirtless on a table and felt antiseptic burn into my shoulder. I couldn't keep from uttering at least one "Ouch!"

Sister Trudy cleaned my wound with a damp cloth. "Hol' still. You men be such babies. Brother Thomas say to go easy on you. He say you kinda soft." She was at least fifty and wore a brightly-colored dress over a very full figure. Her thick black hair was curled and pinned up.

While she worked she hummed a gospel tune I knew from attending Brother Thomas's church. My dirty T-shirt was wadded up in my hands and I gripped it tightly as she finished wiping my injury, using more pressure than necessary, in my opinion.

"There you go, hon," she said. "Good as new." She touched my face with a latex-gloved hand. "You mus' spend a lot of time outside. You get any darker you gonna have to check a different box."

Brother Thomas belted out a laugh from the doorway. "Sister Trudy sure clean up a cut good, don't she?"

"Yeah," I said. "Real swell."

"Glad you still with us," he said. "The po-lice are here. Wanna ask you some questions, mm-hmm."

I hopped off the table and walked into the main hall of the church, draping my shirt over my good shoulder.

The same two detectives that showed up when Willa Mae got shot stood amongst the chairs in the open room. Detective Warrez watched me with some interest. Her partner, Crawford, folded his arms across his chest.

"Nice to see you guys," I said. Nice to see her, I meant.

Warrez asked, "Are you trying to live up to your reputation?"

"I was only the victim of a drive-by," I said.

Detective Crawford asked, "You recognize who did the shooting?"

Visions of a soon-to-be blown up Lexus danced in my head. "I was too busy ducking."

"So you didn't see anything?" Warrez asked.

"Not enough for you to make an arrest," I said, avoiding outright lying to her.

"Excuse me, detectives," Brother Thomas said. "Could I steal Mr. Pelton away for a minute?"

Warrez said, "We're not going anywhere."

Brother Thomas waved me to him, curling his meaty index finger in a condescending fashion as if calling a child.

A child is what I must've been because I followed him.

"I know you know who done it," he said. "I can read you like yesterday's paper. Don't be thinking about starting your own war with those kids. Let the po-lice handle it."

I smiled. "I wouldn't wanna be called a rat, now."

Brother Thomas leaned in, putting his arm on my good shoulder. "We're supposed to be looking for Willa Mae. Remember?"

He was right, and I knew it.

"How much you want me to say?"

"Everything. What we were doing there. Who we were looking for." He paused. "Everything except describing the john with Mary Ellen, that is. I don't want you using that for evil."

I opened my mouth to say something but he held up his hand, then pointed to the outside room where the detectives waited.

I spent the late afternoon at the gym working out with my personal trainer, the dispatcher Marlene's husband. With my shoulder wound stinging from sweat, I spent the two-hour session reflecting on Willa Mae's life. Drugs. The skin trade. The connection to Jon-Jon, Trevor, Mary Ellen and Kali.

Detective Warrez and her partner had unconditionally instructed me and Brother Thomas to "stop any and all inquiries regarding Willa Mae outside of the police department." If we didn't, we'd be arrested.

They'd also promised to roust D-Go and his gang.

After the workout, I passed out in a lounge chair on the beach below my bar. Shelby slept on a towel under an umbrella. I hadn't had a full night's sleep since Friday, the night before Willa Mae got shot. The Rolling Stones tune on my cell woke me. With one eye open, I reached for the phone and looked at the caller I.D.

"Hey, Brother Thomas," I said, still half asleep.

"Brother Brack? You okay? You don't sound too good."

I coughed. "I was just napping."

"The police found Willa Mae," he said. "She the one got burnt up in that barrel."

What he said caused me to sit up. "Then that story about it being a short Latino man was false."

His voice broke. "We ain't gotta look for her no more."

"Does Darcy know yet?"

"How should I know?" He sounded like he'd snapped.

It was then I realized he had convinced himself she was still alive, if only to continue to have hope—which was now lost.

"Sorry, Brother. You gonna be all right?"

"She ain't the first one from my flock gone to see the Lord. We plannin' on havin' the funeral tomorrow."

A lone pelican circled overhead and dove into the water.

I said, "Wanna help me find who did it?" He's got a date with the business end of a pistol, I thought but didn't say.

"I ain't in the revenge business, Brother Brack."

"You're into finding the truth, aren't you?"

He cleared his throat.

"I thought so," I said. "Listen, lemme make a few calls. Keep your phone charged and close."

I hung up before he could come up with a good reason to talk me out of anything. Willa Mae took the bullet for me and Aphisha. And for that she would be avenged.

So I did what I always seemed to do in these situations—I called Darcy.

"I already know," she said.

"I figured you did. It now appears that we are investigating the same crime."

She didn't reply and I wasn't sure if it was excitement or dread. Probably the latter.

I said, "The funeral's tomorrow. I got to make a few arrangements in the morning. How about I pick you up at nine?"

The next day, Friday, opened with an exceptionally burning heat, proving once again that man's greatest invention was air-conditioning. Especially since the Church of Redemption didn't have any. Attendees awaiting Willa Mae's funeral service to begin fanned themselves with the preprinted announcements they'd received upon entering the sanctuary. Three heavyset, African-American women in black dresses and large veiled hats sang a scorching version of "Amazing Grace."

Darcy and I sat at the back of the church, she in a conservative black dress that ended just above her knees, and me in a new, charcoal, Italian two-button suit. My favorite news girl helped me pick out the tie.

Willa Mae had stooped to extremely low places to flee the very people who were now the only mourners of her death. Aphisha and her grandmother, Mrs. Clara Jasper—whom I'd so far let down in my investigation of Willa's death—had been escorted by Mutt, and all three sat in the front row. Mrs. Jasper held her head high in defiance of her deceased granddaughter's shame.

The clicking of heels on the cheap linoleum floor caused me and most of the congregation to turn toward the sound. A woman in her early twenties wore the black pumps echoing in the church. Her black, sleeveless dress stopped a few inches shorter than Darcy's, exposing shapely legs in black hosiery. The whiteness of her face and arms glowed against the sea of brown and tan skin of most of the mourners. Shoulder-length, dark hair and eyes framed by black-rimmed sunglasses completed the package.

Darcy whispered, "You can pick up your jaw off the floor now, Romeo."

I watched the newcomer take a seat behind Aphisha. "Who do you think she is?"

"My guess is a colleague of Willa Mae."

By colleague, she meant fellow prostitute. That would be my guess, too. Still, it took a lot of stones to show up here amongst this crowd.

Aphisha ran to the object of our interest, shouting, "Camilla!"

The young woman now identified as Camilla bent down, wrapped her arms around Aphisha, hugging the little girl tight, and kissed her forehead.

Darcy and I looked at each other.

She whispered, "That's Willa Mae's friend from the diary."

"We need to talk to her," I whispered back.

At ten A.M., Brother Thomas stood in front of the closed casket I'd purchased for Willa's remains and gave a moving eulogy of life and death and rebirth. I thought about the efforts Willa Mae had made before the end of her short life to pull herself free of the consequences of her earlier poor choices, only to be gunned down, dismembered, and burned in a trash barrel. The more I contemplated it all, the angrier I got.

Rebirth? Someone robbed Willa Mae of her rebirth in this world.

And someone would pay.

After the service, Camilla gave us the slip. More like she just vanished. And not because I wasn't looking out for her. Darcy and I stood outside the church and watched everyone else exit. Across the street, I spotted someone I recognized—Trevor. He wore a suit and covered his eyes with sunglasses. But it was him. He saw me watching him and walked away.

Brother Thomas came up to us. Taking Darcy's hands in his, he said, "It sure was nice of you to attend, mm-hmm."

She asked, "Who is Camilla?"

"I ain't seen her before."

Aphisha and her grandmother exited behind us.

I waved them over and introduced Darcy.

Mrs. Jasper said, "I know. I seen you on TV. You such a pretty girl."

Darcy said, "Thank you."

I knelt to speak with Aphisha. "How are you today, sweetheart?"

She kissed my cheek.

Darcy knelt. "Aphisha, who's your friend Camilla?"

"She Willa's friend."

I asked, "How do you know her?"

"Willa Mae and Camilla took me shopping," she said. "They got me my purse." The child proudly held up her pink handbag for us to admire.

Chapter Eleven

Before we left the funeral, Brother Thomas mentioned another lead, this one a long shot. Desperation could be defined as grasping at straws, like this one now.

With Darcy having to film a news segment, I asked Mutt to join me. While I had a manager running the daily operations of my bar, Mutt had no one. But his regular clientele followed a pattern. During the first week of the month after receiving their stipend, the patrons packed the place. But by the middle of the second week everyone had spent most of their money and needed to stretch what was left until the next check.

Since it was now into the last week of May Mutt had some free time on his hands. He and I stepped through a doorway with no door into an old apartment building in North Charleston. We turned right and headed down a corridor that smelled like the men's room at a busy truck stop, one that hadn't been cleaned in a long time. Light fixtures jutted from the walls like gargoyles, most of them lacking bulbs. Some apartment doors had four inch black script numbers screwed to them. Others were missing theirs. We stopped at number two-nineteen.

I gave the door two swift raps. The sound echoed down the hall.

Brother Thomas had said the old man living at this address tried to file a police report about some gangbangers shooting up the parking lot. The police had brushed him off as some disgruntled old crank. While I think Brother Thomas wanted us to check in on his friend, the lead part was finding out any connection to Willa Mae. Not sure how he would help connect those dots, but desperate times called for desperate measures.

We waited twenty seconds and I rapped again.

A scruffy voice spoke through the unopened door. "Yeah, yeah. Whadda ya want?"

Mutt said, "Mr. Porter?"

"Who wanna know?"

"Brother Thomas sent us come talk to you."

"What about?"

"Can we come in, sir?" Mutt asked.

Another few seconds passed—enough for a long sigh. "Okay."

Locks clicked and chains scratched and banged. When the door opened, a hot sticky breeze blew past us carrying the musty smell of old age, tempering the stench of feces in the hall. Mr. Porter stood in the doorway, his black wrinkled face tinted with a permanent gray pallor. He wore no shirt, but suspenders held up his pants.

"Come on in if you're comin'," he said.

Mutt and I entered a time warp. Drawn curtains kept the glare of the sun out, but not the heat. In this part of town, air-conditioning was a working ceiling fan and prayer. The foyer of the small apartment doubled as the dining area and contained a small metal card table and two worn chairs with duct-taped seats. A red light on an old Mr. Coffee glowed and a half-full glass pot warmed on the burner.

"Can I get you guys some coffee?" the old man asked.

"Love some," I said.

Mr. Porter took out two cups and saucers. He set the cups in the saucers and poured our coffee. I noticed a faint flower pattern around the top of the cup and felt the rim of the underside of the matching saucer when he handed it to me. It was smooth which told me it was not cheap.

"Nice china," I said. "I can tell it's good stuff."

Mr. Porter looked me over and said, "It was a wedding present from my wife's parents when we was married. Nineteen sixty-six. Cancer got her. What can I do for you?"

Mr. Porter sat in one of the taped-up chairs. Mutt grabbed the stool by an old wall telephone whose once spiral cord had long given up its struggle with gravity. I took the chair opposite the old man.

Mutt said, "Mr. Porter, the reason we here is, well, we heard you was the one called the po-lice on those boys shootin' guns in front of your building."

"Two night ago," the old man said, "I was tryin' to watch the 'leven o'clock news. They was givin' highlights on the president's trip and I wanted to catch them. As soon as the president came on, it sounded like I was back in Nam. Those boys was raisin' all kinds of ruckus, with them little guns they got popping all over the place." He shook his head. "If they wanna shoot each other, why not sign up for the Marines?"

"Pay's not that great," I said.

His clouded eyes met mine. "You was in?"

"A couple years ago," I said. "Afghanistan. Mutt was in Kuwait."

Mutt said, "I thought I had enough shootin' to last me. But Opie, I mean Brack here, seem to bring it wit him."

The old man's wrinkled face stretched smooth as he chuckled. "Only white folks come round here're either givin' handouts or collectin' taxes. You don't look like you doin' neither."

"He own a bar, like me," Mutt said. "But he don't drink no more."

The old man nodded. "So what you wanna know about them troublemakers?"

"You know a girl named Willa Mae?" I said.

He took a drink from his coffee. I did, too.

"That the girl Brother Thomas been lookin' for?"

I said, "She's dead. The police found her body burned up in a trash barrel. You think she had something to do with the boys shooting up your parking lot?"

"Wouldn't surprise me," Mr. Porter said. "But I never saw her around."

"What about her friend, Mary Ellen?"

Mr. Porter put a hand on the table and used it to push himself up. Mutt stood and helped him.

The old man waved him off. "I got it."

He walked to the back of the apartment—only about ten steps.

I whispered, "I hope it wasn't anything we said."

We heard the old man shuffling things around. After a few moments, he made his way the ten steps back to the table. He handed Mutt a picture. "This who you axin' about?"

Mutt took the photo, looked at it, and handed it to me. It was Mary Ellen. A younger version, looking directly into the camera, her hair pulled back and a big smile on her face that showed she'd been innocent once. I wondered how the girl in this picture could be the same one we saw prancing across the stage at the Treasure Chest, and how she'd decided on the path to get from one place to the other. The question of paths chosen by all these young people, girls and boys, deserved answers.

"That her," Mutt said.

"She my niece," Mr. Porter said. "Mary Ellen was a smart girl. Then she got to runnin' wit the wrong peoples. Now God knows where she is."

Mutt's eyes met mine. We knew where she could be found. I shook my head no. We weren't here for that.

"Why you wanna get mixed up in all this, anyways?" the old man asked, eyeing me.

"Brother Thomas asked me to. I owe it to him."

Mr. Porter frowned as if in thought, then nodded as if he understood.

We left Mr. Porter's apartment after a second cup of coffee and a few war stories. In the parking lot of the apartment complex, a Crown Victoria idled past as Mutt and I climbed into my truck. Twenty-four-inch diameter wheels and purple paint told me it wasn't a police car, or wasn't one anymore.

Mutt said, "Hold on, Opie. Let's see what they doin'."

The windows of the purple people eater were tinted too dark to be legal. It passed, pulled out of the drive, and rolled up the street.

I started the truck, backed out, and sped down the street in the opposite direction. A hundred yards ahead at the next intersection, two more large American cars with huge rims looked like they were waiting for us.

Mutt said, "They might just be trying to scare us."

I slowed to assess the situation.

When the distance had shrunk to fifty yards, the doors opened on the cars ahead. I stopped the truck. The purple car was coming up behind us fast. A long brick building stretched to my right. To my left hid a narrow alley between two homes blocked by trash. Beyond the rubbish I saw a clearing. I slammed the gearshift into low, cranked the wheel, and floored it. We shot up the drive.

"Oh man!" Mutt braced himself.

The Ram's bumper did its job, scattering an old mattress and boxes of junk.

The alley ended just ahead. More like it dropped off. I shifted into second and we bounded over the edge of the drive, landing seconds later on the other side of a ditch. The truck bounced once and then settled. I gunned it and the rear wheels bit through dead undergrowth. The clearing ahead was a football field.

Mutt looked back. "You crazy!"

"They still back there?"

"Naw. They out of their cars though. Looks like they got machine guns. Better get us outta here."

He didn't have to tell me twice. I cut across the fifty-yard line. We sped past worn bleachers, rumbled down a cracked, concrete sidewalk, and hopped onto an empty parking lot. Lucky for us the gate was open. Not so lucky that another huge-rimmed rolling jukebox was on a collision course with my front bumper. I slammed on the brakes, threw the transmission into reverse, and floored it again. The parking lot had separate openings for cars to enter and exit. We sailed out the entrance backwards. The street was empty. Ten years racing everything from go-carts to stock cars had taught me a thing or two about vehicle control. At full speed in reverse, I threw the gearshift in neutral and spun the steering wheel left. The front of the truck slid perfectly around and I caught it when we faced in the other direction, put it in drive, and mashed the gas pedal.

The chase car was no match for the power of my Hemi and we rocketed away. At the last minute, I sliced down a side street. Machine gun fire peppered a stop sign we overran. Mutt hung out his window and fired several return shots. I didn't look back to see how true his aim was.

At the next intersection, I hung a sharp left and gunned it again.

"We lost them," Mutt said. "but don't let up just yet."

I didn't argue.

"You did what?" Detective Warrez stood beside her unmarked car in the Church of Redemption parking lot, arms folded, mouth open. The reason I'd called her was not all that clear to me. If I looked hard enough, I might find that I wanted an excuse to see her again. But I also knew that Mutt and I had stumbled onto something and she needed to know.

"Opie is one crazy white boy," Mutt said. "I ain't never jumped in no car before. Pick'em up, neither. Then we go full speed in reverse, musta been doing a hundred. He spins the wheel and here we go facing the other direction."

She shook her head.

I patted the fender of my truck. "It was a pretty good bootlegger reverse, if I do say so myself. Junior Johnson and Jim Rockford would have approved."

She said, "You could have gotten killed."

"They tried," Mutt said. "We outran the bullets."

She opened her car door, leaned in, and grabbed the radio. Mutt and I listened as she asked for a BOLO so all the cop cars would be on the lookout for each of the vehicles we'd described. She returned the radio to its cradle and straightened up.

"I don't think we're going to get much from that but it's worth a try," she said. "The real question is what you were doing in that part of town. I know you aren't still looking into Willa Mae's disappearance, because, Mr. Pelton, you have been unconditionally warned to stay away from it and to let us handle things."

I said, "Speaking of that, how far have you gotten?"

"We're treating it as important as any other case."

"Yeah, right," Mutt said. "And a white man invented the cotton gin."

Detective Warrez put her hands on her hips. "Now what is that supposed to mean?"

My phone vibrated and I ignored it.

"It means," I said, "the people around here have been getting hosed by the police force long enough to develop a slight mistrust."

She said, "I haven't been anything but honest with you."

"You're a minority, and not because you're Latina," I said.

Her dark face reddened and her darker eyes stared into mine. She was very attractive, in a hard-working, natural kind of way. I know Mutt liked her. I liked her, too.

She dropped her eyes and sighed. "You're right. I am the minority. I'm the only one who seems to care. Everyone else wants to get back to business. Sweep this whole thing under the rug."

"Then we're on the same side," I said.

She shook her head. "No, we're not. You guys are wild cowboys without the hats. I'm trying to conduct an official investigation and you're not helping."

"There wouldn't be no investigation without us," Mutt said.

Detective Warrez looked at him. "Yeah, well tell that to Willa Mae's family when the prosecutor can't use anything you find because it wasn't obtained by a legal search."

Mutt kicked a bottle and stormed off.

"Look," she said to me, "unofficially I appreciate what you're doing. Everything you're uncovering. But next time let me talk to the witness. Let me do the things the city of Charleston is paying me to do." She pointed to a busted headlight on my truck. "It'll be a lot less damaging."

A new headlight unit from the Ram dealer cost a lot more than I expected. In my converted factory, I replaced the busted pieces and set about touching up a few scratches in the paint. All things considered, it could have been a lot worse. Shelby helped by snoring in the corner of the shop. A Miles Davis tune ended and the Wurlitzer switched to U2's *Sunday Bloody Sunday.* I thought about how Willa Mae turned and faced the man with the gun while all I could do was run.

My cell phone vibrated and the caller I.D. displayed Darcy's number. Since I'd forgotten to return her last call, having been preoccupied playing twenty questions with Detective Warrez, I figured I'd better answer.

When I did, she asked, "Wasn't there a TV show in the eighties about some stuntman jumping his pickup truck all over the place?"

I thought about it a moment. *"The Fall Guy."*

"That'll be your new nickname," she said. "You can read about it in tomorrow's paper."

"What?"

"That's what happens when you ignore my calls and I don't get an exclusive. You get a nickname. The Fall Guy is better than some of the others I considered."

"That sounds like a load of what's left in the toilets when we close the bar after a busy Friday night."

"Gross," she said. "But if the shoe fits—"

"Very funny."

"Are you going to let me in or do I have to drive through the door like they do on the TV show?"

I hung up and went to press the inside button. The door to my factory opened silently on roller-bearing wheels and lubricated hinges. Darcy drove in and parked beside my Mustang.

I pressed the button to close the door. "How do you know about eighties television anyway? Weren't you just an embryo?"

"It's not like you were old enough to be at Woodstock," she said, "yet you play Jimi Hendrix all the time."

Pointing to the neon-lit jukebox, I asked, "Does that sound like Jimi Hendrix?"

"No," she said, "but it's still U2 before my time."

"Come to think of it," I said, "the Fall Guy had a blond sidekick. Not very bright, but she did have a certain presence."

"Whatever." She sat on the stool. "So why didn't I get a call after your shootout at the OK Corral?"

I couldn't think of a good reason so I grabbed a clean rag from a box next to the workbench and ran it across the front grill of my truck to remove my dirty fingerprints.

She said, "Not talking, huh? That's all right. My anonymous source says you ran over three little kids playing in the street."

I didn't bite.

"They also said you're wanted for speeding."

With the chrome polished, I stopped and said, "Is that all you got?"

She folded her arms across her chest. "I've got you and Mutt trenching the local football field."

I waited.

"And I've got a source that says there's money for your head."

"How much?"

"I'm serious, Brack," she said. "A gang wants you. Dead or alive."

"They started it."

She looked at me for a long while. "So what did the old man have to say?"

The fact that Darcy knew about Mutt's and my visit to Mr. Porter meant the gang knew, too. And probably the killer.

"Not much," I said. "Remember I told you about a friend of Willa's named Mary Ellen? Well, the old man's her uncle. Brother Thomas said it might be a long shot. I just think he wanted us to check on his friend."

She nodded and took out a notepad. "I found out about the owners of the property."

"This ought to be good. You want a Diet Coke?"

"Sure."

After tossing the polishing towel into a trash barrel, I got Darcy's drink out of an old refrigerator, opened it, and handed it to her.

Darcy accepted it, took a sip, and set it on a worktable next to her.

While she flipped through a few pages, I got a drink for myself.

She said, "Jonathan Langston Gardner the third . . ." she looked up at me and said, ". . . that would be Daddy and current primary candidate for state treasurer," and then continued reading, ". . . inherited the developing business from his father, Jonathan the second, thirty years ago. They lost big in the economic downturn of oh-eight but seem to have recovered."

After a big swallow from my drink I said, "How much did they lose?"

"My source says forty million."

I sat on a stool and blew out a long breath.

"Exactly," she said, "and didn't go bankrupt. That should tell you something."

"They have a lot more than most people know about. How much are they worth today?"

Darcy took another sip of her drink. "A hundred million in the accounts I found, and don't ask how I found them."

"How did you find them?"

"Very funny. The interesting point here, if you'll let me finish, is that ten years ago the business was only worth twenty million."

"Big daddy knows what he's doing."

"No," she said, "he knows how to surround himself with smart people."

"If they're so smart, why are they in business with him?"

"He had capital and equipment. The Gardner name was a selling point. They had a hand in just about everything built on the north side of Mount Pleasant in the last two decades."

I slowly turned the drink in my hands. "What are they saying about the torched body found on their building site?"

"Not much. But as far as I can tell they're cooperating with the investigation. So is the buyer."

"They already have that lot sold? Who's the buyer?"

"Custom spec house. That's the other juicy tidbit." She picked up her drink and sat back.

I watched her take a long drink and finish with a smile.

"Let me guess," I said, "the house is for Jon-Jon."

The smile vanished. "How did you know?"

I leaned forward. "I was right?"

She nodded.

"How many other people know?"

"It's in the public records," she said. "Anyone can find out. You just have to know who's behind the companies that own the properties, which is what I've been digging up. The senior Gardner has quite a lot of businesses."

"You really think Jon-Jon murdered Willa Mae, stuffed her in a drum at his new house, and torched her?"

"No, but someone may want people to think that."

I leaned back again. "This just gets better and better." After a moment, I said, "There's one thing I can't figure out."

Darcy was used to my introspective moments. "What's that?"

"Why was Willa Mae on that particular street when I ran into her last Saturday night?"

The bombshell reporter set her drink down. "That's a pretty good question."

My eyes focused on her. "Only pretty good?"

"Okay," she said. "Better than that. We should have been asking ourselves why from the start."

"Trying to get straight, and she goes right back into the lions' den."

Darcy snapped her fingers. "Aphisha. We need to talk to her and right now."

Chapter Twelve

A quick call to Brother Thomas and Darcy, Shelby, and I met him at his church, the only place of worship that seemed to allow dogs. Or at least my dog. He rested a hand on the lectern facing the empty sanctuary. "What you want to worry that poor child for?"

I said, "You know why."

The pastor turned his head slowly from side to side, mumbling something to himself. Shelby nuzzled his pant leg and Brother Thomas reached down and scratched behind his ears.

Darcy said, "We need this, Brother Thomas. I think you know that."

"All I know is that poor child been through enough."

I said, "I can't help it if you don't like where this is headed."

"Brother Brack," the preacher said, straightening up, "you of all people should know I don't truck to being no victim."

Shelby moved and stood beside Darcy.

Brother Thomas gave another head turn and mumble. Then he said, "Okay."

"Where is she?" Darcy asked.

"Come on." Brother Thomas walked past us to the door. "At her grandmother's. I already called and told them we was comin' over, mm-hmm."

Darcy's eyes met mine. I nodded at her unspoken question. Brother Thomas was not happy. The three of us, Darcy, Shelby, and me, turned and trailed him outside.

"You better ride with me," he said.

We got in his donated Volvo. It was an expensive car before it had gotten riddled with bullet holes. Brother Thomas had accepted the car and had the local kids fix it up. They'd done such a nice job I couldn't tell where the damage had been done.

With me and Shelby in the backseat and Darcy in the front, Brother Thomas drove the two blocks to where Aphisha now lived. We could have walked there but I got the impression that Brother Thomas didn't feel up to it in this heat. Clara Jasper opened the door to greet us, holding her cane. Aphisha ran to Brother Thomas and gave him a hug.

He said, "Hey, little girl."

"Sorry to bother you this evening, Mrs. Jasper," I said.

Aphisha spotted Shelby and stuck her hand in her mouth. Shelby inched close to her, lowering to a crawl. When he was a foot away, he rolled over on his back. Aphisha tentatively reached her hand out and gave his belly a pat. He licked her face and before long, she had both hands working his fur, his back leg going a mile a minute.

Clara Jasper said, "Brother Thomas be tellin' me you doin' all you can to find out what happen to Willa Mae. He say you wanna ask Aphisha somethin'."

She gave a slight chuckle. "Depend on what it is you wanna ask, now don't it?"

"It might help us figure out what happened to her sister," Darcy said.

"Then I guess you better ask your questions." The elderly woman called to her granddaughter. "Aphisha, come inside, hear? These people wanna talk to you."

Aphisha finally stood and approached me. "Hello, Mr. Brack."

She wore a pink T-shirt and green shorts and looked at me with her bright eyes.

I knelt and put a hand on her shoulder. "Hello, Aphisha. How are you?"

"I'm okay," she said. "I like stayin' with Grams."

Brother Thomas said, "Let's go inside before the neighbors start talkin', mm-hmm."

"Do you mind if my dog comes in?" I asked. "He won't bother anything."

Clara said, "He's a good-lookin' dog. I don't mind."

Aphisha let me pick her up and carry her in. Darcy, Shelby, and the preacher followed. Mrs. Jasper closed the screen door behind us. The small home did not have air-conditioning and it was still eighty-five degrees outside. We crowded into a spotless living room. I set Aphisha down and she and her grandmother sat on a worn couch. Brother Thomas leaned against the wall because there weren't any other seats in the room.

Darcy sat herself on the threadbare carpet. I followed her lead, surprised by her humility.

Shelby found a spot beside Darcy and rested his head in her lap.

Brother Thomas said, "Aphisha, honey. These folk wanna know about that night you was with Willa Mae."

The little girl crossed her arms and tapped a foot. "Uh-huh."

I asked, "How did you get there?"

Her bright eyes took me in but she didn't say anything.

"What Brother Brack means," Brother Thomas said, "is what were you and Willa Mae doing?"

She said, "Willa Mae?" It was a question.

"Yes, dear," Darcy said, rubbing Shelby behind his ears, "Willa Mae."

"Um, we was walkin' around."

"At midnight?" I asked.

Aphisha dropped her head.

Brother Thomas stooped down to her. "Aphisha, you ain't in

no trouble. We just wanna know what you all was doin'. It might help us find what happened to Willa Mae."

"Grams said she with Jesus."

Mrs. Jasper said, "That's right, chile. She is. We all miss her so much." The old woman choked up. "Talk to these people, Aphisha. Tell 'em why you was with Willa."

"Um, Willa said we needed to get something."

Darcy stiffened.

It took all I had not to react.

Brother Thomas said, "You know what she needed to get?"

"No. She didn't tell me."

I asked, "Can you tell us which house you were at?"

"Towanda's."

Darcy looked at me. Not knowing who Towanda was, I shrugged and figured Brother Thomas knew her.

He patted her head. "That's real good, girl."

"How'd you get there?" I asked.

"We walked," she said.

Darcy asked, "Did you go for a ride in Willa's car?"

"Yeah, she got a brown one."

Brother Thomas stood. "Thank y'all for your time. Sister Darcy, Brother Brack, we can go back to my office now."

My favorite reporter opened her mouth to say something. Brother Thomas put a finger to his lips and pointed to the front door.

In the car outside Mrs. Jasper's, I asked the obvious question, "Who's Towanda?"

"The local midwife. Unofficially, of course, mm-hmm."

I said, "Well, we know where we need to go next."

Brother Thomas faced me.

"Stop wasting time," I said. "Let's go see this Towanda. Then we've got to find Willa's car."

Five minutes later, Brother Thomas pulled the Volvo to a stop in the exact spot where I'd parked my truck the night Willa Mae was shot. We got out and went to the door of the house I'd ducked behind while running with Aphisha. The same house where the police had found and dug out the bullets that missed me and Aphisha. Bullets that had been fired from the gun found in the back of my truck.

The preacher walked up the two steps and onto the concrete pad that made up the front porch. At the door, he paused and faced us. "Remember, let me do all the talkin'."

I nodded.

Darcy remained silent.

He knocked on the screen door.

Through the screen and the thin front door, we heard a woman's voice say, "Hold on."

After a moment of clicking locks, the door opened. Standing in the yellow light was a thin, light-skinned black woman. She was Darcy's height with shoulder-length curly black hair that fell in rolls. Streaks of beige colored her white T-shirt. The smell of freshly applied latex paint wafted out the open door.

She said, "Hello, Brother."

"Sister Towanda, sorry to bother you this evening. This here's Sister Darcy and Brother Brack." Pointing to my dog, he said, "And that is Mr. Shelby. He doin' some volunteer work at the church."

Shelby sniffed Towanda's hand and she patted his head.

"Please come in." She held the door open for us. The lighting cast the age lines of her face in shadows. Her eyes were clear and her gaze determined.

Ceiling fans blew full blast along with two floor units she'd set up on the weathered hardwood plank floor. The house was small and Towanda was in the middle of repainting her living room a light beige, the same color staining her shirt.

We stood in a small entryway.

"Thanks for letting us interrupt your work," I said.

She wiped her forehead with her arm. "It's okay. I need a break. Can I get you all something to drink?"

"Um, no thanks," Brother Thomas said. "Towanda, the reason we here is 'cause Aphisha told us she and Willa Mae had been here visiting you the night Willa got shot."

Towanda studied my face for a few seconds. "You're the one who saved Aphisha, aren't you?"

I nodded.

She looked at Darcy. "And you're a news reporter."

"Yes, ma'am," Darcy said.

"I enjoy your segments. And anyone who protects Aphisha is a friend." She took a deep breath. "Yes, they came to see me that night."

"What for?" I asked, impatient that I had to ask it.

Shelby offered a paw to Towanda.

She took it and gave him another pat. "This is hard to talk about."

Brother Thomas said, "We buried her this morning. Anything you have to say might help us find out what the police don't seem to want to."

The midwife straightened up. "Don't you think I know that?" She took a deep breath. "Okay. Willa Mae had been coming to see me because she got pregnant."

Shelby circled the floor by Darcy's feet and plopped down. His eyes were closed soon after.

"Pregnant?" The question slipped out before I could stop it. Her diary had talked about her trying to play Jon-Jon, but I didn't expect her to actually turn up pregnant. Of course, why else would she be visiting a midwife?

"Yes," Towanda said. "But she lost the baby that night."

"You mean she had a miscarriage?" Darcy asked.

Towanda nodded.

I said, "We checked out her apartment and found that she had been sick."

"She had been trying to detox," Towanda said.

Darcy asked, "So you knew about her drug use?"

The midwife looked at Darcy when she answered. "Of course. I told her I wouldn't help her unless she got clean."

"Did she have a relapse?" I asked.

"More like she'd weaned herself off."

Brother Thomas asked, "What does that mean?"

The midwife picked up a sweating plastic cup and took a long drink. "Willa was snorting a gram a day when she got pregnant and came to see me. She cut her daily fix a little each day for ten days."

"We saw her apartment," I said. "It was not a pretty sight."

"She had morning sickness on top of everything else."

Darcy asked, "How was she paying her rent?"

The midwife gave us a tight-lipped smile.

We waited for a reply that didn't come.

Brother Thomas said, "Towanda, Willa Mae's dead. Someone killed her and burned her up in a trash barrel."

"I told you I know that," she said, her voice rising.

"These two friends of mine are the only ones tryin' to find the one who done it. Please talk to them."

"Are you in danger?" I asked.

Towanda sat down on an old green couch and wiped tears from her eyes. "Willa was trying. The baby changed her. I saw it in her eyes. She stopped working for her madam."

"So then help us," Darcy said.

A thought came to mind. One I didn't want to believe. I said, "She was still turning tricks, wasn't she?"

Towanda glared at me. "Yes. You happy now that you know?"

"So, who were her clients?" I asked.

The midwife to the poor said, "I don't know."

Brother Thomas asked, “Where she meet them?”

“I don’t know.”

“Can you think of anything that might help us find who killed her?” Darcy asked.

“All I know,” Towanda said, “is she got a lawyer to work for her. Someone named Sykes.”

Darcy took out a pad and wrote down the name.

I wondered what she needed a lawyer for. Unless it had been for the baby. “One last question,” I said. “Do you know why Aphisha was with Willa Mae that night?”

“Not sure,” the midwife said. “Aphisha normally stayed with her grandmother. I guess Willa wanted to spend time with her. Something told me she hadn’t been there for her much before.”

We tried to find Willa Mae’s car and struck out, even with Darcy’s limitless resources. Willa Mae must not have registered it, therefore leaving no digital or paper trail. However, the lawyer, if one could call him such, was named Gordon Sykes. Early Saturday morning, I had Chauncey Conners, my lawyer and fellow Isle of Palms resident, look him up for me, and the report was not good.

Chauncey said, “Your Mr. Gordon Sykes, Esquire, as he likes to be called, gives ambulance chasers a bad name.”

“I wasn’t expecting Perry Mason,” I said.

“I’m not quite sure what his client base is, but the few inquiries I made had him representing low-end drug dealers and prostitutes. Probably the absolute bottom of the barrel, and all of their cases beginning with an arrest of some kind.”

“Anything else?” I asked.

“His office is on the outskirts of town. I have the address here if you want it.”

After I got it, I hung up with him. Paige called soon after.

She asked, “Where have you been?”

"Guess," I said.

After a pause, she did. "You've been looking into the murder of that dead girl, haven't you?"

I didn't respond.

"Of course you have," she said. "Well, I'm not even going to comment on that. You see, we have another problem now."

"What's that?"

"Somehow all our purchasing records have been wiped out. Normally that would just be an inconvenience except that since we've applied for another license to sell alcohol, we need to show proof that we're obtaining it legally. We can't do that now. The state has placed a hold on our request for a new license pending investigation, as they put it. It's still pending, but now flagged for further inquiry."

"This keeps getting better and better." I said. "Call Chauncey and let him know. See if he has any suggestions."

Chapter Thirteen

The afternoon was just as hot as the day before. Brother Thomas, Darcy, and I watched through the windshield of my truck as a skinny white guy we guessed to be Gordon Sykes, Esquire, stepped out of Sykes & Associates, a grungy steel and glass structure book-ended by two vacant offices for lease. He wore a light-colored suit that looked as if he'd slept in it. Since it was Saturday, maybe he lived at his office. His bald head boasted a few long strands he must have greased into place because they gleamed in the sun when he looked up and down the street.

I tapped the steering wheel. "He feels us watching him." With his client base, Sykes probably had the clichéd eyes in the back of his head.

From the backseat, Darcy said, "You don't know that."

We were parked across the street from his office in a lot where most of the vehicles looked abandoned. If Mr. Sykes knew what he was looking for, such as a brand new chrome-laden pickup truck with three of the strangest carpoolers this side of a flea market, we wouldn't stand a chance at fulfilling our plan. Lucky for us he didn't know what to look for and spent a few more seconds glancing around before locking up. He made his way along the cracked sidewalk, past the rundown storefronts his law firm shared space with, stopping at an old Pontiac Grand Prix with a sagging headliner. Scanning the street one last time, he got in the car and drove away in a cloud of blue smoke.

When he turned left at a four-way stop, I started the truck, pulled out, and punched it, heading in the opposite direction.

Darcy asked, "Where are you going?"

I ran a stop sign, hung a right, floored the accelerator, and did the same thing at the next intersection. Another stop sign ahead would put us perpendicular to Sykes. As we approached the corner, his Grand Prix crossed in front of us. I flipped on my left turn signal, came to a complete stop, let a car get behind Sykes, then followed when it was my turn to go.

Brother Thomas said, "Except for the two stop signs you didn't stop for, nice doing."

"You got lucky," Darcy said.

I looked at her from the rearview mirror. She was smiling.

"Thanks a lot," I said.

"Any time," she said. "Just don't lose him."

Sykes pulled into a turning lane.

I trailed behind and realized where our mark was headed. Mutt and I had been there five days ago. "It couldn't be that easy."

"Easy?" Brother Thomas said. "Nothing about this been what I call easy."

The Treasure Chest was open but not very busy. It was still early.

I said, "We may have to go get Mutt."

We watched Gordon Sykes, Esquire, pull into the parking lot of the one place I should have known he'd eventually head to. Willa Mae must have had prior contact with Sykes somewhere. Anyone looking in the phonebook or on the internet for an attorney wouldn't have found him listed. Chauncey said Sykes's clients lived under rocks and didn't come out until after dark. And they usually didn't call him until they needed to get out of jail.

I said, "I wonder who's headlining tonight."

Darcy said, "I'm surprised you don't already know."

"Quiet, you two." Brother Thomas did not suffer fools.

I drove past the strip club and no one spoke for a half mile. Brother Thomas ended the silence.

"I believe Brother Brack is right. Any of us go in there and it won't be pretty." He dug out his cell phone and searched his contacts.

I turned at the next side street and headed for Mutt's house. He'd said to call him if we needed any help. Otherwise he'd be playing dominoes with Willie.

"So lemme get this straight," Mutt said from the backseat of my truck. "You want me to go inside and sweet-talk a crooked lawyer?"

"Close enough," I said. "You think you can get around the manager we beat up?"

"Yeah," Mutt said, "he got fired 'cause of that. How'm I supposed to get this lawyer outside?"

I handed him a hundred-dollar bill. "Show this to him. Tell him you need to talk and you'll give it to him outside."

Mutt said, "You think he'll bite?"

"He's a starving vulture," Darcy said. "He'll probably lick the bathroom clean for a twenty."

Mutt laughed. "What happen when we get outside?"

"We be watching," Brother Thomas said. "When you get him out the door, bring him over here and we'll have a talk."

"He see ya'll and he'll run," Mutt said.

"Then he loses the hundred and we go to plan B," I said.

Mutt shook his head. "Plan B? You got a plan B?"

"I got a few ideas," I said. "Most of them will violate his civil rights if it comes to that." Handing him more bills, I said, "Here's for the cover charge and the drink minimum."

"There's a drink minimum?" Darcy asked and chuckled.

Mutt folded the bills and stuck them in his pocket. "Opie, I always said you was one crazy white boy. Now you got Twiggy and Fat Albert in wit you." He opened his door and got out, letting the door close on its own. We watched him enter the club.

Darcy asked, "Did he just call me Twiggy?"

"Naw," I said. "You're Fat Albert. Twiggy's up here riding shotgun."

Brother Thomas said, "Who in the Good Lord is Twiggy?"

The clock in the dash said 5:05.

At 5:09, Mutt and Sykes walked out the front door of the strip club. Mutt guided the lawyer beside my truck and the three of us got out.

Sykes said, "I didn't know it was going to be some kind of white trash reunion."

"Mr. Sykes," Brother Thomas said, "we'd like a moment of your time."

"The hundred bucks or I'm leaving," Sykes said. "This goes past two minutes and it's another hundred."

Sykes was Darcy's height, which meant he was a few inches shorter than me. Half a foot shorter compared to Brother Thomas and Mutt.

Mutt handed him the hundred.

Sykes smiled, showing an almost full mouth of teeth, took the money, and slipped it into his shirt pocket. "Now, what can I do for you fine people?"

Darcy said, "Why did Willa Mae Johnson retain you?"

"I'm afraid I can't divulge any information about my clients," Sykes said. "Attorney-client privilege."

"We're not cops," I said.

"Still," Sykes said, looking at his watch.

I handed him a twenty.

"The deal was for another hundred," he said.

I said, "That's for good faith on our end. Why not return the sentiment and give us something?"

Sykes looked at the folded money clip in my hand thick with more twenties, licked his lips, and wiped beads of sweat off his forehead. He checked his watch and seemed to be contemplating something.

Finally, he said, "I represented her."

I handed him another twenty.

Darcy said, "In what capacity?"

"As legal counsel," he said.

"I figure that's what's meant by her retaining you," Brother Thomas said. "Come on, Mr. Sykes, tell us something we don't know."

"Look, my girl comes on in five minutes. I been looking forward to seeing her dance all day."

"You answer a few more questions and I'll make sure you have enough for a trip to the champagne room," I said. "Mutt and I already know how much it costs."

Sykes's beady eyes seemed to brighten at the prospect. He licked his lips again. "Okay, but make it fast."

"Why were you representing Willa Mae?" Darcy asked.

"She was pregnant," he said.

I asked, "And?"

Sykes smiled. "And she wanted to make sure the father was going to pay his fair share."

Brother Thomas said, "How much was she thinkin' his fair share was?"

"Normally," Sykes said, as if he handled paternity cases all the time, "it's based on the financial means of the father."

Already knowing where this was headed, I asked, "Who was she thinking the father was?"

"You say that as if there might be some doubt," Sykes said.

"Well," I said, "she was a drug addict who stripped and also used prostitution as a means to fund her lifestyle."

Darcy said, "Did you get a paternity test?"

"We were going to make the father ask for one," Sykes said.

"And pay for it," Darcy said.

"Of course," Sykes said. "Now if you don't mind, I need to get back inside."

Brother Thomas said, "We ain't done yet."

Darcy said, "How did she pay you?"

"That's not relevant here," Sykes said.

I snatched his shirt collar and lifted him off the ground. "Make an exception."

"Hey!" His feet scissored in midair trying to find where the earth had gone. "Get your hands off me."

"I suggest you answer the questions we axin', Mr. Sykes," Mutt said. "Else we might have to go to plan B."

Sykes's eyes bulged in their sockets. "Pl-plan B?"

"Plan B," Darcy said.

I lifted him higher.

"Okay! Okay!" he said. "I'll answer your questions."

As soon as I lowered him to the ground, he tried to run.

Brother Thomas grabbed him. "You don't want to do that, Mr. Sykes. Mm-hmm."

"You people're crazy," Sykes said, his beady eyes now large and bloodshot.

Mutt grinned, showing his missing teeth. "Now you gettin' the picture."

Darcy said, "How much did Willa Mae pay you?"

The shyster ran a hand over his head, repositioning an errant strand that had shifted from its perch. "My end would be covered with the settlement."

Darcy said, "Again, who was the father?"

Sykes said, "Where's the rest of my money?"

I held up another hundred.

"Uh-uh," Sykes said. "This one's gonna cost you."

Mutt stepped forward and Brother Thomas stopped him.

"How much?" Darcy asked.

"Ten grand," Sykes said.

"Yeah, right," I said.

"I got a deal for you, Mr. Sykes," Darcy said. "You can tell us here for five hundred dollars or you can tell the police for free. Your choice."

"Ten grand," Sykes said. "That's my price."

I took hold of his shirt again.

Brother Thomas said, "Let him go."

I did and Sykes took off, ducking fast inside the Treasure Chest.

Darcy said, "I guess we better make our exit before the bouncers come after us."

"You kiddin'?" Mutt said. "Them guys too busy watching the show to worry about anything out here."

"We still didn't get what we came for," I said.

Darcy tapped her chin. "You think Sykes might be playing the other side?"

Brother Thomas asked, "What you mean by that?"

"Blackmail," I said. "Sykes probably already cut a deal with the father."

After another two-hour session with my personal trainer and then a shower, Shelby and I made our way to my bar.

Bonny flew over and landed on my shoulder.

"Hey, pretty girl," I said.

She nibbled at my ear. "Hi, Brack. *Squawk!*"

"I wish all women treated me as good as you do," I said.

Paige came through the doors from the kitchen. "Don't listen to him, Bonny."

Bonny flew up to her perch and whistled.

"She's just playing hard to get," I said. "What's the word from Chauncey?"

"He says we can still operate as long as our application for a replacement license is still pending."

"Good. What about actually getting it in our hands?"

"He's still working on that, but said the state operates at its own speed and it's never as fast as you want it to be."

"Hear, hear," I said.

Paige reached underneath the bar and pulled out a box that she set on the bar. "This came today. Think we need to call the bomb squad?"

Though she said this with a smile, having been a target already I didn't find the remark all that funny. I gently lifted the box and looked at it. It showed the markings of being one of an express overnight delivery. The sender's address read the Church of Redemption. "You saw the delivery driver leave it?"

Her smile faded. "I signed for it. Don't be so melodramatic. Brother Thomas probably cooked up another one of his schemes to keep us coming to Sunday service."

The box weighed only a couple of pounds so I wasn't too worried about a bomb. I pulled out my cell and called Brother Thomas.

He said, "Brother Brack."

"Hey, Brother. You send me a package?"

" 'Scuse me?"

"An overnight package arrived at my bar today. The sender is your church."

He didn't say anything.

I looked at Paige. "I'll take that as a no."

"As far as I know, no one here sent any packages. You think something hinky is going on?"

"Thinking that way's kept me alive this long," I said. "I'm calling the police."

★ ★ ★ ★ ★

Detective Warrez and her partner, Crawford, showed up an hour later. I'd had the single mom army close up early, but most had stuck around to see what would happen. As soon as Crawford saw the group of attractive women that made up the bar's wait staff, his disposition brightened significantly.

Warrez carried a navy blue canvas bag slung over her shoulder and set it on one of the barstools close to the package. From the bag, she pulled out latex gloves and put them on. Then she took out some hand-held device. "This sniffer will check for anything toxic, like anthrax."

A few of the waitresses gasped.

The device was similar in size and shape to one of those supermarket scanners that do inventory counts. Warrez turned it on and moved its green light over every inch of the box, keeping it close to the package and taking extra time at each end. Nothing happened.

She looked at me. "It's not detecting anything."

"The box is pretty light," I said. "Maybe a pound or two."

Warrez put the scanner down on the bar and picked up the box. She pulled the strip that opened one of the sides and bent the flaps back. As she peeked inside I noticed everyone lean in for a closer look. Then Warrez said, "Detective Crawford, get me one of the large evidence bags."

He dug into the navy blue canvas bag, snapped on a pair of latex gloves, and pulled out a plastic bag that opened to the size of a pillow case. Warrez emptied the contents of the box into the bag. What dumped out was clothing. It appeared to be women's things. The last item to drop out was a gold chain. I couldn't tell for sure, but it looked like it held a pendant. I think I glimpsed a heart with a red stone and immediately thought of the gift Brother Thomas had said he'd given Willa Mae for her sixteenth birthday.

Warrez looked at Crawford and then at me. "Recognize any of this?"

I met her eyes and nodded yes.

Chapter Fourteen

The evidence bag filled with the contents of the box was sealed tight and sat on the desk in my office. Warrez, Crawford, Paige, and I stood around it.

"All right, Brack," Warrez said. "What do you know about this stuff?"

I pressed a button on the office phone that activated the speaker, then dialed a number I'd memorized.

"Church of Redemption," said a woman's voice.

I said, "Merlyne, this is Brack. Is Brother Thomas around?"

"He is but he's busy with someone right now."

"I hate to impose, but could you tell him it's important? It will only take a minute of his time."

"I'll see," she said. "You know he don't like interruptions." She put me on hold.

Warrez said, "How is this going to answer my question?"

I held up an index finger, telling her to wait.

Brother Thomas's voice boomed over the speaker. "What's up, Brother Brack?"

"Sorry to bother you," I said, "and I want you to know you're on speaker phone. I've got Detective Warrez and her partner, Detective Crawford, with me, along with Paige."

The preacher said, "How y'all doin'?"

"Fine, sir," Warrez said.

"What I want to ask you," I said, "is to tell me again what you gave Willa Mae for her sixteenth birthday."

I picked up the evidence bag and turned it so we could all see the chain and pendant while Brother Thomas described each item to us over the phone.

Warrez asked Brother Thomas, "Did you get anything engraved on it, like her initials or a message?"

"Um, no," he said, "but if you opened it up, it would have a picture of Jesus inside."

Crawford snapped on fresh gloves, opened the evidence bag, and took out the necklace. Each of us watched as the detective unlatched the locket, revealing two tiny heart-shaped frames. One held a very small picture of Jesus. The other held a photo of a child, Aphisha.

Paige said, "I don't believe it."

I sat down in the chair that used to be my uncle's.

Brother Thomas said, "Are you still there, Brother Brack?"

"Yes, we're still here."

He asked, "Did you find the locket?"

"You could say that," Warrez said. "We're going to need you to identify it for us in person, Reverend."

"It's Brother Thomas, and I'd like to say I'd be glad to, but it will probably break my heart."

"I understand," Warrez said. "When is a good time?"

"I have to finish up something here," he said. "I can be ready in about an hour and a half, if that's okay with you, mm-hmm."

Warrez looked at her watch. "Mr. Pelton and I will see you at your church then. Thank you."

None of us gathered in my office said a word. Eventually I looked at Paige and she said, "Why would someone send this to you?"

I shrugged.

"Could be many reasons," Crawford said. "Intimidation. Whoever it is might be taunting you."

Warrez said, "If that is Willa Mae's necklace and her clothes, whoever sent it knows you've been looking into her murder."

"Everyone in the projects knows that," I said. "Brother Thomas announced it in his service."

Detective Warrez left her partner behind together with their cruiser and the Cove's attractive group and rode with me and Shelby to the Church of Redemption.

Whoever sent the package was one sick individual. It didn't make any sense. Why send it to me? Why not have just burned it up with the body?

Whatever the reason, at least Warrez couldn't say I wasn't playing fair. If I'd thrown caution to the wind and opened the box myself, the contents would have been next to useless in court. Or they could be used to try and nail me for the murder. At least this way, the evidence followed a more incontrovertible chain of custody. And I'd sidestepped the proverbial landmine.

Inside the Church of Redemption, Warrez and I sat with Brother Thomas in his office. The necklace and pendant rested in a separate plastic evidence bag.

Warrez said, "I'm sorry to have to ask, Brother, but are you sure that's her necklace?"

Brother Thomas nodded when Detective Warrez handed it to him. "Yes. There ain't none others like it. I bought it in the Market about five years ago. There was a local woman. Made it herself. She still live here in town. She can tell you about it."

Warrez touched his massive shoulder.

Brother Thomas wiped his eyes and took a deep breath, seeming to gather an inner strength. It looked to me like he'd faced this kind of grief before and knew he had to pull himself together and keep going.

On the drive back, Warrez said, "So why are you still involved in this, anyway?"

"Brother Thomas asked me to. And Willa Mae earned it when she took the bullet for me and Aphisha." I passed the entrance ramp to the bridge that would take us back to the island, continuing instead down East Bay Street.

Warrez asked, "Are we taking a detour?"

Turning onto Market Street, I found a parking spot on a side street. "I had the sudden urge for a double scoop of Pralines and Cream. How about you?"

Shelby barked his approval. I opened my door and let him out. He waited dutifully while I snapped on his leash. Warrez still sat in the truck. Through the open rear door, I asked, "Well, are you coming?"

"I guess I don't have much of a choice," she said and opened her door.

"On the contrary," I said. "We have all kinds of choices. It's the one thing we've got free and clear. I learned that from Brother Thomas."

Warrez offered her hand and Shelby gave it a friendly lick.

"Your dog is one well-trained chick magnet," she said.

"He told me so when I found him in the shelter," I said.

We walked to the ice cream parlor and I handed Warrez the money to get us our cones so I could stay outside with Shelby. Even in the middle of the week the shops around the Old City Market were busy. People talked and laughed as they passed us, and a few, mostly women and children, stopped to pet Shelby.

Warrez came out of the shop, handed me my cone, and set a small cup of what looked like vanilla on the ground for Shelby. He licked her face before diving into the treat. She had gotten herself a single scoop of chocolate, I had my Pralines and Cream, and we stood there, quiet, and enjoyed the evening.

At least, we tried to enjoy the evening. We both knew that a killer had sent me the trophies of his victim, a twenty-two-year-old who had been trying to get herself straight so she could be a responsible mother to one child, a good sister to another. Her killer's gift to me was a mocking gesture and only stirred the coals burning inside of me. And my friend was back in his church picking up the pieces of Willa Mae's life.

After finishing our ice cream, we sat on the tailgate of my pickup. Detective Warrez phoned her partner and told him not to wait for her. Shelby slept behind us in the truck bed.

When she hung up, Warrez turned to me and said, "He's still at your bar."

"Of course he is," I said. "I just hope he likes kids."

Warrez laughed. "I heard about your manager's propensity for hiring single mothers."

I caught the sight of a late model Crown Victoria creeping past us for the second time. Dark tinted windows hid the occupants. Purple metal-flake paint shimmered in the street lights like glitter. And like one of the cars that chased me and Mutt. The twenty-four-inch rims it rolled on were so ten years ago, but that didn't bother the current crop of gangster wanna-bes. Fat exhaust pipes angled out from under each side of the back bumper.

On this second lap past us the passenger window of the car rolled down and something poked out. I shoved Warrez down onto the bed of the truck to shield her with my body, and grabbed Shelby's collar to hold him down.

A staccato round of bullets fired from a submachine gun. It busted the back window of my truck. Shelby went nuts barking. I heard the Crown Vic's engine rev and speed away.

Immediately Detective Warrez pushed me off her, jumped down from the truck, and pulled her Glock in one fluid motion. She stood in the middle of the street, squinting, apparently trying to get a plate number. I had a hunch that the light bulbs illuminating the license would not be functioning, if the car even had a plate.

Luckily, because it was a side street there were no tourists. Shelby was shaking and whining as I stroked his fur to calm him down. For his sake I kept my reaction in check, thinking it was time to pay the gangbangers a visit of my own.

The police were nice enough to impound my truck. It was evidence, though I had a feeling that the damage caused by the bullets was about to multiply as the crime scene technicians attempted to dig out each one. I would feel every dollar of my insurance deductible on this one. My history of claims for damaged vehicles already had me on the probationary list.

The Mayor arrived not too long after. After a long discussion with Warrez and her commanding officer, they decided damage control was in order. For the good of the city. Surprisingly, it included the truth, which was that this was a specific gang-related issue and not some kind of terrorist attack. The fact that no innocent tourist had been involved helped.

Of course, Darcy showed up with her camera crew and did a segment.

While Detective Warrez and I watched Darcy from the sidelines, Warrez said, "You don't seem fazed by almost getting shot just off Market Street."

"I'm getting kinda used to it," I said.

Her partner, Detective Crawford, arrived and gave us lifts home.

Chapter Fifteen

The next morning, Darcy picked me up at my house. Using every resource at her disposal, she'd tracked the girl from Willa Mae's funeral, Camilla, to a rehabilitation center in West Ashley. How Willa Mae's friend got there and who was providing financial assistance were unknowns that even Darcy's deep pockets hadn't unearthed yet.

A woman with short hair, a middle-age paunch, and inquisitive brown eyes asked us to sit in a waiting area while she requested permission for us to speak with Camilla.

After ten minutes, someone else, this one a tall woman wearing a gray business suit, white blouse, and low-heeled shoes, greeted us. She introduced herself as Dr. Townsend.

Darcy and I explained why we wanted to speak with Camilla.

"In situations like this," Dr. Townsend said, "it is up to my discretion as to whether or not it is appropriate for our guests to have contact with outside influences."

"Neither of us knows Camilla," I said. "She attended the funeral of the woman whose murder we are looking into."

"Shouldn't the police be leading that investigation?" Dr. Townsend asked.

"Yes, they should," said Darcy. "Unfortunately, the victim was from the poor side of town and not exactly a model citizen."

"I see," the doctor said. "And how do you think Camilla can help you?"

"We'd like to discuss her relationship with the victim," I said.

"If she knew Willa Mae well, Camilla might be able to give us better insight."

We played it straight with the good doctor, something I wouldn't necessarily do. But in this case, we figured the truth would earn us more points. And it did, as Dr. Townsend agreed to our request.

Darcy and I waited for Camilla underneath a pavilion at a picnic table on the grounds. Ten minutes passed and then we saw her. Black hair to her shoulders, the same black-rimmed sunglasses, and ivory skin. Camilla was blessed with a very full figure—sort of a white Mariah Carey. She sat at the table in front of us, removed a Camel Light from a pack of cigarettes, and lit it with a purple Bic lighter. "You're with Channel Nine News, aren't you?"

"Yes," Darcy said, "But the camera crew isn't here."

"I can see that," Camilla said. She looked at me closely. "I know you, too."

I raised my eyebrows and felt my blood tickle my ears and cheeks.

In all of my inconsolable escapades after I returned from war, I never woke up with a woman like Camilla. At least, not one that asked me for any money afterward.

"Not like that," she said. "I mean, I know you from somewhere."

"He's been on TV almost as much as I have," Darcy said. "I report the news, but Brack has a habit of making it."

Camilla smiled. She had a really nice smile. It seemed genuine.

"I've been there." She took a drag from her cigarette.

I really wanted to find out what news she'd made, but figured Darcy knew or could find out.

"Thanks for agreeing to meet with us," Darcy said.

"We have a lot of group therapy here," Camilla said. "It's a nice break not to have to listen to another train wreck. I've heard enough on ways to self-destruct to last me quite awhile, thank you very much."

I said, "We would like to know what you can tell us about Willa Mae."

"What makes you think I know someone by that name?"

"We saw Aphisha hug you at her sister's funeral," Darcy said. "And you seemed to have an effect on Boy Wonder, here."

Camilla gave me another big smile and turned back to Darcy. "Okay, so how'd you find me?"

"Darcy has sources all over this town," I said.

Camilla took a deep drag on her cigarette. She let the smoke turn around in her lungs, exhaled, and seemed to go deep within herself. After a few seconds, she took off her sunglasses and looked at me. Brown eyes showed resolve. "Me and Willa Mae were special. Caroline used us for her higher-paying clients. The men liked Willa Mae because she looked like she came right from the islands. Tie some towels around that girl and they thought they were with an Amazon princess or something. I'm not sure why they liked me so much."

"I can think of a few reasons," Darcy said. "I'm sure Brack can, too."

Camilla gave me that grin again and I felt my ears heat up.

"Anyway," she said, taking a last puff before she stubbed the butt out on the concrete floor of the pavilion, "there was really about six of us. Caroline sent us all together a lot. Parties. Conventions. Elections. A lot of the time it was the same group of men. Very exclusive. I'm not sure how much she got but we were making a lot of money. Enough to support a very expensive coke habit, anyway."

"Who's Caroline?" I asked.

"My employer."

Darcy said, "You think she's connected to Willa Mae's death?"

Camilla frowned. "I don't know. When Willa dropped out, I was shoving a gram a day up my nose. My only thought was for the next party. We were all just simple, stupid girls. Willa Mae from the projects. Me from the trailer park. All that mattered was how we looked."

I asked, "How did you end up with Caroline?"

Camilla's dark eyes brightened. "You mean instead of walking the street with a crack pipe in my purse?"

"Um—"

Camilla touched my arm. "I'm sorry. That was uncalled for."

"He deserved it," Darcy said.

"No," Camilla said, "he didn't. I know the path I took is just another version of the same story. At least, I realize that now. I honestly can't answer the question."

Darcy said, "Do you mind telling us how you got started?"

"I'm nothing but a cliché," Camilla said. "Bad home life. Stepfather started spending the night in my room instead of my mom's. At first, she acted like nothing was going on, then blamed me for taking her man, which might have been true except I was thirteen. So, I ran. All the way from North Charleston. Met up with a group of other runaways. We stole to get money for nice clothes. The nice clothes got us into the nicer clubs. The nicer clubs got us rich boys. The rich boys gave us good drugs. The good drugs got us hooked. And that got me tricking. Rafe found me in the clubs and got me to join their 'organization,' as they called it. Suddenly, I had a great apartment and didn't have to steal any more. And the rich boys became older rich men."

Darcy asked, "And Rafe is . . . ?"

"Caroline's underling. He does whatever she needs him to do. And I mean anything."

I said, "Tell us about Willa Mae."

Camilla lit a second cigarette. "Most girls are too easy. A few shots of vodka and they're ready to give it up on the dance floor. Girls like Willa Mae and me, we knew what to look for. Money and attitude. The ones that liked paying for it. Liked thinking they owned us.

"Willa was really smart, ya know? Like street smart. At least, up until the moment she fell in love and dropped out of sight."

Darcy said, "Fell in love?"

Camilla blew out a stream of smoke. "Yeah, like she had the look." She touched Darcy's arm. "You know what I'm talking about . . . the look? Like everything all of a sudden is a bag of candy."

"So who was the lucky guy?" I asked, wondering if she knew about Willa Mae's diary and that she'd been in it.

"Not sure," Camilla said. "She just wasn't into the johns any more. Her regulars started complaining. Caroline tried to talk to her but it was a lost cause. Like telling the cat not to touch the catnip."

Darcy asked, "She continued to work?"

Camilla held her cigarette between the two fingers of her left hand. "I'm not a hundred percent sure, but I don't think it was too much longer after all this started that she left."

I asked, "How long ago was this?"

"Maybe a month. I OD'd right after the funeral and here I am." She waved her arm around.

"Better than the alternative," I said.

Camilla's eyes met mine. "You fought in Afghanistan, didn't you? And now you own a bar or something on one of the islands."

"Yes."

The smile returned to Camilla's face. "Aren't you a little old to be going to war?"

"I had a death wish," I said. "Kind of like doing coke and tricking."

I expected her smile to leave, but it didn't. Camilla just kept smoking her cigarette and I realized she'd already made the association between our self-destructive behaviors. She wanted to see if I had. Any time a beautiful woman was involved, I always seemed to take the bait. And be at least a few steps behind.

"Wow," Camilla said, "a judge and a gentleman."

"And that's not the half of it," I said.

Camilla said, "No kidding."

"Can we get back on track, please?" Darcy had more than a hint of annoyance in her voice.

"Absolutely," I said.

Darcy asked, "Why would someone kill Willa Mae?"

Camilla shrugged. "I don't know."

I said, "You got any idea who might have?"

"There was this guy," Camilla said. "About two years ago, we're in this club doing our thing and this guy grabs Willa and tries to drag her out of the place. The bouncers and a few others beat him up. It was ugly. We didn't make any money that night."

"He got a name?" I asked.

Camilla reached over and touched my cheek. She retracted her hand and said, "I asked Willa, but she just blew it off. Said he was some guy from her old neighborhood. Terrance or something like that."

"Trevor?" I asked.

"Could be. I'm just not sure."

After we ran out of questions, Darcy and I stood to leave. I handed Camilla a Pirate's Cove business card. "My number's on the back. Give me a call if you think of anything else that might be helpful."

She took the card and looked at it. "I've never been here before."

"Come by when you get out of here," I said. "I'll buy you a

shrimp cocktail."

We walked away.

In the parking lot by the car, Darcy said, "I'll buy you a shrimp cocktail? That was a pretty lame line, Romeo."

"You should be more concerned about what she didn't tell us."

Darcy paused at the driver's side door. "Like what?"

"Like the names of the johns."

After she dropped me off at my house, Shelby and I went for a run.

Later that afternoon, sitting on the upper deck of my inherited dive of a bar overlooking the Atlantic Ocean, my cell phone vibrated in my shorts. I grabbed it and looked at the caller I.D. before answering.

"Hey, Darcy," I said.

"They got to Camilla," she said.

"Who? What are you talking about?"

"She's gone. Left the clinic not too long after our visit," she said.

"She's a big girl," I said. "If she wanted to leave, I guess that was her right. What makes you think someone got to her?"

"Gee, Brack. You know me. Always flying off the handle and spouting conspiracy theories."

Cussing myself because I'd taken the bait, again, I asked, "She called you, didn't she?"

"Bingo."

"What did she say? She need help?"

"She's hiding at a friend's house. That's all she'd tell me. I didn't get a chance to ask if she needed anything. She said she'll call me later. In the meantime, I think we need—"

"To get over to the rehab center and see who paid her a visit," I said.

"Two for two," she said. "You're on a roll. I don't know what I'd do without all that cunning brainpower of yours."

At the rehab center, we pulled into the same visitor parking spot we'd been in earlier. Darcy got out and walked inside. Our plan was for her to do the sweet talking.

I got out, stretched, slid a new cigar out of my pocket, clipped the end, and lit up with my uncle's Zippo. There wasn't a cloud in the sky. The heat from the asphalt baked my feet while the sun overhead cooked the rest of me. A regular convection oven. Shorts and a T-shirt were still too much clothing. I tapped the toe of a sandal on the hard road surface to get a pebble out from under my foot while I puffed away on the stogie.

"Excuse me," a young voice said. "Are you with the News?"

I turned around. A little white girl who looked about twelve, with thick glasses, twin pigtails, and freckles, stood ten feet away. Her navy T-shirt carried a private school logo on the front. Khaki shorts, brown sandals, and a backpack rounded out her ensemble.

"No," I said. "Apparently I'm the brains of the operation."

"That was Darcy Wells with you, wasn't it?"

I nodded. "Yeah. We're here in sort of a non-official capacity."

The girl asked, "She checking you in?"

Lots of thoughts spun around in my head. One of them wondered why I looked as if I needed rehabilitation. "No. A friend of ours was staying here."

"Who? Maybe I know them."

"Are you a guest?" It came out sounding like disbelief—not that I doubted a twelve-year-old who should be home doing her homework needed to be in rehab.

She kicked at a loose chip of asphalt. "For the second time."

Around the cigar, I asked, "Second?"

"First time was about a year ago. My parents caught me with a bottle of vodka."

"And this time?"

"My mom noticed some of her Percocet missing."

"You didn't learn from the first time?"

She shrugged. "I couldn't get to my dealer and I needed a fix."

I took a puff of the cigar and blew out a cloud of smoke. A slight breeze took it away.

"You needed a fix," I said. "Of course."

"I slipped up and now I'm back here again."

"Have we learned anything since the second time? And don't say something stupid like 'Yeah, I learned not to get caught.' "

Pulling on a strap dangling from her backpack, she said, "So, are you going to tell me who Ms. Wells is investigating?"

"Actually, we found out the person is no longer here. Her name's Camilla."

The girl's eyes widened. "I know Camilla. She was nice to me." She unslung her backpack, set it on the ground, unzipped the top, and pulled out a leather-bound journal. "She gave me this before she left. It's for my poems."

"You write?"

She nodded. "Isn't this nice?"

The book was lavender-colored.

"It sure is."

"Camilla was the only one who ever asked to hear my poems."

I smiled.

She said, "Are you sure you don't need to check yourself in? You look like you've got some problems. I can tell."

"My wife died a few years ago," I said, not sure why I was telling this to a stranger—and a kid, no less. "Last year, my uncle was killed. Between those two losses, I spent some time in Afghanistan." I looked down at the cigar. "I don't have problems. I have baggage." Two storage containers full—one with my wife's belongings, the other with Uncle Reggie's.

The girl laughed and said, "You're funny. That's good. You'll need it. One of the first things we learn here is not to take ourselves too seriously. You do and you're dead."

"So why the booze and pills? Cookies not cutting it for you?"

She shrugged again. "My parents do it. I wanted to see what was so great about it."

"And what'd you find out?"

"They seem to think it's okay for them to drink all day and take pills, but I'm a disgrace if I do it."

"When my wife died, I didn't want to hear another person tell me how sorry they were. I was just really angry. I drank a lot for a couple of months. Started out as one drink before bed to help me sleep. Then it was one when I got home from work and one before bed. Then it was several. Then it was all night. One day, I looked in the mirror and decided that killing myself slowly wasn't enough. I wanted to kill someone else. Or be put out of my misery. So I joined the Marines and got what I asked for. More than enough."

Birds chirped in the trees.

She asked, "Is this supposed to be a pep talk or something?"

"All I'm saying is that you can blame your parents all you want. Unless they poured the drink for you and shoved the pills down your throat, you're just lying to yourself."

The cute little smile on her face tightened. I puffed on my cigar some more. She looked away. I wondered if she still thought I needed to check myself in.

"You're not a very nice person," she said, wiping tears from her eyes.

"And you're too smart to be doing what you're doing." I took a business card for the Pirate's Cove out of my wallet and handed it to her. "When you get out, come by. We make the best Cherry Cokes around. Hamburgers, too. My name's Brack. I'm the owner."

She looked at the card and then up at me. "I've been here before. My friend Kristin's birthday party."

"Did you like it?"

"My mom and dad got drunk in the bar and I had to spend the night at Kristin's."

I said, "Oh."

"My favorite part was the parrot."

"She's a macaw," I said. "Her name is Bonny."

"She's really pretty." Her expression changed, her eyes getting this dreamy look to them.

"You like animals?"

She nodded. "I want to be a vet some day."

"Good. The next time you want to use, decide for yourself what is more important, helping animals or getting loaded. You can't do both."

"Jeez. I know, already."

Locking my eyes with hers, I said, "Then I want you to say it."

She took a step back. "Say what?"

"I want you to say 'I can't do both.' "

She huffed.

I waited.

Finally, she said, "I can't do both."

"All right. And when you get out, you and Camilla can come meet Bonny."

She asked, "Do you know where Camilla is?"

"No. Do you?"

"She came by my room and gave me the journal. She hugged me and told me to be strong. Then she whispered that she was leaving but that she would stay in touch."

I took a second card from my wallet and found a pen in

Darcy's car. On the back of the card, I scribbled a message and handed it to the girl. "If she comes by and sees you or calls, can you give her this?"

"Okay." She looked at her watch. "I've got to go. I'll be late for my group."

"Wait," I said. "You never told me your name."

Her cheeks became big dimples. "You never asked. I'm Megan."

I shook her hand and watched her walk away.

Darcy stormed out the front door. "The guy at the front desk was a real piece of work," she said. "A first class jerk."

I dropped the cigar butt on the ground and got in the car. Darcy hadn't opened her door yet. Her hand was on the handle but she seemed troubled.

I said, "He didn't respond to your feminine wiles, huh?"

"No."

"Wow. The guy must not be an Elizabeth Shue fan."

"I do not look like Elizabeth Shue! She's like thirty years older."

"Actually, you look better than she did at your age."

"At my age?" Hands on hips, she said, "What is that supposed to mean?"

"Nothing. I—"

"I'm a lot younger than you are."

"Um—"

"And that jerk back there kicked me out."

I decided I should stop baiting her and let her calm down.

She said, "He wouldn't tell me anything. Maybe he thought I was too old, too."

Frankness grenaded any semblance of a working relationship with the fairer sex. Loose lips sank ships. I tried to give her nothing else to rile her—no tell. No hint of what I was thinking or wanting to say. Nothing. Nothing but a big black hole. That was me, a big black hole.

Darcy got in the car and shut the door. Then she slapped the steering wheel.

I decided to take a risk.

"I might have found a lead," I said.

Chapter Sixteen

At the offices of the *Palmetto Pulse,* Darcy and I sat across from my Aunt Patricia in the conference room. Miss Dell, a heavyset African-American woman about fifty who worked as the receptionist, walked in with a tray of iced coffee.

"Thank you," Patricia said. Her business suit was dark, wrinkle free, and looked very expensive. Over sixty, but I wasn't sure by how much, she kept herself in great shape with a healthy diet and personal trainer appointments.

Miss Dell said, "I didn't do it for your old wrinkly butt. I did it because we got us a man in here, yessir."

"You can have him," Darcy said, still riled up. Not her usual response to broken leads or bureaucratic obstinacy.

Miss Dell set the tray down and looked at her. "So can you if you'd just get over yourself. A man like that don't grow on no tree."

My favorite news girl opened her mouth to say something, then closed it, reconsidering. Probably a good move.

Patricia, Darcy, and I watched Miss Dell walk out, her large hips swaying with serious attitude.

Patricia turned back to face us. Her expression was anything but ecstatic. "So, anyway, the big lead you managed to get after losing the only good source we had is a twelve-year-old junkie?"

"Alcoholic junkie," I said. "And she's really a sharp kid."

"Not sharp enough to stay out of trouble," Patricia said.

I clapped my hands together. "It must be nice to walk around on water all day."

Patricia tapped a finger on the table. "You said it, yourself, Brack. She's twelve years old with a substance abuse problem. That doesn't lend itself to Emmy award–winning journalism."

I said, "Is that what this is all about? I thought we were trying to solve a brutal murder."

After the unproductive meeting, Darcy dropped me off at the airport. My reluctant insurance company had arranged for me to have a rental car while my bullet-strafed truck was being torn apart by the police.

The next day, around noon, a certified letter arrived at my residence by mail. The envelope bore the letterhead of the state of South Carolina. My cell phone rang as I read the notice that my license authorizing me to sell alcohol was being suspended. Disheartened, I didn't look at the caller I.D. but simply answered.

"Well," I heard, "if it isn't quick-draw McPelton."

I lowered the sheet of paper that announced my bar's demise. "Detective Wilson. To what do I owe this honor? It's not every day we little people get to hear from an honest-to-goodness hero."

Wilson had pulled the trigger ending the life of a shady character named Michael Galston and had to resign from the Charleston Police Department. Lucky for him, he'd gotten a job with the Myrtle Beach P.D.

He said, "All I gotta say is the more things change, the more they stay the same."

I tried to think of what that might mean, but most of my mind was on my bar. "Huh?"

"I got a buddy that works for the state. He said you got a mess on your hands. Don't answer your door. They suspended your—"

"Liquor license," I said. "I've got the notice right here." I crumpled the notice. "I can't close my place. Too many people relying on the income."

"I heard the Gardners are behind it," he said.

"Just great."

"Don't worry," Wilson said. "I got an idea."

I called Paige at the Cove and when she answered said, "Remember going over the profits with me and the accountant?"

"Yes."

"Remember what she said we make the most money on?"

"Yes, Brack. Liquor sales. What are you—" She cut herself off.

"That's right. Well, guess what we can't sell anymore?"

The phone was so quiet I heard crickets.

I said, "Not even a peep, huh? Well, that's okay. Save it up for later. I got a plan. Actually, it's Wilson's plan, but it's a good one." I laid out the details.

Paige listened without saying anything, even when she gently hung up.

My next call was to Chauncey. He did not like Wilson's idea but would pursue an appeal of the suspension immediately. While I knew he would fight the good fight, something told me we were in trouble.

Wilson's idea had an air of "sticking it to the man" that I found most appealing. If they were going to fast-track my license suspension through the usually lethargic system, they didn't know who they were messing with.

Paige put the kitchen to work cooking up as many hors d'oeuvres as we had supplies for. She mobilized her single-mom army to get the word out via social media that we were having a BYOB party. All anyone had to do was show up with the beverage of their choice and we'd take care of the rest. The party started at eight.

By ten the crowd was so thick, the only way I could get to the back deck was to walk around the outside and climb the back stairs. Over the sound system, I heard Paige say, "Make sure you support your servers. Just because the grub's free doesn't mean their service has to be."

I watched wallets open and cash flow into the pockets of the wait staff.

The Isle of Palms Police Chief wove his way through the crowd and approached me. "You better explain to me what's going on."

Before I could respond, Paige came up behind him and tapped him on the shoulder.

"Hey Chief," she said. "If you open up the backseat of your car, we've got some trays of food to take back to the station."

Chief Bates looked at her, then at me. A big grin crawled across his face. He said, "You better do whatever you can to keep this one, Pelton."

"You bet."

"This isn't going to help your cause with the state, you know."

"But it sure is fun," I said.

I spent the next morning picking up trash on the street in front of my bar. As the owners of the neighboring businesses and their employees arrived for work, they saw me and grabbed trash bags to help. All had enjoyed themselves freeloading at my place last night. It didn't take long before we were laughing and cutting up while we made our way down the sidewalk, filling our bags with trash and singing the Toby Keith lyrics about red Solo cups.

An unmarked cruiser came up Ocean Boulevard, slowed when it got to our group, and parked.

"You're in trouble now, Pelton," said Jesse, a woman who works as concierge for the hotel down the road.

Meredith, one of my waitresses, said, "Looks like our little stunt caught up with you."

Detective Warrez got out of the car and leaned her elbows on the opened driver's door.

One of the men behind me whistled.

I smiled, waved at the detective, and announced, "My ride's here."

With everyone's eyes on me, I approached my new favorite detective.

Detective Warrez watched me walk up to her car. "I got one question," she said when I was close enough.

"What's that?"

"How does someone who gets his liquor license suspended think it's a good idea to throw a party and close down the whole street?"

"Seemed like a great idea to me."

"You can't afford to go to jail."

I smiled, then said, "Sure I can. Got a good lawyer."

"I know." She rested her foot on the rocker panel of her car. "You doing okay?"

"Yes, ma'am. The state doesn't know what they started."

"I'd say last night gave them a good idea. I heard you had members of the Isle of Palms police force swing by for a plate of food, and even shipped some back to the station with the chief."

I nodded.

"Smart move."

"I know it's early," I said, "but I still have some food left, if you're interested. We make a mean burger."

"Well, I haven't had breakfast yet." She shut her car door and walked with me into the bar. My helpers had not left yet, nor had they bothered to pick up any more trash. They stood and stared.

Detective Warrez stopped and faced the gawkers. "Get back to work!"

The authority of the badge was evident as everyone bent in unison to gather more trash.

Inside, I carried a barstool into the kitchen for her. Two of my waitresses were cleaning up when we walked in. They looked Detective Warrez up and down, then gave me a thoughtful eye as they left.

I set the stool down at a table in the middle and fired up the grill. "So how do you like your burger cooked?"

"Well-done," she said. "Sorry about your license suspension."

In the fridge sat the platter that at the beginning of the evening held a mound of uncooked patties. Two remained and I set them on the grill. Her dark brown eyes watched me as I sliced two potatoes and dropped them into the still-hot fryer. When she didn't say anything else, I said, "You come here to ask me some more questions about Willa Mae?"

"No."

Not knowing how to respond to that, I kept my mouth shut and prepared two plates for us with buns, lettuce, tomato slices, and jalapeños. A hunt in the shelves netted bottles of ketchup, mustard, and hot sauce, and some packs of mayo if she went that way.

The fries and burgers got done at the same time and I loaded our plates and slid one across the table to her. It occurred to me she didn't have anything to drink so I left the kitchen and came back with two cups of ice and a quart of spicy V-8. "Hope this'll do."

She looked at me, the cups of ice, and the plate of food in front of her.

Her expression made me uneasy. I said, "Is everything okay?"

After a pause, she said, "It's been a long time since anyone cooked for me."

I set the glasses on the counter and poured the juice. "Well, you better eat before it gets cold."

Afterwards, we took a walk on the beach. Detective Warrez removed her shoes and socks and walked barefoot. It was still way before ten A.M. so the few people on the beach were mostly retirees getting their exercise. We didn't speak to each other during the walk, just took it all in.

When we returned to the Cove she left. I felt that more had happened during our silence than in all the conversations we'd had.

After heading home for a long nap, I returned to the Pirate's Cove with my dog. With no leads on Willa Mae or Camilla, and my bar now in jeopardy, I thought I'd lay low. At least until later. Besides, it wasn't as if Paige didn't have things under as much control as possible.

Two regulars sat at the bar, Jim and Tony. I had no doubt they'd been amongst the crowd the night before.

"Didn't get enough last night, huh?" I asked.

Since they weren't female, Shelby ignored Jim and Tony, trotted behind the bar, and curled up on his mat.

Jim waved a half-eaten chicken wing in the air. "Ha." He was fifty but looked sixty with his sun-weathered skin and gray hair. His T-shirt said "Hollywood Hot Rods."

Tony said, "So when we gonna be able to drink in here again, Brack? You got the best bar on the island except for the no-liquor part."

I said, "You New York guys got more money than the Port Authority. Why don't you see what you can do to help?"

Jim was involved in some pharmaceutical breakthrough that earned him something like three hundred million dollars, so the story goes. Tony had owned night clubs but sold out before the economy tanked. Rumor had it he was connected with the mafia. His bright green Lamborghini was the only car I'd ever seen distract men to the same extent as the women walking around in bikinis.

"I tried," Tony said. His New York accent had him enunciating every letter. "I don't know how anything gets done around here. This state moves slower than my mother-in-law and she's dead ten years." He threw another picked-clean bone on the dish between him and Jim.

Thinking the state had moved pretty darn quick on suspending my license, I went behind the bar and pulled out two Corona long necks from the cooler. I popped the tops and set them on coasters in front of my regulars. "On the house. I can't sell it, but I'm not above giving it away." Which was another violation, but I didn't care.

Jim picked up his bottle. "I always said you was okay."

"No, you didn't," Tony said. "Before he walked in here, you was telling me what a schmuck he was for losing his license."

"Jim is right," I said.

"Yeah," Jim said, "but I can be bought with beer. All is forgiven, Brack."

"I just hope Chauncey can fix this," I said. "Or we're in trouble."

I opened up an IBC Cream Soda for myself and we toasted the future demise of all state inspectors.

At the entrance to the bar, the chief of police for the Isle of Palms was entering as a family that had eaten dinner was leaving. He held the door for them, then came over and nodded at me and took a stool next to Jim. Chief Bates noticed the beers on the bar.

I asked, "You on the job or off?"

Dressed in his summer uniform of a gray short-sleeved shirt

and dark trousers, Chief Bates looked up at me. "Just got off."

I pulled another beer out of the cooler and placed it on a coaster in front of the chief.

Tony said, "He can't sell it, but he's not above giving it away. Right Brack?"

"That's what I said."

The chief's eyes went from his beer to Tony, to me, to Jim cleaning his hands with a wet wipe, and back to his beer. While he was deciding his next move, I cut up a lime and gave each of them a wedge.

I said, "You want some wings or something, Chief?"

He pushed the piece of lime into the bottle, put his thumb over the top, and gently turned it upside down so the lime went up to the bottom of the bottle. After right-siding the bottle, he eased his thumb off slowly, releasing the built-up pressure. Then he drained half of it down his throat before saying, "Yeah. Make 'em hot. None of that pansy stuff like the last time."

"You got it." I put in his order.

The chief said, "Gardner's got me running ragged with security for that fundraiser he's got at his house Saturday night."

Tony said, "Gardner's a putz."

"Which one?" Jim asked.

"Both," said the Chief. "Senior and his brat-of-a-son."

"I wouldn't vote for him," Tony said.

"Me either." The Chief looked at me. "But the reason I'm here is I heard you been interfering with a CPD investigation."

"You could say that."

Tony said, "You holding out on us?"

"And," the Chief said, "been shot at by some gangbangers."

"You like how the city soft-pedaled that one through the media?" I asked.

"Why didn't that hot Channel Nine chick spill the beans?" Jim asked. "Aren't you and her an item or something?"

I'd love to hear Darcy's reaction to that comment.

From the doorway, we heard, "No, we're not an item, as you so eloquently put it."

We all looked in the direction of the voice.

Shelby jumped up and ran to Darcy.

"Wow," Jim said. "Wow."

Darcy scratched behind Shelby's ears, then strode with him to the bar, the pink sundress she wore accentuating her moves, her hair tied up to keep her neck cool in the lowcountry heat.

Wow, I thought and almost said.

The chief stood and pulled out his stool for her between himself and Jim.

"You on the clock or off?" I asked her.

"Does it matter?"

I guessed not and poured her a Grey Goose screwdriver.

"And to answer your question, Jim," she said, "we soft-pedaled the drive-by story because neither Brack nor Detective Warrez, nor the mayor, I might add, wanted the headline."

"That's right." I handed her the drink. "On the house."

She said, "Of course, I know why the mayor wouldn't want it turning into a media circus. And I can figure out why the detective might not want the exposure."

All the men were silent. Captivated was more like it.

"But," she continued, "I'll give you guys one guess as to why Mr. Brack here wanted it hush-hush."

The chief said, "If I didn't know better, I'd think he wanted to get even."

Darcy said, "Bingo."

"He's not the brightest bulb in the fixture, is he?" the chief asked.

"No, he isn't," she said.

I said nothing because defending myself would only prove them right, which they were.

★ ★ ★ ★ ★

After locking the doors at ten P.M. and saying goodnight to the staff, I took Shelby home. With the focus the Marines had drilled into me, I put on a black shirt and black jeans and laced up an old pair of my uncle's boots I'd found in the closet. It was time for some payback.

In Afghanistan, I'd gone on missions where the chance of success was less than fifty percent. I was actually told that. Still, I went. Tonight was one of those missions. I got in the Korean rental car and drove downtown to the edge of the projects. Behind a dumpster at a closed-down gas station, I parked and used shoe polish to darken my exposed skin. With my wallet locked in the car, I hid the keys in the driver's side wheel well and took off through a back alley.

Keeping to the shadows, every so often I pulled out my iPhone to guide me to my target—the garage behind D-Go's grandmother's residence that Brother Thomas had told me about. Lucky for me, the house was dark. It was now past midnight so I figured the grandmother was in dreamland. I eased past her house as silently as I could. Light escaped from the cracks around the door to the building in the backyard. As I got closer, the beat of rap music vibrated the ground beneath my feet. I kept away from the closed door and circled the building. The smell of marijuana grew strong as I got closer. Around the corner I found a window unit air conditioner protruding from a makeshift hole in the wall. Whoever had installed the unit had not deemed it necessary to seal around it. A nice inch gap gave me a good view of the interior.

D-Go and three of his buddies huddled around a ratty folding table playing some kind of card game. A pile of money lay in the center. Beer bottles and pills and opened clear plastic bags of marijuana littered the edges.

The kids were arguing over some rule and who should have

won. Behind them, much to my delight, a late-model Crown Victoria sat, its metallic purple paint glimmering under the exposed lightbulb hanging from the ceiling.

Ten minutes later, I was back at my rental car, using a disposable cell phone called a burner to drop the dime on the delinquents. Feeling good I didn't have to shoot it out with them, I wiped off as much as I could of the shoe polish from my face and hands and drove home.

Chapter Seventeen

The next morning after a jog around the island with Shelby, I stretched out in a chair on the back patio of Uncle Reggie's place and realized I missed the view at my old house. The little oasis of two palmetto trees and a small fountain I'd added to my uncle's backyard was not as calming as the intracoastal waterway had been out my previous front door. As much as I didn't want to admit it, I needed to move. I needed to see the water.

The morning paper had a small story about a police raid of a house in the poor section of town. In addition to the arrest of four men with outstanding warrants, drugs were found on the site as well as several weapons linked to other crimes. The men, alleged members of a local gang, were being arraigned today.

Mission accomplished. D-Go and his buddies wouldn't be a bother for a while.

My cell phone sitting on the small table next to me vibrated, making a terrible racket. Shelby, who had been fast asleep on the ground beside me, jolted awake and almost knocked the table over. I grabbed the phone and a bottle of water before they fell off.

The number in the caller I.D. was not familiar. I answered anyway. "Pelton."

"Yeah, hi. This is Camilla. Megan gave me your card and said you wanted to talk to me again."

"Camilla?" I said, "You doing okay?"

"Yeah, I'm still clean if that's what you mean."

"How are you fixed for money? I mean, you got a place to stay?"

"Why? You wanna pay me to come over?"

I cleared my throat. "Sorry. Not like that. I mean . . ." Think, Brack. "I mean, I only want to make sure you are okay."

She laughed. "I know. I just wanted to hear you squirm over the phone. Pretty good, huh?"

"Yeah. Real funny. Anyway, we heard you checked yourself out of the center."

"We?"

"Darcy and I. We stopped by to see if we could ask you some more questions."

"You can ask me anything you want."

My ears started heating up again. "Come on, Camilla. You know I really want to find out who killed Willa Mae."

The lightness in her voice changed when she said, "Me, too. That's why I'm calling."

"I'm sorry. It's just been quite a week."

She didn't reply.

I looked at my watch. It was almost noon. "Have you eaten yet?"

"Coffee and cigarettes."

"How about I take you to lunch?" I said. "It's the least I can do."

I found Camilla sitting on a bench in Battery Park. Her beauty seemed at home amongst some of the most expensive houses in the country. She wore a lavender T-shirt and white shorts and she'd gotten some coloring from the sun. Her hair was pulled back and her eyes were bright and clear behind black-framed eyeglasses.

She said, "Where's your sidekick?"

"You told me not to tell anyone," I said. "So I didn't."

She stood and tucked her arm in mine. "You think we can behave ourselves without a chaperone?"

"For the past couple of years I haven't been too good at the whole self-discipline thing. I was banking on you being the responsible one."

"Oh, I see," she said. "You're the one trying to be funny, now. Maybe a little payback for my phone call?"

"Maybe a little." I escorted her to my rental car and held the door while she tucked in.

When I got into the driver's seat she said, "I figured you for something like a muscle car."

I smiled. "I've got an old one tucked away in a garage. This is a rental."

"I knew it," she said. "I'll bet you like classic rock, too."

She was right.

With a chuckle, she said, "What can I say? Men are my specialty."

If she hadn't been a prostitute, and if I hadn't already developed an interest in a woman who legally carried a gun for a living, as well as a news reporter supposedly heading to Atlanta to get married, I'd have driven off into the sunset with Camilla and never looked back. But some things were not meant to be, and sometimes even I knew when to keep my pants and my libido zipped.

After lunch, which was awkward because I wasn't sure what to say to her, especially in the restaurant, we meandered along Market Street. She put her arm in mine again. With the tourist season ramping up, people were everywhere.

"You can at least pretend like you're having a good time," she said.

"What do you mean?"

She hooked her free arm across her stomach and over my

arm, connecting her hands together. "I know men. It was my job for way too long. You have a big problem with what I am, don't you?"

My eyes stayed straight ahead but I felt her looking at me.

"It's all right," she said. "I understand. It's just nice to be out with someone who didn't pay me for sex."

A woman walking in front of us with two toddlers stopped and turned around, her mouth contorted into the shape of a question with more than a little bit of edge to it.

I held up my hand as a peace offering and said, "Please excuse my sister. She's out on bail for murder."

The woman grabbed her kids and stormed away.

Camilla watched the woman's exit. "I'm much too pretty to share genes with you, you know."

"I know," I said. "It was the best I could come up with on short notice."

"We'll have to work on that," she said.

"In the meantime, why don't we move on from playing this game and tell me what you wanted to tell me."

Her smile could slice through the Red Forest. "My, my."

I waited her out.

"Okay," she said and we kept walking. "I knew Willa Mae was trying to get straight."

"You know why?"

"Yeah. She was pregnant."

"She know who the father was?"

"Yep."

"How?"

"You want the Disney version or triple X?"

"Whichever one gives me what I need to know."

"We always use condoms. Every time. No exceptions."

"Okay."

"If one breaks, it is a big deal on a lot of levels."

"Who'd it break on?"

A crowd waited for the light to change at the corner of Market and Meeting Streets as we turned right and headed up Meeting. Once we were alone, Camilla said, "Jonathan Langston Gardner."

"Junior or Senior?"

"Junior, I guess. What do people call him? Jon-Jon? That one. But both of them have a history with Caroline's girls. At least up until last summer. Something happened and I seem to remember Caroline thinking she was going to be arrested."

"What happened?"

"I'm not sure. But then, it was like it all went away."

"And you knew this before when Darcy and I talked with you but pretended like you didn't." Something occurred to me. "You sent Darcy the diary, didn't you?"

She didn't say anything.

"So why all the games? Why not just tell us when we visited you?"

"I was going to tell you over the phone," she said, her face turning red. "You were the one who asked me if I wanted to go out. Why? You didn't have to do that. Was it some sort of warped fantasy? Going out with a pro without actually going out with one?" She stopped and tapped me in the chest with her fist. "Are you going to go brag to all the boys, now? Tell them how you rode in on your white horse and saved the poor defenseless hooker from the mean streets?" She wiped tears from her eyes. "All you men ever do is use. But you're worse. At least the johns didn't lie about what they wanted. They paid me. You take me out. Treat me nice, make me feel almost normal again. Then you jerk the rug out and the real reason comes out. You're pathetic."

"I am," I said, facing her, keeping my voice neutral. "But do you expect me to believe you aren't playing your own little game?"

"I don't care what you believe."

"Sure you do. You dropped Jon-Jon's name without too much coaxing. Either it's the truth and you want something, or you got something against him. If you tell me he screwed you over, I can buy that. He's a real piece of work. The dentist mistakes his silver spoon for a filling." I grabbed her arms and looked into her eyes. "Just don't tell me you're doing this out of the kindness of your heart."

"Let go of me!" She jerked her arms loose and slapped me. It was a pretty good hit, too.

I massaged my jaw and was glad no one was around. "Not bad. Not bad at all."

"No one grabs me like that. Ever."

I said, "If you don't start talking, I'm leaving your cute behind right here."

She watched me wipe my mouth with a handkerchief from my pocket. Her voice turned kittenish. "You think my behind is cute?"

"I'm a man. We're worse than dogs. Some of us are even worse than that. And, having a cute behind doesn't say anything about what's in the heart."

She slapped my other cheek.

Five seconds passed before the sting went away. "That was pretty fast. You've got good reflexes."

She narrowed her eyes. "You won't hit a woman." It was a statement.

"There's a first time for everything. Keep it up if you want to find out."

She popped me again, softer.

I said, "Is this some kind of warped form of foreplay?"

She grabbed my face and kissed me. "Is that what you want?"

"What I want is Willa Mae's killer in jail." Or dead.

She kissed me again, longer, and said, "Is that all you want?"

I inhaled deeply through my nose and then exhaled. Detective Warrez came to mind. Her chin-length hair and dark skin. And then there was Darcy. And Jo. God, I still missed my wife.

Camilla traced my ear with her finger and leaned in closer. "Tell me."

I pulled away from her. "What I really want I can never get back."

CHAPTER EIGHTEEN

I dropped Camilla off at a house on Folly Beach where she said she'd been staying, then I phoned Darcy while driving home.

She said, "Have fun with the hooker, lover boy?"

"How . . . Where . . ." I gave up. She knew more about what was going on in this town than I could ever imagine.

She laughed. "So, what did she tell you?"

"Jon-Jon was the father of Willa Mae's baby."

"All we need now is a little something called proof."

The stoplight turned red and I slowed. It gave me some time to think. A car horn blew directly behind me. I looked in the rearview mirror. Darcy waved from the driver's seat of her Infiniti convertible. The first thing that came to mind was how stupid I'd been to miss a tail.

"You were easy to follow," she said. "Must have been distracted."

The light turned green and she sped around me before I could pull ahead. Dead air came through the phone still held to my ear. I threw it on the passenger floorboard and stomped on the accelerator. I was out-horsepowered and out-handled but I did what I could. She drove with a heavy foot and lots of speed all the way to the parking garage next to her condo.

We didn't say anything as we walked inside her building. She pressed the button to call the elevator. We remained silent for all seven floors. Inside her apartment, she went to a small bar in the corner and poured herself a double vodka. Having been here before, I got a bottle of water from the fridge and we went out onto the terrace that overlooked the Cooper River. The wind was warm. Sulfur off the wetlands filled the air. Not as strong here, seven stories up, as it had been at my old house on Sullivan's Island with the marsh only fifty yards away, but I savored the memory.

Darcy watched the river. "Why didn't you spend the night with her?"

I took a sip of water and wiped my mouth with the back of my hand. "She is a junkie prostitute and I wasn't going there."

"You two looked pretty cozy to me. At least, after she was done slapping you. What did you say to make her do that?"

"I told her the truth."

Facing the water, she said, "I could see how that might not go over too well with some people. Present company included."

"Present company included," I said.

She turned to me, and her hand reached out to my chest.

A chime came from somewhere inside the apartment. Darcy went in and answered her phone. I leaned forward and rested my arms on the railing. The million-dollar view from the balcony reminded me how far I'd come.

"Your girlfriend's on the move," Darcy said from the doorway.

I was about to ask which one she was referring to but knew better than to poke that beehive. Sometimes it was better to allow things to unfold, so I turned around and gazed at the river again.

Darcy said, "When she gets to where she's going, I'll get another call."

"Why did you have a tail on me?"

I could feel the grin spread across her face without even looking at her.

"How many times have I told you I have sources all over this town?" She stood beside me and showed me her iPhone. A grainy video clip played and I watched the whole scene on the street with Camilla replay. When it finished, she scrolled down some more and said, "That was sent to me thirty seconds after you drove off with her. After that, I got minute by minute texts on where you went and how long you stayed."

The phone chimed. Darcy read the text message she received. "Camilla's at the bus station."

I stood up straight. "What?"

Darcy's eyes met mine. "It looks like she's leaving."

I started for the door. "We've got to stop her." When I got to the door, I turned around. Darcy had not followed. "Come on!"

"Let her go."

"We need her."

She approached me. "No, we don't. She pointed us in the right direction, but she doesn't have anything that we can use. Her testimony won't hold up in court. It's all hearsay."

I opened the door. "She's the one that sent you the diary."

Darcy touched my hand. "Let her go, Brack. She's old enough to make her own decisions."

The first thing that came to mind was Camilla's lack of good judgment. Drugs and prostitution. "She hasn't made any good ones that I can see. Running away is another bad one."

Darcy let go of my hand and I ran out the door.

The car's little engine screamed its curses at me the whole way to the bus station. It might have had something to do with the abuse my right foot was giving the gas pedal. For a family sedan, it really wasn't a slug, but Camilla was right—it wasn't for me.

The antilock brake system kicked in as I braked hard at the terminal. I ran to the entrance. The building was old, in a sixties-style government architecture kind of way, meaning basic and drab. My footsteps echoed as I double-timed it to the waiting area. A single woman with three toddlers took up half the section with strollers and bags and toys. The other half was taken up by two black men in their fifties. No one else was there. I found the ticket kiosk. A bald white man worked the counter. He smiled at me with brown and rotting teeth. His nametag said Fred.

He said, "Can I help you?"

"I'm looking for a girl," I said. "Black hair, dark rimmed glasses. Built, you know? You'd remember her if you saw her. Here about a half hour ago."

The jagged toothed smile remained. "She was. But she caught her bus already."

I said, "Where was she headed?"

Fred rubbed his chin. "Well, I can't really say."

I pulled out a twenty and laid it on the counter.

He put the twenty in his pocket. "She gave me fifty and said that if anyone asked, I was to tell them I didn't know who she was."

I laid a fifty on the bar. "I appreciate your remembering her. See if you can come up with a destination."

The fifty joined the twenty in his pocket.

"I seem to recall her asking for the next bus out of town. Now, that would have been the one headed to Atlanta."

"Thanks," I said and turned to walk away.

"Of course," the man said, "I also seem to recall her adding another fifty and asking for me to say she was heading to Atlanta, and then she buys a ticket to somewhere's else."

I walked back to the counter and rested both hands on the worn Formica. "You wouldn't be shucking me, would ya, partner?"

He rubbed his chin again. The smile was still there, giving him an innocent quality that belied his greed. I wanted to reach over the counter and strangle him.

From behind me, Darcy said, "She's gone. Let her go."

I gave Fred one last glare and then walked to the exit. Darcy joined me.

Outside the bus station, she said, "I told you not to bother chasing her down. You just spent seventy dollars for nothing. We'll get the real proof we need somewhere else."

I leaned against her car and lit a cigar. After a few drags, I said, "Why do you think she ran?"

"Is that what this is about? Are you after the hooker, now?"

"I'm not after the hooker," I said. "Not like that."

"Then, like what?"

"I just want to help her."

"Get your head out of your pants and let's return to finding Willa Mae's killer and getting your liquor license back."

"You don't cut any slack, do you?"

"Slack is for those who lack focus. We, or at least I, have focus. I want the story."

The killer was still out there and I didn't have a clue who he was, where he was, or what his motives were. That he was linked to Jon-Jon and Willa Mae, I was sure. I just didn't know how. It was time to tighten the screws on him. But I needed to exercise precaution first, so I made a phone call first thing the next morning.

My call was answered by Trish, the wife of my favorite lawyer, Chauncey Connors.

I greeted her and she said, "Hey, Brack. Nice to hear from you. How's Shelby?"

She loved my dog as much as she loved her own two Labrador Retrievers. She'd taken care of him the last time I ran around trying to solve a murder.

"He's fine," I said. "In fact, he's the reason I'm calling. I was wondering if you'd mind watching him for a few days . . . a week, tops."

"Of course, Brack," she said, a little too eager. "The groomers are coming this afternoon so this is perfect timing."

Gritting my teeth, I said, "I really appreciate it. If you and Chauncey ever need a dog-sitter, you know who to call."

Thoughts that leaving Shelby might be a bad idea lingered. But, I knew Shelby loved her as much as she loved him and he would view this as a mini-vacation. That's what I told myself, anyway, as I drove him to the Connors house. He seemed to know where he was going and gave a few quick barks, the same as he gave in anticipation of anything he enjoyed, like our walks on the beach, rides to the bar, or his favorite ball. Sometimes my presence didn't make the cut. Especially when a woman was nearby.

When I parked in the driveway and opened the door, Shelby, shot out of the car and ran to Trish before I could get his leash snapped. She knelt and made a fuss over him while he licked her face, then rolled onto his back so she could scratch his belly.

I carried a sack of his food and his two bowls and set them in the garage.

Trish led us inside and I said, "You're the only other person he'll eat for."

She nodded and petted him again, cooing, "He's such a pretty boy, yes he is."

Shelby gave her a paw to shake and a gleam came back in her eyes—the one that told me to not leave him here too long. Her dogs barked from another room and she made no attempt to go to them.

Using the Bluetooth connection in the rental car, I called Mutt as I drove into Charleston.

"Yo," he said.

"You still got your thirty-eights?"

"You know that's right."

"I'm heading your way. See you in twenty." I ended the call and sped up.

Fifteen minutes later, I parked in front of his house and got out.

Mutt sat in a worn-out rocking chair on his front porch. A teenage girl stood on the sidewalk with a baby stroller. It looked like they were talking.

"This here's Shamiqua," he said.

I shook hands with the young mother and watched as she pushed the stroller up the walk.

He said, "Poor girl got gang-raped by them bangers that just got arrested. She got pregnant and now she havin' to raise the child on her own."

Brother Thomas had mentioned her to me earlier. It was sad to put a face and name with the tragedy.

Mutt took one look at my ride and shook his head. "This here car will not do, Opie. We need us something with a little more muscle than a hamster."

"We need stealth, like the Navy SEALs. That's what this is. And the cops still have my truck."

"This ain't no Navy SEAL."

That was all I would get out of him at the moment.

He went inside the house. Thirty seconds later he came out carrying a paper bag tucked under an arm, locked the door behind him, and got in the rental car. "Let's go."

I drove to North Charleston and parked in front of Plug It and Stuff It, my favorite gun range and taxidermy. The owner, an old man named Jed, wore long-sleeved flannel shirts and jeans year long and smoked unfiltered Camels. His ball cap sported the rebel flag to announce which side he'd be on if another war between the states broke out. Lucky for me and for Mutt, Jed's daughter had married a black man and their union produced a granddaughter. Every time I'd been in to buy ammo or to practice my shooting, she sat behind the counter playing with her dolls. She had apparently softened the old man, who'd been providing day care while running his business.

I introduced Mutt and we bought several boxes of thirty-eight rounds. The price of ammo was at record levels with no sign of coming back to reality. Fifty was the new twenty when it came to cost.

"How you doin' down there, little lady?" Mutt asked the granddaughter.

She looked up and gave us the prettiest smile this side of a sunset, albeit one showing two missing front teeth. Her bright brown eyes and milk-chocolate skin reminded me of my vow to always protect the good and innocent.

The old man led us downstairs to the basement where the range resided. We had our choice of targets: Arabs with turbans, Somali pirates wearing bandanas, or Asian army soldiers. An equal opportunity target selection. I wasn't sure if the last one was People's Republic of China or North Korea.

Mutt selected an Arab. I chose the North Korean.

"You can shoot the pirate if you want, Opie," Mutt said. "I won't be o-ffended you shoot a brother."

"Thanks, Mutt, but I prefer to support our South Korean allies by taking pot shots at the dictator of their northern neighbor." I removed a Swiss Army knife from my pocket—the big one that had every tool except a two-way radio. From the handle, I pulled out a small ink pen. On my target, I drew a rough bowl cut on the head of the soldier.

We hung our targets and loaded our revolvers.

Mutt said, "Watch this, Opie."

He extended his arms with the gun clasped between both hands and fired six shots, pausing long enough between each one to steady the recoil.

The target was thirty feet away and his shots were grouped in the center torso.

"Not bad," I said.

"Not bad at all," said the old man.

"Not bad, huh?" Mutt said. "Lemme see what you got Opie."

I turned to my target, raised the thirty-eight with both hands like Mutt had done, and put all six shots in Junior's head. Mutt and the old man looked at the target with me. Four of the shots formed a vertical line. Two flanked the second hole from the top, forming a cross.

"Jesus," the old man said.

Mutt said, "Jesus is right. Always gotta be a showoff, don't you Opie?"

Reloading, I said, "Some people are going to get some religion if it's the last thing we do."

"Amen to that." Mutt flicked open his revolver, dropped the spent shells into a bucket, and grabbed a box of ammo.

Chapter Nineteen

After we emptied several boxes of ammo, I took Mutt to my bar for dinner. Our favorite Charleston restaurant, Cassie's, had closed when Cassie decided to move to Atlanta and open a place with one of her siblings. I missed her shoulder massages and her fried chicken, both of which I could enjoy at the same time nowhere else.

The gun range had focused my thoughts. I was tired of trying to find the killer. It was time to turn the tables. I mulled that over while sitting at a table on the back deck of my bar with my friend.

He seemed to study my face. "You look like the cat what ate the canary."

I watched him put two French fries loaded with mayo in his mouth, wash them down with a draft beer, and belch. "I think what we've been doing is chasing our tails in this investigation."

"How!" he said. "That's the first smart thing you said today."

The plate of chicken tenders sat untouched in front of me. I reached in a pocket, found a cigar, and lit up.

Mutt wiped his plate clean with a french fry, ate it, and pulled out his Kools. "What we got here," he said as he knocked one out of the pack, "is a real killer."

"So how do we catch him?"

The cherry on Mutt's Kool glowed as he took a deep drag. He jutted his bottom jaw out on the exhale and blew a stream of smoke straight up. The passing breeze wafted it away.

"You know," he said, "back when I was a boy, we dint have nothin'. Sometime the only way we got food on the table was we went out and hunted it. If we dint get any, after a day or two you get to where you ready to eat your own arm. I remember one time, me and my Pa was out. I had this twenty-two rifle. But like I said, we dint have no money. Every bullet counted. And I missed this possum. Twice. After Pa beat the devil out of me, he showed me a trick."

My chest bumped the table. I hadn't realized I'd been inching closer.

Mutt continued. "We set out bait and hid behind a tree. Wouldn't you know it, not too long after, that fat little bugger hobbled out and started eatin'. I plugged him with one shot and we ate good that night, yessir."

I thought about Mutt's story as I headed back to the island after dropping him off at his house. And then I thought about the Senior Gardner's fundraiser soiree tonight. The one that the Isle of Palms police chief Bates had tipped me off to. And I knew what I needed to do. A quick stop at my inherited shack for a shower and a change into some nicer clothes and I was on my way.

The security guard at the entrance to the private resort let me through on the ruse I was going to feed my dog at the Connorses' place. That was half a truth. I parked my car there and walked.

The Gardner house was what one would expect of someone with a net worth of a hundred million dollars. At least, one who believed in flaunting what he had. Framed in that context, big and gaudy suited the jerk-off.

Like all homes on the island built after Hurricane Hugo, it was elevated. Two large white staircases extended from either side of the grandiose front porch, also painted in white. The hue of the home struck me as appropriate—yellow.

Tony greeted me at the top of the stairs. "Brack! How are ya?"

"Just came to see how the other half lived," I said.

"You remember my wife, Marlene, dontcha?"

No man who'd ever come across Tony's second wife Marlene could ever forget her. Six-foot-two in her bare feet, platinum blond curls, she'd had a few alterations. Those alterations preceded her through doorways. Tonight's low cut ensemble took advantage of everything Tony had paid his hard-earned money for.

Her crystal-blue eyes took me in and she held out a hand. "How you doin', Brack?"

I kept my eyes on hers, except for a quick glance around the room. Several men would need a pry bar to get their own eyes under control.

"Nice to see you again, Marlene." I motioned to Tony. "You keeping him in line?"

She squeaked a giggle.

Tony patted her bottom. "You got that right."

Jim approached holding a tumbler filled with what probably was twenty-year-old scotch. "Brack! Didn't know you'd be here tonight."

"Me either. How's it going?"

"Typical rich snobs." He used his drink glass to motion to the crowd. "They're all afraid of embarrassing themselves. I guess that's why they invite common folks like me and Tony."

"Don't forget me," Marlene said.

"I don't think anyone ever could," Jim said. He put an arm across my shoulders. "Let's talk business." Guiding me to an open corner of the porch, he faced me. "I'm guessing you weren't invited to this."

"You guess right."

A grin crossed his face. "Excellent. I can always hand it to you to keep things interesting. What can I do to help?"

"I think you might want to stay out of this one."

"Where's the fun in that?"

I scanned the porch and through the windows into the living room. "Okay. Point out Gardner's goon squad."

Jim took a sip from his drink and looked around. "There's one by the front door. Tall guy with the open-collared black shirt."

Glancing toward the door, I saw a guy a few inches taller than me, flat-top haircut, with a military stare.

"The other one I know of is in the front room. Looks like he's talking to Estelle Gardner."

Estelle was the senior Gardner's wife. She always seemed to be primed and ready to be in the society pages. Attractive, thin, and with a reputation of always being in control, she was the treasurer candidate's perfect model spouse.

The guard with her was a slightly shorter version of the guy at the door, who thankfully hadn't seen me yet. Or didn't know I didn't belong.

"You know where the candidate is?" I asked.

"I think he's holding court on the upper back deck."

"I guess I need to at least thank him for his hospitality, even if I wasn't invited."

Jim chuckled. "I love it. What else can I do?"

"Your mission, should you choose to accept it, is to keep the door man busy. See if Tony and Marlene can take care of the inside guy. I'll try to slip in around Mrs. Gardner."

"This is gonna be funny."

I laughed. "I need you on the town council."

He raised his glass in a toast and went over to talk to Tony and Marlene. After a few seconds, all three turned to me, grinned, and nodded. I watched as Marlene adjusted her dress to drop lower in front, which I hadn't thought possible. Tony escorted her inside and all eyes went to her. I could have strolled in behind them and never been seen.

Jim put his hand on the doorman's shoulder and pointed to the full moon above with his drink. I took the opportunity and walked past both of Gardner's men, knowing that I gave Tony and Jim something to talk about for the next month.

What I noticed first about the inside were twelve-foot ceilings, big crown molding, and hardwood floors. The furnishings in the foyer looked like real antebellum pieces.

My immediate problem was that everyone recognized me. It didn't help that they all were customers of the Pirate's Cove. I nodded and waved and worked my way upstairs.

Gardner was exactly where Jim said he'd be, on the upper deck holding court. And lucky for me his court was not that large. I chose an empty section of wall to lean against and watched him work his audience. Gardner was the image of success: tall, tan, and well-dressed in a silk shirt, linen pants, and loafers, sans socks. He called attention to a very large watch on his wrist by periodically giving his hand a few shakes.

Since I was outdoors, I thought it a good opportunity to grab a quick smoke. I pulled out a Dominican I'd started earlier in the day and saved. It occurred to me that I was probably the only attendee of this soiree that saved and relit his cigars. That's because, well, they cost ten bucks a pop.

I lit up with my uncle's Zippo and snapped it shut, which got Gardner's attention. He cut himself off in mid-sentence and stared at me. His security detail would be in for a thrashing later, I was sure.

The group who'd been listening to Gardner blow smoke turned, one by one, to watch me. I exhaled a mouthful of Dominican.

"How you fine folks doing this evening," I said.

Jesse Tinsdale, the wife of state senator Doug Tinsdale, said, "Hey, Brack! Sorry to hear about your bar. Any idea when you'll be open again?"

My eyes didn't leave Gardner's. I said, "Thanks, Jesse. We're still open and serving food. Just can't sell alcohol. But don't worry, we'll be back to a hundred percent in no time."

Josh Frist, a trust-fund baby in the body of a middle-aged man, said, "I can't wait. Yours is the only decent bar on the island."

Knowing him as I did, his reference to decent meant bar with the most women in swimwear.

"Thanks, Josh."

No one said anything else. But silence seemed to make the group uncomfortable, and one by one they slipped away to freshen their drinks. Soon, it was just Gardner and me.

He said, "What are you doing in my house?"

"Crashing your party."

"This is trespassing."

I pushed off the wall and stood straight. "I've got a question for you."

"What's that?"

"Why were you dumb enough to burn up Willa Mae on your own property? And why do anything this close to the primary?"

Before Gardner could respond, the security guard who'd been manning the steps downstairs stepped onto the deck. "Is there a problem here?"

Gardner said, "I don't know. Is there a problem here? Or are you going to leave quietly?"

The desire to deck both of them told me it was time to leave.

"No problem," I said. "Just know that I'm connecting enough dots to make the rest of your life difficult."

The security guard said, "Come on, let's go."

As I turned to go inside I said, "There's proof her baby was Jon-Jon's."

"I don't know what you're talking about," Gardner said. "Get out."

A stiff hand rested on my shoulder, nudging me along. I shrugged it off and walked down the stairs and out the front door.

Jim and Tony started to approach but I shook my head no. They'd already done enough. I didn't want them mixed up in this any more. The risk was too great.

My exchange with Gardner had fired my pulse up. I needed to calm down and decided a cruise through downtown with the windows down might do the trick. I took the new bridge across the Cooper River and wound my way around the Market and then Broad Street. The last time I'd tried this I got chased. Just thinking about that made me check my rearview mirror. A late-model white Cadillac with chrome wheels and a big chrome grill stayed a few car lengths behind but seemed to make the same turns I did. On a hunch, my next two turns were as random as rolling dice.

"You've got to be kidding me," I said to no one but myself.

The saying, "If you play the other man's game, you'll always come up short," came to mind. So, thanks to the hours I spent with Brother Thomas and Mutt, I was able to lead my tail onto my adopted turf. Driving down a side street in the projects, I reviewed my options. I could maybe outrun the Caddy, but only if there were more turns than straight-aways. Another option was to stop and shoot it out. Tempting, but not advisable. After all, I didn't have a gun.

We approached a stoplight that had just turned red. A plan formed, one that could be expensive if I was wrong. I slowed to a stop at the light behind a car already waiting.

My tail also stopped—immediately behind me, no car between us. That seemed odd but to my advantage. Especially since all four doors on the Cadillac opened simultaneously and four men stepped out. They didn't look friendly, either. Big, serious, and armed. And I'd seen two of them before.

Chapter Twenty

I threw the rental into reverse and floored it. My rear bumper crunched into the grill of the Caddy. Through the back window, I saw all four men get close-lined by their own doors. With my foot still on the gas, I pushed the car and my targets backwards. With no one behind the wheel of the Caddy it swerved and bounced over the curb, dragging the four men with it. It stopped when it ran out of sidewalk and hit a building. I pinned the car in with mine, threw the rental car into park, and jumped out.

The stoplight changed and the car in front of me took off, its driver no doubt afraid of the crazy white man in the Korean sedan. Probably a good thing. I'd rather not have any witnesses for what would happen next.

The Cadillac was a mess. Steam spewed out of the crushed radiator. Groans from the men got my attention. The first one I came to, the driver, had managed to get on his hands and knees. So I picked up his pistol from the ground and smashed it across the back of his head. The man who'd been sitting behind him was pinned under his door and unconscious. He'd been the one guarding the front door at Gardner's. I slid across the hood, Dukes of Hazzard style, and found the front passenger crawling from the car. This one had escorted me out of the house earlier. A quick check revealed the other rear passenger was breathing, but otherwise still. With three down, I focused my attention on the one still moving—a pitiful sight. He dragged his legs lifelessly behind, using his elbows to move. One hand was crushed.

I said, "Stop."

"Screw you," he said through gasps.

"Why'd he send you after me?"

He grunted and didn't answer.

In war, we were allowed some leeway when interrogating a known terrorist. And I was pretty good at getting intel. I moved and stood in the path of the man. "We can do this easy or easier."

He swung a fist at my legs.

"I guess you want it easier." I stomped on his good arm and felt his bone break.

The man howled and groaned and I used the time to check the other goons. They were still lying where they'd fallen. And still out cold.

"What were you supposed to do with me?"

Through gasps, he said, "When I heal, I'm coming after you and your whole family." He coughed. "Friends, too."

A siren howled in the distance. I reached down and pulled the man's wallet out of his back pocket and flipped through it. He had pictures of a pretty woman and two cute kids. I said, "If you want to come back and settle this man to man, that's fine." I knelt, and dropped the photo in front of him. "But if you touch anyone close to me, your kids will lose a father."

The siren wail got closer. I kicked the man in the head and he collapsed. Then I dove into the rental car and sped away.

At an IHOP in North Charleston, the farthest place I could think to go without actually leaving town, I sipped coffee dispensed from a bottomless carafe. The two phone calls I'd made requesting an impromptu meeting had me waiting for the other attendees.

I didn't have to wait long. Within an hour, both Darcy and Detective Warrez sat across from me in the booth. I wanted to kiss, well, both of them. Apparently neither felt the same toward me.

Detective Warrez said, "Charleston P.D. issued an A.P.B. for a white male approximately thirty to forty years old driving a silver sedan with a crashed-in trunk. Know anything about this, Brack?"

I said, "You guys want something to eat? I was thinking of ordering pancakes."

The waitress came to the table and poured coffee for Darcy and the detective. They didn't order anything else. I asked about the specials and chose a short stack, bacon, and scrambled eggs.

After the waitress left, I said, "They work for Jonathan Langston Gardner, Senior. He sent them after me after I crashed his party."

"Why would he send them after you like that?"

Sitting back, I raised my arms, clasped my fingers together and rested my hands behind my head. "He's an idiot, I guess. What are the goons saying?"

Detective Warrez said, "They're not talking. Someone else made the partial identification of you and your car. No plate number, though."

"Good," I said, "but I'm going to have to ditch the car now."

Darcy asked, "What do you think they wanted?"

"I'm not sure. Gardner is going to be upset his boys were unsuccessful. He was stupid to send two of them I could identify."

"This close to the primary," Darcy said. "It doesn't make sense."

"I asked him about Willa Mae," I said. "He threw me out."

Warrez asked, "Did you have to beat them up so bad?"

"It was better than killing them." I looked at Darcy. "Why don't you tell her what happens when you let guys like this slide."

She turned to the detective. "You get shot."

★ ★ ★ ★ ★

The next morning, Mutt answered my knock at his open door, a beer in one hand and a cigarette in the other, wearing shorts and no shirt. "Opie! Come on in."

All the windows were open but there was little ventilation, which made his wardrobe choices, or lack thereof, sensible.

He asked, "Wanna root beer?"

"Sure."

He rummaged in his fridge, ultimately finding the right can. "This was left from when my daughter came to visit over Christmas."

I held the cold can to my head for a few seconds, then opened it and chugged.

My friend said, "I heard some dudes in a Cadillac had to be hauled off in an ambulance last night. Word is you ran them over."

"That about sums it up." Feeling a little tired, I took a seat on his couch.

Mutt took a drag off his Kool. "You make me so proud, Opie."

Shaft played on his TV. I said, "You studying up for our next adventure?"

"What you talkin'—" He stopped himself and seemed to get my joke. "You real funny. I suppose when you need to brush up, you pull out James Bond or sumpin' like that. That ain't real." He pointed to the TV with his cigarette. "Not like this."

While I would have loved to engage in a discussion on the reality of James Bond clobbering Shaft, I didn't have the time. "We need to get rid of my rental. The police are looking for it. Any ideas?"

"Why not just turn it back in?"

"It's got a few new scratches on it and I don't want to have to explain how I got them."

The rental agency didn't deserve the total loss on the rental car, which they'd have to take because I'd signed up for full coverage, but I had more important things to worry about. Like catching a killer.

Snapping his fingers, he said, "I know a guy who runs a place. Takes cars on the down low. No questions."

"How much?"

"Nothin'. He strips them for parts. Makes a lot of money doin' it, too."

"We can't take it to him. The car's probably got a tracker on it. Call him and tell him he can have it, but explain the problem."

"How we gonna get around, then?"

That was a good question. My vintage Mustang was not coming back out of the garage for a while. "Ask him if he's got anything fast he wants to sell. Something that's clean and legit. I don't need to get pulled for stolen wheels."

Mutt made the call and then said, "He's got a car might work for you. Wants twenty in cash. Said he'll meet us in North Charleston. I got the address."

Standing, I said, "Let's roll."

We smoked Dominican cigars while we waited in the back parking lot of an abandoned strip mall for the man to take the dirty rental car away and hand us our new wheels. Lucky for us the two patrol cars we passed didn't seem to notice or weren't interested enough to pull us over. That was good because I didn't have a good explanation of why I matched the description of the A.P.B. in their system. A flatbed truck pulled into the lot when we were half through with our stogies.

I looked at the car on the hauler. "I don't believe it."

Mutt said, "No way."

The flatbed truck carried a gray Audi S4, similar to a car we'd chased down a killer with and almost died in previously. Mutt's friend was dark-skinned, wore grease-stained overalls, and smiled with fewer teeth than Mutt.

"Lemme get this one down so you can look at it," he said, "and get that one loaded so I can find the tracker."

"Where'd you get the Audi?" I asked.

"Police auction. Belonged to some drug dealer, what they told me. I got it for a good price 'cause it's a standard. You can drive a standard, can't you?"

I nodded, thinking this could even be my old car.

Mutt said, "Batman and Robin ride again."

The tow truck driver asked, "Who is which?"

"I'm Batman, of course," said Mutt. "Already got the color."

The man drove the Audi off the truck and we exchanged keys. While he loaded the rental car, I sat in the Audi and revved the motor a few times. It sounded fine. I shut the door and took off hard. After two laps around the lot, I sped up to sixty and slammed on the brakes. Everything worked like it was supposed to. I drove back to where Mutt and the man stood watching, got out, and handed over an envelope with twenty thousand dollars, gotten from cash I kept on hand at the Cove.

The man took the money and held up a small black box. "We gotta get gone. They could come lookin'."

After the old man signed over the title to the Audi to me, Mutt and I got in and sped away.

That afternoon, Mutt and I took up a post by the pavilion at the Market. He lit a cigarette and offered me one, trying to return the favor of the cigar. Though tempted, I knew the stogies were already doing a number on my lungs. Adding another vice wouldn't help my jogging.

In response to Gardner sending his goons after me, Patricia turned over the copy of Willa Mae's diary to the Charleston police chief. It didn't take him long to find Jon-Jon's name in it and decide that, maybe, the case wasn't only about the murder of some worthless hooker. I guess it helped that the Gardner name meant the case would turn high profile and put him and his department in the limelight. Darcy's source had tipped her when and where the takedown would be, which is why Mutt and I happened to be standing partially hidden behind a street vendor, getting a clear view of what was about to occur. I got a call from my old friend Sergeant Wilson.

"Kind of busy right now, Detective," I said.

Wilson said, "Yeah, right. I forgot how good you think you are at solving crimes."

I laughed. "What's up?"

"Get up here. I got something for you but I'd rather give it in person."

He wouldn't normally just ask me to make the drive. Something was up. I looked at my vintage Tag watch. "Okay, Mutt and I will be there—how is two hours from now. Where you wanna meet?"

Wilson told me where and hung up.

"When this is all over," I said, "my dog and I are going to Mexico for a month."

"You ain't gonna go without me, are ya?" Mutt asked.

"Or me," said a voice from behind us. A female voice. One that sounded a whole lot like—

"Detective Warrez," I said. "Did you come to watch all the fun?"

Almost under his breath, Mutt said, "Whoa."

My friend was right. With her black hair tucked behind her ears, her unblemished face, and her piercing eyes, she had our attention.

She said, "I got word that you were in the vicinity, and darned if my intel wasn't spot on."

"We wouldn't miss this for anything," I said. "I thought you'd be the one snapping the cuffs on the spoiled brat."

"Conflict of interest," she said. "I might accidentally shoot him, and who'd want to have to explain something like that?"

Mutt chuckled.

"My real concern is what you two are doing here." She crossed her arms over her chest. "And why."

"It's a free country," I said.

"Freedom I believe in," she said. "Coincidence I don't."

Jon-Jon and his buddies came out of the restaurant they'd been in.

Mutt said, "Check this out."

We watched the awaited event unfold.

As soon as the rich punk reached the sidewalk, the police were on him like flies on a dog turd. The first officer spun Jon-Jon face-first into the wall and wrenched his right arm behind his back. I couldn't see Darcy, but I was sure she was capturing all this in digital.

Jon-Jon yelled, "What are you doing?"

From experience, I knew cops didn't like being questioned while they violated your rights. The second uniform pulled out a card and Mirandized Jon-Jon.

Jon-Jon's entourage took a few steps back, and stared, speechless. Then, one of the other privileged brats said, "You can't do that. My dad's a lawyer. He'll have you fired."

The cop turned to the smart-mouth. "Well, since I'm going to get fired, I guess I'll haul you in, too."

The smart-mouth reeled back and said, "Hey man, just sayin'."

The cop smiled. "Well, you can say it at the station or shut up."

As an officer slapped the cuffs on Jon-Jon, another searched his pockets, pulling out his keys and wallet. Then they escorted him to their waiting cruiser. Jon-Jon's entourage followed close behind, as if in a trance, crowding the officers trying to do their jobs. In the commotion, the police told them to stay back or they'd be coming with their friend. The brat-packers looked at each other, shrugged, and backed away. Each took out his phone and snapped photos.

Jon-Jon looked at his friends as the police loaded him into the cruiser and drove off. I almost felt sorry for him. His picture would be all over the web before the cruiser made it through the first traffic light.

"Well," I said, "Jon-Jon's used to being chauffeured."

Mutt took a drag off his smoke. "They're gonna love him in lock up. Cute white boy like that."

Detective Warrez said, "Remember, stay out of the way unless you want to ride with your friend Jon-Jon."

We watched her walk away.

"Ma-an," Mutt said. "She got some nicc action." He turned back to the scene. "You see them po-lice officers drop somethin' when the kids tried to stop them?"

"No. What was it?"

Mutt walked over to where the arrest had just concluded. He stooped down and picked up something small, shiny, and metallic. Cigarette dangling from his lips, he examined the item, then raised his eyes to meet mine. The lines of his mouth stretched into a smile that created the best imitation of the Grinch who stole Christmas I'd ever seen, if the Grinch were a middle-aged, Kool-smoking black man with a boxed afro.

I spread my palms. "What?"

Mutt held up his new treasure. I saw the shiny yellow keychain and knew exactly why he was smiling. The cops had dropped Jon-Jon's key fob.

Jon-Jon had parked his Ferrari diagonally across two spots in the public lot. It sat low and mean in the nastiest shade of blood red.

"Man," Mutt said, "I hate it when people park like that."

"Did you notice the sign out front of the lot?" I said. "It read full." I stood by the driver's side. "I think we need to do our part to support Charleston tourism."

Mutt stood across from me. "You mean free up two spots for the good peoples what came down to support our fair city?"

"Something like that."

He tossed me the keys.

"You think this is what Detective Warrez meant by getting in the way?" I asked.

"Naw."

I pressed the button to disengage the alarm and opened the door. Mutt ran his hand across the smooth leather seat before getting in.

"I ain't never been in one of these," he said.

"Me either." We sat and my fingers curled around the steering wheel, getting the feel of it. "If the cops stop us, we found the keys and were looking for the owner."

"Yeah," Mutt said, "that'll work."

The Italian V-8 barked to life with the fury of a thousand gunshots going off at once.

"How!" Mutt yelled.

"How is right."

I tried to remember what the car magazines had said about how the automated transmission worked and finally found the right sequence. Lucky for us, the attendant was nowhere to be found and I inched out of the lot to avoid scraping the front spoiler on the dip at the exit. Once on East Bay, I opened up the throttle. The "waaaaa" of the engine located behind the seats as it went through the gears sounded like something that should be in a fighter plane. With no cars in front of us as we headed onto the new bridge, I got it up to a hundred and glanced at Mutt. "You look a little white."

Then I really pushed it. The force made time stand still—like in the Star Wars movies when Han Solo put the Millennium Falcon into warp drive and the stars became lines. Air turbulence baffled the cockpit. I felt every groove in the road surface through the steering wheel but the car tracked straight and true.

What seemed like seconds later we descended into Mount Pleasant. At the first traffic light, Mutt's hands shook as he fumbled to light a cigarette. He took a long drag and exhaled slowly. His eyes looked straight ahead. "Opie," he said, "this is one bad whip."

The light turned green. I took a quick glance around, then floored the accelerator again.

Luck was on our side. Anyone dumb enough to steal a bright red Ferrari belonging to a murder suspect and speed through busy suburbs needed something to counteract his lack of brains. We spotted no police and were in Georgetown, fifty miles north of Charleston, before the next challenge occurred. A light appeared on the dash.

I said, "I think we need to stop for gas."

At the next intersection I slowed and pulled into a filling station, hoping the gas cap would be easy to find. It was and on my side of the car, too. I found one of Jon-Jon's dorky visors stuck behind the driver's seat, added a pair of wraparound sunglasses from the glove box, and went inside to pay the attendant fifty bucks. In high-test dollars, that equaled not very many gallons at the pump. We'd be stopping again.

Chapter Twenty-One

Detective Sergeant Wilson had said he'd meet us at the Dirty Laundry Bar in Myrtle Beach. He was late. Mutt spent the time shooting pool with some local sharks. I smiled when he let them take him the first two games for ten bucks and suggested doubling up the next one. If Wilson didn't get here soon, Mutt would own these guys.

Wilson walked into the bar dressed in a yellow knit shirt and cotton trousers with more wrinkles in them than Hugh Hefner's face. He looked like he'd lost a few pounds off his stocky frame, along with a little more hair off his head. A Glock sat in a holster clipped to his belt. His eyes scanned the room until they found me.

I stood and shook my friend's hand.

From the pool tables, I heard Mutt yell, "How!"

Wilson looked over at him.

I said, "The sharks just met a killer whale."

"Don't tell me Mutt's cleaning out the local guns?"

I smiled.

"And," he said, "don't tell me you and Shamu over there drove up here in a red Ferrari owned by a certain individual I just learned got popped today?"

I said, "Okay. I won't tell you that."

The bartender asked if we wanted anything.

Wilson said, "Iced tea. And make sure I get one of those plastic umbrellas."

The bartender said, "Plastic umbrella?"

Wilson smiled. "Yeah, like the ones y'all put in the mixers."

"We don't have those here, sir," the bartender said.

"Well then surprise me," Wilson said.

The bartender smirked and walked away.

Wilson turned to me. "About that certain red sports car. There ain't an A.P.B. on it or anything. But, if I knew its owner was in jail and had wondered why it was a hundred miles north of where it outta be, I'd have to call it in. Lucky for me, I didn't get a good enough look."

I said, "Now that we have that settled, why don't we get Mutt out of here before it gets ugly?"

"Probably a good idea. A couple of those guys have records."

The bartender returned with Wilson's iced tea. The lemon had a toothpick stuck in it.

Wilson said, "That the best you could do?"

He said, "Surprise."

Outside, the sun was so hot I felt the hair on my head begin to singe. The three of us walked along the sidewalk, passing the tourist shops and bars.

Mutt said, "Two more games and I'da owned those guys."

I said, "Two more games and we'd have had to shoot our way outta there."

Wilson said, "You guys wanna stay here and complain or you wanna know what I got for you?"

"Since you brought it up," I said, "why are we here?"

Without replying, Wilson led us to his unmarked Charger.

"You arrestin' us for stealin'?" Mutt asked.

Opening the driver's side door to his Dodge, Wilson hesitated before getting in. "I could do that. It'd be a good collar, too. Grand theft auto of a Ferrari." He smiled and inhaled through his nose. "Don't get opportunities like that around here very often."

The three of us stared at each other for a moment. Mutt lit a Kool. Detective Wilson stuck a toothpick in his mouth. I put my hands in my pockets.

Finally, Wilson said, "Two uniforms rolled a scumbag for selling Ativan to kids and getting a little too friendly with the teenage girls. On a hunch, a buddy of mine got the perp in the box and sweated him out a little. We got him on possession of a controlled substance with intent to distribute, and of course it ain't his first rodeo. He was small fish and we really wanted his source. Lo and behold if he don't start talking about a dead, high-priced hooker in Charleston."

Sweat dripped into my eyes and I wiped my head and face with my T-shirt. The distraction kept me grounded. My mind spun faster than the engine in Jon-Jon's Ferrari.

"Well spill it!" Mutt said.

Wilson said, "This is way off the record."

"Of course," I said.

"For a 'get out of jail free' card," Wilson said, "he'll give a name."

"Why aren't you talking to Charleston P.D.?" I asked.

Wilson's eyes met mine. "We did. They weren't interested in what some drug dealer in Myrtle Beach looking to cut a deal had to say."

"But you believe him?" Mutt asked.

"Something about it rings true," Wilson said. "He said the guy was an amphetamine freak and a gun for hire. Any job that paid his rate, which is not cheap. No questions."

"How's he know this?" I asked.

"My snitch's supplier was also the killer's."

"Was?"

"He's dead."

I asked him if he knew Detective Warrez.

"You betcha," he said. "I tried six ways from Sunday to get into her pants. I think she may hit for the other team."

"Either that," I said, "or she's actually got taste."

He laughed and said, "You're not the only one that has a grudge against Jon-Jon. She can't stand him."

"What's the connection?"

"Warrez's got a daughter. Must be twenty, now. Anyway, a couple years ago Jon-Jon gets hold of her and next thing you know the teenager's pregnant. Wonder boy finds out he's gonna be a daddy and pressures the girl to have an abortion. Her mother didn't find out until after the fact. Last I heard the poor girl had a nervous breakdown. She's in treatment in some facility near Columbia."

That was why Warrez couldn't be involved in Jon-Jon's arrest. Her "conflict of interest" comment made sense.

What Wilson provided was good information, but I wondered why he couldn't give it to me over the phone. Especially since that seemed to be all he had. In any event, it was good to see my friend again. Because I thought it would be funny, we left the Ferrari in Myrtle Beach. Let the punk figure out how his car got there. Mutt and I spent twenty minutes wiping our prints off the interior and door handles. I stuck the keyfob in the glove box and walked away. Detective Wilson assured us the lot where we'd parked it did not have camera surveillance, and he gave us a lift all the way back to Charleston.

The beeping of the Audi's rear bumper sensors sped up to one steady hum as I backed into a spot about fifteen cars up the block from Mutt's Bar. I thought I had another inch until I heard a crunch. After pulling the emergency brake, Mutt and I got out to assess the damage. It was just an old trash can that someone had left too close to the curb. I'd pinned it to a telephone pole also too close to the curb. I got back in the car, pulled forward to release the can, and killed the motor.

As I moved the crushed can away from the street and picked up the spilled trash, a brown Cayenne SUV—a dead ringer for Jon-Jon's—sped past us heading for Mutt's Bar. The only time a Porsche ventured on this particular street was if the driver was lost or trying to score drugs or prostitutes. Mutt and I watched it double-park in front of his bar, too far away to read the tag number.

Wearing a white visor, a white male who could have been Jon-Jon got out of the SUV carrying what looked like two liquor bottles. While I contemplated how he could have been released so soon from the clutches of the police, the figure lit a rag or something sticking out the top of one, opened the screen door, and threw it inside.

I screamed, "No!" and ran toward the rich snot.

He lit the second bottle and threw it at the front of the bar. It shattered against the siding. The contents ignited in a wave and the white bastard jumped in his SUV and sped away.

In seconds, an explosion blew the screen door off its hinges. It landed on the sidewalk in front of me.

Immediately behind me, Mutt screamed, "Willie!"

Flames engulfed the narrow building. Mutt ran across the busted screen door to the inferno. I grabbed him and dragged him away.

He pushed and punched, screaming, "Willie's in there!"

A second explosion erupted. The front of the bar collapsed in on itself with the most god-awful groan.

"Willie!" Mutt yelled, struggling to get free of my grip.

Another wall fell in. The abandoned house next door burst into flames. A lone siren pierced the roar all around us.

"I'm right here, Mutt," Willie's voice came from behind us.

★ ★ ★ ★ ★

Covered in black soot, Mutt and I sat on the diamond-patterned step-bumper of the fire engine. The firefighters had succeeded in saving the surrounding homes, but Mutt's Bar and its neighboring house were toast. Willie had been smart enough to jump out the back door. When the police questioned me, I described the arsonist and the SUV in as much detail as I could, even dropping Jon-Jon's full name.

While I couldn't positively identify him, Jon-Jon more than fit the profile. But I knew how slow the police could be at times. Especially if some on the force viewed anyone's torching of a dump like Mutt's a community service.

Hearing about the fire at Mutt's, Darcy had called. While getting the details, she informed me that Jon-Jon had spent less than an hour in lockup. His father had pulled a lot of strings and gotten him out. So, he had opportunity and motive to do this.

Well, the punk would not get away with it. He would pay. No one decides to lob a fireball into my friend's place. If the police were going to let him off the hook, I wasn't.

Chapter Twenty-Two

I left Mutt with Willie and the firemen and sped home to shower off the smell and soot. With a change into clean clothes in what a district attorney could describe as a premeditative action, I raced back across the bridge into downtown. I parked the Audi in one of the multi-level garages, but the short trek from the garage to where I was headed did not calm me down, nor talk me out of what I was about to do. At the entrance to the Cradle, the anger coursing through my veins barely let me notice the doorman, a massive kid with juice-induced arms. I gave him a twenty, the going cover charge these days, and strolled past.

Strobe lights bounced off dimly lit brick walls and dry ice haze. Jon-Jon, the jerk-off, was here, I could feel it. I made my way through the mob of twenty-somethings, scanning the room in all directions. But too many bodies were here to sort through.

When all else fails, ask a bartender. I knew a lot of them in Charleston. They'd come to my bar on their days off for the beach and live music. The one working tonight, a white guy named Jim, had been to the Cove a few times. I stood at the bar behind two short girls waiting for their drinks.

Jim spotted me when he brought the girls their order. "What are you doin' in this place?"

"I came to see how the other half lives."

"I can answer that," he said. "Lousy."

I asked, "You know a guy named Jonathan Langston Gardner, Junior?"

Jim rested a hand on the bar. "Jon-Jon? What d'you want with him?"

"I need to give him something."

"I'd like to give him something, too," Jim said, wringing out a bar towel. "He likes to stiff his friendly neighborhood bartenders on their tips. Last time I saw him, he was with some bottle-job blonde with a tramp stamp. Check out the dance floor."

"Thanks." I turned to walk away but came back. "You may get your wish."

He smiled and nodded.

The moving lights leapt over the gyrating throng. At the edge of the dance floor, I stopped and checked every face on the dance floor. Two guys next to me were ogling a pair of girls dancing together a little too close and friendly. The song ended and the slow-dancing girls left, apparently not liking the new selection the DJ chose. I couldn't blame them—I didn't like it either. As soon as they moved away, I spotted Jon-Jon grinding with the bottle-job and wondered what had happened to Eve White, the aspiring actress/model I'd seen him with.

My dad always said you could tell a lot about a man by his shoes. Jon-Jon had on pointed Italian jobs that stuck out a few extra inches. On his lanky figure, they looked like they belonged on a clown. In other words, a perfect fit.

Jon-Jon grabbed the girl's breasts with both hands.

She slapped him and stormed off.

He laughed, standing alone in the midst of others still dancing.

I pushed through the crowd, came up beside Jon-Jon, and shouted in his ear, "I'll give you something to laugh about, sport!"

He spun around and his fist came at me. I took the hit directly on the jaw. But Jon-Jon's punch was more show than go and merely reenergized my anger. I hit him hard in the stomach.

His eyes bugged out and he doubled over.

The people dancing stepped away, giving us the floor.

"That's for Mutt's Bar," I said. Then I slammed my fist into his face. Jon-Jon fell backwards into some barstools lined up against a side bar, knocking them over.

"And that one's for me."

Something in my right periphery distracted me. I looked just in time to see a guy running for me. Stepping aside, I shoved him on top of Jon-Jon. Next, I picked up one of the barstools, planning to get serious about giving Jon-Jon the beating of his life but I got hit by a freight train. Quicker than a blink I was on the ground. The barstool I'd raised crashed against the wall. My arms were pulled tight behind my back. The figure on top of me had to be the front door beefcake because even gung-ho cops didn't tug this hard. My face stuck to the beer residue on the tiled floor. I managed to lift my head in time to see Jon-Jon standing above me. He looked down, smiled, and kicked me in the face with one of his clown shoes.

I sat in a lounge chair facing a cop.

The officer, a white guy with a short goatee, shined a light in my eyes. "How many fingers am I holding up?"

I said, "I could tell if you'd get that light out of my face."

He angled the light away. "How many?"

Focusing on his fingers, I said, "Three."

"What's your name?"

"Brack Pelton."

"What day is it?"

"Wednesday."

The cop leaned toward me. "How you feeling, Brack?"

The room was fuzzy but getting clearer. I smiled. "Tops."

He said, "Great, 'cause I've got to read you your rights."

"He hit me first."

"We're still interviewing witnesses. Not sure how it's gonna play out yet. So, I figure better safe than sorry."

I said, "Yeah, well where's the jerk-off with the clown shoes? He getting the first-class treatment, too?"

The cop didn't say anything.

I frowned. "His daddy came and got him, didn't he? That's okay. Do what you gotta do. I want my lawyer."

To his credit, the officer escorted me out without the embarrassment of handcuffs. Still a little hazy, I offered no resistance. On my way to the door I spotted Jim, the bartender. He gave me a thumbs-up, then moved his fingers across his mouth, imitating a zipper. Even though the left side of my face ached, I smiled.

At the cop-shop, they put me in an interrogation room and left me alone. I sat in one of the chairs, put my head on the table and fell asleep. Sometime later, the click of the door woke me up. I wasn't sure how long I'd been out.

"As many times as you have been in here," a female voice said, "you should know that falling asleep only makes you look guilty."

I lifted my head up off the table and rubbed my right eye. My left one had closed up. When the room came into focus, I saw Detective Warrez watching me from the doorway. She wore a light-gray shirt and dark pleated slacks.

Standing across from me, she said, "You feel like talking?"

"Yeah," I said, "to my lawyer. Just as soon as you people let me call him."

She looked at my face, then left the room and returned with an icepack and a first-aid kit.

Snapping on latex gloves, she pulled a chair close to me, sat, and wiped the sticky dance floor residue off my cheek with sterile towelettes, a serious break in protocol.

Watching her with my good eye, I decided that I liked her being this close. I liked it a lot.

Her focus was on the side of my face. “The officer on the scene already said you lawyered up. I called Chauncey for you. He’ll be here for the arraignment.”

She stopped wiping, examined her work, and handed me the icepack wrapped in a towel. “Hold this above your eye. It should stop the swelling.”

“Thanks,” I said. “And thanks for calling Chauncey. How did you know he was my lawyer?”

“Like I said, this isn’t your first time in here.”

Of course.

Thursday morning, after my arraignment, Chauncey escorted me out of the courthouse and into his twelve-cylinder German sedan. He handed me a piece of paper.

“What’s this?” I asked.

“I have a conflict of interest here,” he said, his Charlestonian drawl emphasizing every syllable. “That’s the name of a lawyer I’m referring you to.”

I looked at him. His navy silk custom-tailored suit. His starched white shirt. And his burgundy bowtie. “You represent the Gardners?”

He nodded.

I did my best to glare at him with one eye. “And you’re picking them over me.” I reached for the door handle. “Don’t worry, I’ll find my own ride.”

He grabbed my arm. “Brack, I’m removing myself from both sides. Ethically, it’s the only thing I can do. But I don’t think much will come from this. The officers I talked to back there said they couldn’t get a straight answer from anyone.”

When Chauncey pulled up to the entrance of the parking garage where my Audi sat, he said, “I recommend you not say another word to me or anyone else about this except the lawyer written on the paper I gave you. In fact, before you do anything else, call and set up an appointment. He's expensive but worth it."

I nodded, said, "Thanks," and went to get my car.

When I arrived at my house on the Isle of Palms, I found Darcy's car in my drive.

She asked, "Did Jon-Jon do that to your face?"

"Not without help."

"Tsk, tsk, tsk," she said.

"The worst part," I said, "is Chauncey also represents the Gardners, so he recommended another lawyer."

Darcy said, "Who is it?"

I read the card. "Lester Brogan."

She whistled.

Thanks to the *Palmetto Pulse,* I knew of Brogan. Though my father may have looked at what kind of shoes someone wore, I tended to judge people by what they drove. The new Aston Martin I'd seen Lester piloting around the islands told me he was a winner.

"How's Mutt?" she asked.

"I need to call him," I said. "His friend Willie barely made it out of the place alive."

"Jon-Jon really did it, huh?" she asked.

"I'm pretty sure. He'd threatened to do it before, but I didn't take it seriously."

"What a piece of work."

After Darcy left, I called Mutt. Brother Thomas was with him and he seemed to be doing all right. Next, I called Lester Brogan's office. A breathy receptionist took my information. She seemed professionally eager to please because she said the attorney had an opening at two o'clock that afternoon.

Chapter Twenty-Three

I showered the scent of jail off and changed into khakis, a starched white shirt, and leather loafers, clothes more appropriate for meeting with the most expensive lawyer in town. Even if I wore no socks.

Lester Brogan's firm occupied the top floor of one of the few tall buildings in Charleston. When the elevator doors opened with a chime, I was greeted with a tasteful combination of stainless steel and glass, and light gray walls with matching wall-to-wall plush.

The receptionist, a gray-haired woman wearing a white blouse asked, "May I help you?"

Lucky for me, the swelling in my face had gone down a lot and I could see out both eyes again. "My name is Brack Pelton. I have a two P.M. with Mr. Brogan."

"Welcome, Mr. Pelton." She motioned to a group of leather chairs. "Please have a seat and Mr. Brogan will be with you shortly."

"Thank you." I did as she asked.

Before I had the opportunity to attempt chit-chat with her, Lester walked into the reception area. Five-five, shaved head, and five-figure suit, he greeted me with a big grin and firm handshake. "Mr. Pelton, good to meet you."

Lester led me back to his office, which copied his lobby's Bauhaus decor. The view of the city was breathtaking. I saw the clock tower of St. Michael's that has given the city the time of day since 1764. Once we were seated, he asked me to replay the previous night's events.

When I finished, he rested his elbows on his desk and laced his fingers together. "Well, at least you didn't kill him."

"No, but I wanted to."

He nodded. "I suggest we not mention that."

"Agreed."

"Anything else you want to tell me?"

I relayed the problems we were having with the Pirate's Cove, starting with the break-in. "The little snot wants my bar." I sat up straight and looked Lester in the eye. "You need to stop him from using this arrest to take it from me."

Later that afternoon, Detective Warrez called to see if I wanted to meet for a drink and suggested a cigar bar downtown. Because of her earlier threats of arresting me, I wondered what she was thinking and arrived early, getting a sofa in one of the semi-private lounge rooms. A large coffee table sat in front of the couch and Picasso prints hung on the walls. For this evening I'd chosen an especially robust Punch cigar and was in the process of unwrapping it when my friendly neighborhood detective showed up. Her perfume, a subtle scent of flowers, cut through the smoke and announced her presence.

I looked up from my cigar. "You look very nice."

And she did. Her chin-length black hair was parted just off the middle and swept back behind her ears, which only accentuated her large, inquisitive eyes. A simple, unadorned silver necklace showed perfect taste.

"Don't laugh." She sat down next to me, straightening the hem of her black sleeveless dress, and put her pocketbook on the coffee table. "I don't get out much and felt like dressing up a bit. I hope you don't mind."

I was glad I'd gone with my first instinct on attire. The dark blue, silk shirt and light-colored, linen slacks felt cool in the heat. My second choice had been ripped shorts and an old T-shirt, which would have gotten me no points this evening, and I needed all the extra credit I could get.

"I like a woman who takes pride in her appearance," I said.

She smiled and crossed her legs. "Thanks, I think."

I waved a waiter over.

Detective Warrez told him, "One-fifty-one, neat."

I added a seltzer and lime for me and the waiter left.

Detective Warrez asked, "You don't drink?"

"I try not to," I said. "It's usually bad news for me." I put the cigar in my mouth and lit it, taking in a mouthful of smoke and blowing it toward the ceiling. "By the way, am I supposed to keep calling you Detective Warrez? I don't mind, but you might get tired of it in a less formal setting."

Her cheeks reddened and her mouth opened, letting me glimpse what she must have looked like as a young girl. "I guess I never did tell you my first name."

"No. You never did."

"Rosalita. My family calls me Rosa but I don't like that."

"I like Rosalita. It suits you."

The waiter came back with our drinks.

She held her jigger up to me. "To making things right."

I tapped her glass with mine. "Amen."

Rosalita sipped her rum and looked around the room we had all to ourselves. "I don't think I've ever been in here on a social occasion."

I took a pull of my stogie and exhaled slowly. "What made you pick it?"

"I know you smoke cigars."

"Yeah, but I'm trying to quit," I said, and hoped I'd mean it someday. "Anyway, you said you had something new on the case."

She took another small sip of her drink. A drop of rum ran down her chin and she wiped it with a cocktail napkin. "Foreplay is over, huh?"

"I could sit and watch you in that dress all night," I said. "But I have more respect for you than that."

She held my gaze for a second, then broke away. I might have even seen her mouth turn into a half smile as she looked around the room again. "Pretty good, Pelton. That was pretty good."

I relaxed on the couch, slouching down an inch or two. "Please call me Brack."

"Okay, Brack," she said. "Here's the deal. I know you don't want to stop looking into the Willa Mae case. I also know you have Patricia Voyels and the Channel Nine News girl in your pocket."

"And?" I felt her trying to read my face but I know I wasn't giving anything away. Her chest rose and fell as she took in a deep breath. It looked to me like she had come to a decision.

She said, "Some people are very nervous about Willa Mae's murder case. They want it closed fast. They would have preferred it remain quiet but you and the media took care of that."

"That first amendment really gets in the way sometimes," I said.

She took another sip.

"Do you know why they're nervous?" I asked, locking my eyes on hers.

"I've got a few ideas."

"Well, you're probably on the right track then."

"Thanks for the confidence." The small pocketbook she'd brought vibrated towards the edge of the coffee table. She picked it up, unzipped the top and took out her smart phone, looking at the caller I.D. "I've got to answer this."

I nodded and watched as she stepped away to talk. She went

toward the rest rooms, one hand holding the phone and the other covering her ear to block out the noise from the bar. While she was gone, I smoked my cigar and thought about what she'd just said.

Rosalita returned but didn't sit down.

"Problem?"

She picked up her purse and dropped her phone inside. "I have to go. Something's come up."

"Work related?"

"We're not close enough for me to be answering questions like that," she said.

"Well, I appreciate your getting all dressed up to come out this evening, Rosalita. Next time, I'd like to buy you dinner so we can get to know one another a little better, feel more comfortable answering those types of questions. Maybe show you I'm not that bad of a guy after all."

She came closer, stooped down, and gave me a single kiss on the lips. "I know you're not that bad of a guy."

I watched her walk away again, this time with the knowledge that she wasn't coming back any time soon. People say, the more things change, the more they stay the same. I have to agree with that. My luck with women was a case in point. I dug out my cell phone and hit speed dial. Darcy answered on the third ring.

I asked, "Any of your sources give you a news flash in the last five minutes?"

"No. Why? Is something going—" She paused in mid-sentence. "Hold on, I'm getting another call." When she clicked over to it, I took another drag off my cigar and waited. Thirty seconds later she was back. "You must be psychic."

"So what happened?"

She didn't say anything.

"Well, spill it, girl."

"Bad news."

Brother Thomas, Mutt, and then Aphisha came to mind. "What?"

"There's been another murder. It's Camilla."

I stared at the wall of the room. "Where'd they find her?"

She told me. I said I'd meet her there, ended the call, and dialed Brother Thomas.

"I just heard," he said.

"You and Darcy have got some wicked sources," I said. "She's going to meet me at the crime scene. You want to come?"

"Since she was a friend of Willa's, I believe I will take you up on your offer."

The Deep South forms its own version of Hades when the thermometer hits a hundred and the hygrometer nears the same. Nights offer some relief, but tonight was not one of them. In the palmetto heat, I wiped sweat off my forehead with my hand and flung it at the asphalt.

The crime scene was a stark reminder to me of events of a year ago. Events I'd rather forget but thanks to this investigation couldn't. My uncle had been gunned down by an old army buddy because he didn't want to sell a hundred acres of undeveloped wetland along the Ashley River. The crime scene was an alley not far off the tourist section of downtown Charleston. I now stood at the entrance to that same alley, with the same crime-scene tape holding back the media, tourists, and other gawkers. And the same news vans were blocking the street.

I found Darcy and a cameraman setting up to film a segment for Channel Nine News not far from where I'd first met her on that dreadful night. Brother Thomas ambled up close behind me. Darcy greeted him in her usual fashion, giving him a hug and a kiss on the cheek. She never greeted me that way.

"Your cop friend is already here," she said. "She showed up in a black dinner dress like she was out on a date or something." Darcy looked me over. "Nice outfit. Must have been blind luck, your calling me asking if something's happened five seconds before I get a call about another murder."

"Must have been," I said. "So what do we know?"

"I know a lot," she said. "And I have a news clip to film. So if you don't mind . . ."

"Actually, I do mind," I said, my voice rising. "Quit the—"

Brother Thomas interrupted me. "Children, children. Let's calm down and take a deep breath."

"I am calm," Darcy said, "and I need to finish this segment. Now, again, pretty please, with sugar on top, get out of here so I can work."

The tone and volume of her voice suggested that she was, in fact, not calm. But I let it slide.

Brother Thomas grabbed my arm and escorted me closer to the barricade. "Officer," he said to one of the men in uniform wandering around behind the crime-scene tape. The man tried to look away.

"Officer, my name's Reverend Thomas Brown. Please tell your commanding officer I'd like to speak with him."

The man raised his head and nodded without so much as glancing in our direction. Then he disappeared in all the activity. While we waited, I watched Darcy give her clip on the murder. Her profile was flawless.

"Darcy Wells, Channel Nine News," she began. "I'm standing in front of Simmons Alley where the body of a twenty-one-year-old woman was found stabbed to death a short time ago. The police are withholding the name of the victim until the family can be notified."

Darcy looked from the camera to me and said: "A year ago, another murder took place in this same alley. That victim was

Reginald Sails, the owner of the Pirate's Cove Bar and Grill on the Isle of Palms. It remains to be seen whether the two crimes are connected." She deadpanned the camera. "All we know is that two murders in the same location in this city usually turns out to be more than coincidental. This is Darcy Wells, Channel Nine News."

My insides burned with anger. She had no reason to go there. I turned to say something to Brother Thomas and found him talking with the C.O.

"Brother Brack," Brother Thomas called. "We need to leave now."

"Just a moment, Brother," I said and started for Darcy.

He stopped me. "No time. They gonna let me notify the next of kin 'cause I used to be a police chaplain. We gotta leave. Now."

It was not a suggestion.

Chapter Twenty-Four

I gripped the steering wheel tight and gunned the motor. "She had no right to do that."

"If you run any more traffic lights," Brother Thomas said, "I'm jumping out."

At the next intersection, I slowed to a stop. "Can you believe she did that to me?"

"To you?"

"Yeah," I said. "Dragging Uncle Reggie's murder back into the spotlight. It's been a year and things were just getting back to normal."

If I thought about why I was really mad, I'd ram a brick wall.

"But another murder happened in the same alley," Brother Thomas said. "What did you expect her to do? Ignore it?"

"It was the least she could do considering all that I've done for—"

"Oh, so it's about you, now? She supposed to forget she's a reporter and look after the poor little Marine who can't seem to get a grip on hisself."

I slammed on the brakes and slid into a parking lot. "You want to say that again?"

Brother Thomas looked at me and spoke in a voice much too calm. "Maybe she was protecting you and Patricia by making the connection tonight. What do you think would happen if she and the TV station tried to hide it? Like the other papers aren't smart enough to find out on their own?"

I hit the steering wheel. "She had no right!"

"She had every right. In fact, I think it was her duty to her employer and as your friend to do exactly what she did. You forgetting one small little fact in all this."

"What's that?"

"That girl loves you."

"She has a funny way of showing it. I mean, she's moving to Atlanta in a couple of weeks to get *married.*"

"Brother Brack, you ever think she really don't want to?"

I didn't respond.

He said, "Why else would she still be coming to see you? Spending time in your bar? Getting you to give her boat rides? You think she don't have enough money to buy a whole fleet of ships?"

He was more right than I wanted to get near to. Still, she was leaving in a month. And I didn't like that at all.

"It took all the strength she had to give that report," he said. "You could see it in her face. Why you think she looked at you when she made it?"

"It still hurts." I wasn't talking about the news clip anymore.

"I miss Reggie, too. That boy had more crazy ideas than the sanitarium. But, he gone and we here. And we need to get going before that girl's family finds out from someone else. If that happens, I'm blaming you."

The police had tracked Camilla's mother without too much trouble, thanks to Camilla keeping her real name. And according to Brother Thomas they didn't really seem to want to notify any family and were glad he'd volunteered. Her mother's last known address was a trailer park in North Charleston. The GPS got us to the park, but we had to roll through at five miles an hour until we found the unit.

I pulled in behind a fifteen-year-old Honda Accord with faded paint and cut the motor. "How you wanna play this?"

My minister friend asked, "What you talkin' about?"

"We gotta find out if they've seen her in the last week."

Brother Thomas wiped his face with a handkerchief.

"Brother Brack," he said, "that is not what I signed up fo'."

I looked at the rusty screen in front of the front door, the dirty siding on the trailer, and the concrete blocks that someone had begun to line the bottom of the trailer with which stopped at only the second course. "You want to find Willa Mae's killer, don't you?"

"Not like this."

"Two people are dead, one of them being Willa Mae. Now, I'm going in there and I'm going to ask a few questions. I liked this girl. I liked her a lot. But she's another victim in this mess that started two weeks ago. This has got to stop, one way or another. No matter what it takes."

Brother looked away from me and wiped his face again. Shaking his head, he said, "No matter what it takes."

I wasn't sure whether he was agreeing or not and didn't really care. With a flick of the handle, I opened my door and stepped out.

Brother Thomas did the same. "Okay. We do this my way. If you start in on those people, like I know you want to, I will drag you out of their home dead or alive. We clear?"

Something told me he was serious. He had the moral high ground covered, so who was I to question it. I nodded and motioned him to take the lead to the door. He cleared his throat and gave the door two good raps.

The door behind the rusty screen was opened by a woman who was the spitting image of Camilla twenty very hard years down the road. Her pale, white skin and long, dark hair and curvy figure were present and accounted for.

She gave me a grin and took a drag on a cigarette. "Well, if this ain't something."

Brother Thomas said, "Sorry to bother you, ma'am. I'm Reverend Thomas Brown, and this here is Brother Brack. We was looking for Dolores Good. Would you happen to be her or would this be her place of residence?"

The woman leaned against the open door.

From behind her, a man yelled, "Who the hell is it?"

Ignoring him, she said, "I am and this is. What's this about, Reverend? You collectin' for your church?"

Now for the bad news.

The preacher said, "Sorry to bother you, Ms. Good. We got something we need to talk to you about and I'd rather not do it through your screen door here. You mind if we come in?"

Her eyes went from my overweight friend dressed in black to my silk and linen duds. I gave her what I felt was a sympathetic smile.

She unlocked the screen. "All right. But just so's you know, Tom's got a shotgun so you best not try anything."

"Yes, ma'am." Brother Thomas held the door open for me and then followed after.

We stood in the sparsely decorated living area of the old, run-down trailer. A small flat screen TV belted out *American Idol.* The gentleman who'd called to Ms. Good must have been in another room. Threadbare furniture and fading wallpaper had the tint of yellow from years of cigarette smoke.

She said, "Okay, now what do y'all want?"

I said, "I'm afraid we've got some bad news regarding Camilla."

Ms. Good said, "I haven't seen her in, like, five years. What's that little tramp done now?"

"Ms. Good," Brother Thomas said, "I'm sorry to say she died this evening."

"Shut up!" she said. "Shut your filthy mouth!"

A man stormed into the living room. He was fat and round and bald. He did not have the aforementioned shotgun. "You get the hell out of my house, you hear!"

The woman put her hands to her face, turned away, and began to cry.

The man looked at her. "What in the hell is going on?" To us, he said, "You two get the hell out!"

Brother Thomas said, "I am so sorry for your loss." He set one of his cards on the counter of a dinged-up end table, turned, and opened the door.

The poor woman's shoulders shook, her breaths coming out as gasps for air.

I said, "Your daughter was trying to do the right thing when she died. I wanted you to know that."

The next morning I called Mutt, figuring that he might not want to be alone what with his bar gone. As I opened the door to leave, an attractive brunette woman I'd seen before was set to knock.

"Oh," she said, flashing perfect teeth. "I'm looking for a Mr. Brack Pelton."

"You got him," I said to Eve White. "Please come in." I waved a hand to direct her inside.

She passed me and stood in my living room, her brown hair pulled back in a clip, and her outfit a peach body-hugging number. "I'm a . . . well, I used to date Jonathan Gardner."

Closing the door, I said, "Junior, right?"

"Yes. My name is Eve White."

I shook her offered hand. "Can I get you something to drink, Ms. White?"

"No, thank you."

Motioning to the couch, I said, "Have a seat."

We sat, her at one end and me at the other.

"What can I do for you?" I asked.

Looking at her hands, she said. "Um, certain things have come to my attention. Things I'm kind of embarrassed to talk about."

"Yes?"

"I know you are looking into the deaths of those girls."

She said girls. Plural. That means she already knew of a connection. The police hadn't gone that far. At least, officially.

Without trying to seem eager all of a sudden, I said, "You know something about them?"

She smoothed out an imaginary wrinkle in her tight skirt. "More like I overheard something I probably shouldn't have."

Waiting patiently was not one of my virtues. I had to dig deep to stay composed.

Continuing, shc said, "I went over to Jonathan's to break up with him this morning. He was talking with his father on the phone when I let myself in. I've got my own key. And actually, they were yelling at each other. I heard him mention the two women who'd been killed, Willa Mae and Camilla, and that they didn't know who killed them." She wrung her hands together. "That's when I let myself back out. I don't think he even knew I was there."

"Smart move. So you're saying they didn't know who'd killed the women and were upset?"

"Yes. But only about how it was going to ruin his father's chances in the election. It was awful. The deaths of those girls only mattered to them in how it made them look. And some link to something that happened last summer. I didn't quite catch that part either."

"Why do you want to stop seeing Jon-Jon?" I asked.

"Are you kidding?" she said, her voice rising. "He was sleeping with prostitutes."

"I could see how that might not be the best thing for a

relationship." I paused and thought. She seemed sincere and I didn't believe she was playing me or trying to cover for Jon-Jon. "So what do you want me to do with what you just told me?"

"I thought you were after him."

"I'm after the killer," I said. "You just gave me reason to believe both Gardners don't know who he is."

"Yes, but don't you see?" she asked. "They knew the girls. Both of them. And they're afraid of what's happening. They might not be the killers, but they're involved. I know it."

Before Eve left, I gave her my card and told her to stay away from the Gardners. She told me she was leaving for California in the morning. As I drove to Mutt's, I phoned Darcy and told her about my conversation with Eve. She agreed it wasn't anything we could use at the present time, but would start looking into anything that happened last summer.

As I stood in Mutt's living room while he changed his shirt, my phone vibrated in my pocket. I pulled it out, looked at the caller I.D., and answered.

The caller sniffled and gasped. "Mr. Brack?"

I thought I recognized the voice as the girl from the rehab center. "Megan?"

More crying. "Yes."

"Are you okay?"

"Ye-yes."

"Where are you?"

Mutt said, "Who's that?"

I waved him off. "Are you still there?"

She said, "Mm-hmm."

"Are you at the rehab center?"

"Mm-hmm."

"Good," I said. "Are they treating you okay?"

Sniffle. Cough. "I found out Camilla was killed."

"Yes. I'm very sorry."

"Can you come here to see me?"

Looking at Mutt, I said, "I've got a friend with me."

Megan asked, "Is it Darcy Wells?" The hope in her voice made her sound like a young teenage girl for a moment. In other words, like her real age for a change.

"Not this time. She's working on a story. Camilla's story. I've got another friend. I think you'll like him." I chuckled. "He's kind of silly."

Mutt said, "You get off that phone and you and me's gettin' into it."

Winking at Mutt, I said, "Hold tight, Megan. We're on our way."

We said our goodbyes and ended the call.

"Silly, huh?" Mutt asked. "Like how?"

After more than a few moving violations, we pulled into the entrance to the rehabilitation center.

Megan sat on the front steps waiting for us, her backpack by her side. Her arms were folded underneath her legs and she rocked back and forth. I parked in visitors' parking and Mutt and I walked over to her. She stood, ran to us, and gave me a hug. I hugged her back. Mutt lit a cigarette.

She cried some more. Apparently she didn't get all of it out over the phone. I gently patted her back.

After more than a minute, her sobbing slowed and she took deep breaths. Holding her at arm's length, I watched her.

Her red and puffy face got redder. "What are you looking at?"

"Just making sure you're not hurt."

She shook me off. "I'd've told you if I was hurt, doofus."

Mutt cackled. "I call him Opie, but I like your name better."

"This is the silly friend I told you about," I said.

Mutt held out a hand. “Clarence Alexander. My friends call me Mutt.”

She blushed again and shook his hand.

“This is Megan,” I said, since she didn’t.

He let go of her hand. “This a nice place, Megan. You like it here?”

“Not really,” she said.

“Then if I was you, I’d do whatever it took to get out.”

That was deep, especially for Mutt.

“We’re here,” I said, “and I’m glad to see you again.”

Her interest shifted from Mutt to me. “I got a letter from Camilla.”

She had my full attention.

Megan dug through her backpack and pulled out a folded piece of paper. “She mentioned you in it.”

Taking the offered envelope, I said, “It’s your letter. Are you sure you want me to read it?”

With straight shoulders and the stare that soldiers got when they’d seen a lot more than their young years should have, she said, “I miss her every day. She was the only one that treated me as a person, and not some screwed-up kid. She was my big sister because my real one doesn’t care enough about me to visit or call. That’s a copy for you to take when you leave.”

I asked, “Do you want us to go?”

“Not yet,” she said. “I’d really like to just walk around the grounds if you have time.”

Mutt said, “We got all the time in the world for pretty young ladies.”

Megan blushed again.

Chapter Twenty-Five

"I really like that girl," Mutt said. "She remind me of my daughter. Headstrong and not afraid of nothing. Just got some problems to get over."

"We should recruit her," I said.

"Maybe you right."

We were cruising on the interstate back into the city at a slow pace, thanks to a lost tourist in a slow SUV ahead of us. When a break opened, I downshifted to fourth and blasted past.

At the Church of Redemption, we caught Brother Thomas sifting through a mound of paper. I read him the letter:

Megan,

I never told you how special you are to me. I am so glad I got to know you and that you shared so much with me. If the only good that comes out of our stay at Serenity Hills is that I got the chance to know you, it was worth it all. Don't take my leaving as a sign I'm giving up. I'm not. I am in trouble and there are bad people out to get me, like they did my friend, Willa Mae.

There is a man by the name of Brack Pelton, who is after the men who killed my friend. You told me you'd met him when he came to see me with Darcy Wells from Channel Nine News. Brack is the only one I'd trust with my life. Call him. Tell him I left town and plan on starting my life over. Tell him Willa Mae wanted the father of her baby to help support her but she was killed because someone close didn't want a black sheep in the family. Tell him I know this because that's who threatened me. Tell him to check out the Courtyard Suites, room 113, on Friday night.

I love you, Pixie. Stay strong!

C.

After reading the letter, Brother Thomas asked, "What you wanna do?"

I said, "I was thinking of hiring some call girls."

Brother Thomas cocked his head as if he wasn't sure he'd heard what I just said correctly.

Mutt got to his feet. "What we waitin' on, Opie? Let's hit it!"

The preacher said, "I think we need to have a talk before you go and do something like that. Sin ain't the answer, mm-hmm."

"You don't want to join us?" I asked.

The big man in the black suit gripped the arms of his chair like they were attached to a servant of the enemy he was about to choke to death. "Join you? What are you talkin' about?"

Knowing that if I kept this dialogue up, my poor friend would have a heart attack, I shifted gears. "How much do we know about how Jon-Jon got involved with Willa Mae? How much do we know about who else knew?"

Mutt folded his arms across his chest. "This is just like at the Treasure Chest. All you wanna do is talk, talk, talk."

"We've run out of witnesses and information. You got any other ideas?"

Brother Thomas got to his feet. "I wish you wouldn't do that, Brother Brack. You almost caused me to have to take a nitro pill."

"And I wish you'd stop thinking the worst all the time. I made a promise to you and Aphisha."

Mutt said, "How we gonna pick up the girls with Pastor Fat

Albert over here riding shotgun? They take one look at him and they gone."

I said, "I've an idea."

We dropped Brother Thomas at a hotel in Mount Pleasant with the instruction to get a suite for the night. Mutt and I headed downtown. While Mutt drove the Audi, I made a call to Caroline—Camilla and Willa Mae's madam. How I got her number was through my Aunt Patricia, Darcy's employer. How she got it she wouldn't say.

When a female voice answered, I said, "My name's George. Last summer I was in town for a convention and hooked up with a couple of your girls. I was wondering if you still had any around from then. Some friends and I'd like company."

From the driver's seat, Mutt said, "Amen to that."

The woman asked, "Did you have anyone in mind?"

"I remember there were a couple ethnic girls and an Oriental. Their names escape me."

"I think we have what you're looking for as long as you plan on treating them well. We have high standards for our girls. Their time is very valuable."

To keep from laughing, I said, "How does a thousand an hour sound for the three. Plus a bonus if the boys and I really take a liking to them."

"You know I will," Mutt said, a little too loud.

"And how many hours will you require?" she asked.

"Four." I asked where I could pick them up and said I'd be there at five o'clock. Before we hung up, she said she ran a cash upfront business.

Mutt wheeled us to the entrance of the condo building on upper King Street the madam had described. He whistled and said, "This is some nice digs."

Feeling glad that I'd stopped at home and changed into a polo shirt and khakis, I nodded and opened my car door. "Don't scare the neighbors, now, Clarence."

He lowered his window and took a cigarette out of his pack. "Call me Clarence one more time and see who gets scared."

"Who peed in your cereal this morning?" I asked.

"You did. We pickin' up three girls hot to trot and paid for and you invite Brother Goody-Two-Shoes to the party."

"I'm sensing one of us might have a problem controlling himself this evening. Let's get one thing clear. We can't touch these girls. All we can do is talk to them. Okay?"

The cherry of his Kool glowed as he lit up and inhaled.

"Okay?" I asked again.

"Yeah, yeah. Now go get them."

It was not easy keeping the reins on Mutt, but it had to be done. One wrong move and we'd be in jail. Our plan to pay for and pick up three call girls flirted with incarceration no matter what happened next.

Inside the building, a man in a suit at a desk pointed me to the elevators. Within thirty seconds, I was knocking on the devil's door.

A white woman answered my knock and I recognized her as Caroline, the madam from pictures Patricia had shown me from her archives. "Do come in, Mr. um—"

"Nelson." I held out a hand. "George Nelson."

She took my hand and my appearance in at the same time and apparently found everything in order. Her black silk dress exposed a healthy figure, even without the long slit up the side.

"Would you like to meet the girls, Mr. Nelson?"

"You said you had ones who might remember me and my friends?"

A grin formed across perfect teeth. She said, "Our girls will remember anything you want them to."

"Super."

She led me to a living room and motioned me to a couch, something not in my plan. The little voice in my head said to watch out.

"Be right back," she said.

The couch was black leather and soft. Thick planks made up the hardwood flooring. Stainless steel track lights provided soft illumination. The sound of someone mixing a drink focused my attention on a granite bar to my left. A slender Asian girl in a red kimono shook a drink shaker and poured the mixture into a martini glass. She set the shaker down, smiled at me, and brought the drink over. "For while you wait."

"Thank you." I took a sip of iced Absolut, the voice now screaming in my head.

Though I'd quit drinking, I reasoned that I couldn't afford to be anything less than a party in search of entertainment in front of this group. Declining the drink would have raised suspicions. At least, that's what I told myself while I finished it off.

As my head dropped and my eyelids grew heavy, I thought it peculiar no other men were in the room with me.

"Get up!"

A sharp pain shot through my side. I coughed and tried to sit up but couldn't with my hands tied behind my back. Someone had been nice enough to bind my feet as well. Blinking a few times, I made out a rough concrete floor, poor lighting, and the shape of someone standing over me.

"I said get up." The voice was male. Not very deep.

Swallowing hard, I said, "Kick me again and I'll rip your head off."

He kicked me again. I grunted, bit back obscenities, and spit on a nice pair of black loafers.

"Aw, man!" said the voice. He raised his foot for another shot.

"Stop." A woman's voice, this time. The madam's, I thought. "Maybe he's ready to talk."

Coughing up a big wad of phlegm, I swore off cigars again. The fancy shoes moved out of range so I settled for a straight shot at the madam.

She sidestepped my projectile loogie. "I guess not."

A stiff blow hit me between the shoulder blades and I saw stars. The bully threw in a few more kicks for good measure.

"Ready to talk now, punk?" The man with the kicking fetish had to be her assistant or whatever he called himself. Whipping boy . . . lap dog. . . .

He said, "What did you call me?"

I didn't realize I had spoken aloud.

Another direct pointy-shoe hit.

Pain shot through my side. "Son of a—" I cut myself off because it wasn't worth another hit.

"That's what I thought," he said. "Time you showed a little respect, old man."

Old man? I had maybe five years on this guy. Take these shackles off and I'd show him what an old man could do.

The madam said, "The license in your wallet says your name is Brack Pelton. I recognize you from the news. Any reason why you lied to me?"

Even through the pain, my brain put together the fact that the madam probably knew I was investigating the deaths of two of her girls. "I didn't realize pimps had an honesty code."

She made a sound like a sigh. I couldn't really tell, so I braced myself for another kick. It didn't come.

"We don't have time for games," she said.

"You mean I don't get to tie you up next?" I asked.

That got me another kick, a hard one. I grunted.

"Rafe doesn't like you much," she said.

"That's too bad," I said through clenched teeth, my shoulder blades aching from the blows. "I was starting to enjoy his company."

The madam sat in a folding chair facing me and crossed her legs, showing almost as much flesh as the customers who wore bikinis in my bar. Certainly more than most clothed women her age would, even the immodest ones. The bindings on my wrists and ankles caused my fondness for the whole situation to wane somewhat.

She said, "Why are you interested in girls from last summer?"

"Why don't you tell me why I should be?"

Rafe raised his foot to kick me again but the madam held up a hand. "Not yet."

I said, "I heard that girl that got burned up in the barrel worked for you two. Care to comment?"

Caroline looked away. "I don't know what you're talking about."

"What about the latest murder?" I asked. "Her name was Camilla Good. I believe she also worked for you. Seems to me your employee retention statistics are taking a beating lately. Especially when they seem to show up dead."

Rafe said, "Shut up, old man."

"What shall we do with him?" the madam asked.

Rafe paced. "Not sure. We've got to think about this. He's in with Darcy Wells. We can't have her snooping around here, either."

Of course, there was only one solution to that dilemma and it wouldn't end well for me.

"I guess there's only one thing to do," he said.

Caroline smiled and nodded.

Here it came.

As Rafe stooped down to lift me off the ground, someone kicked open the door. The madam screamed. Rafe let go of me and reached for something behind his back. I swung my body in an arch and swept his legs out from under him. He fell over the top of me.

Mutt stepped through the doorway. "Opie!"

Rafe scrambled to his feet with a gun in his hand. It was too late because Mutt swung the butt of his thirty-eight into his face and knocked him out.

The madam yelled again, a loud screeching noise.

Training the pistol on her, Mutt said, "You shut up."

She did as he asked.

"Good," he said, "now cut my brother loose."

"Br-brother?" she asked.

"That's right." With the gun still pointed at the madam, Mutt lit a Kool. "He ain't heavy, he's my brother."

A mile down the road, we found a pay phone and made an anonymous call to the police about the mess we'd left. They'd find Caroline and her muscle man tied up in some rundown apartment in North Charleston. That's where they'd apparently moved me to—unseen by Mutt waiting for me in the parking lot—after knocking me out. With the first-aid training Mutt and I received in the Corps, we did our best to patch up Rafe. It wasn't the time to rip his head off, although I secretly wished for a second chance to meet up with him. Instead, I found the four thousand missing from my pocket and then some, about ten grand altogether.

Watching Mutt drive my car again, I asked, "How'd you find me, anyway?"

Before he could answer, my cell phone vibrated and I looked at the screen. "Darcy."

"You best get it, then," Mutt said.

Smiling at the fact that despite all of my character flaws, and there were quite a few, my friends took care of me. I accepted the call from the person I believed had tracked me down for Mutt.

Darcy said, "You all right?"

"Never better," I said. "So how'd you find me?"

"Patricia used her sources and did a check on all the properties owned by Caroline and her company."

"She was incorporated?"

"Yes, but that isn't the point."

"What is?" I knew what was coming but asked it anyway.

"You and Mutt can't go around playing the Lone Ranger and Tonto."

"High ho, Silver."

"Whatever," she said. "We'll meet you at the news office."

She clicked off.

Mutt said, "What was that high ho bidness? High ho what?"

"Silver," I said. "We're playing Lone Ranger and Tonto."

"No, we ain't."

"It's better than Batman and Robin. You don't want to be Tonto?"

"I'm Shaft. You're Opie."

My watch said seven in the morning. "I've been out a long time."

"You sho' have. Where we headed?"

"The paper. And step on it."

He floored the accelerator, humming the theme song of his favorite detective.

Chapter Twenty-Six

At any other place of business, Mutt and I would have gotten quite a few stares. A six-foot-three black man, worn out Dickies, and a stained T-shirt, and me, a handsome specimen, if I do say so myself, except for the cuts and bruises from Rafe's kicks. Both Mutt and I needed showers and changes of clothes.

Miss Dell said, "Patricia expectin' you, sugar."

Mutt stopped in front of her desk, leaned forward, and said, "How you doin', hot stuff."

As he walked away, I caught Miss Dell pick up the small circulating fan and aim it at her face and neck, her eyes locked on Mutt like he was the next best thing to a Porterhouse steak. Love was definitely in the air.

Patricia stood in the doorway of her office, waving us in.

Mutt gave my aunt, the local media mogul, a peck on the cheek. I did the same.

She said, "You guys need showers."

Darcy acted impatient and petulant. She asked, "Why don't you tell us what kind of intel you were able to collect. That is, I hope you got something. Otherwise we all just wasted time."

Leaning against Patricia's mahogany desk, I looked at the two beautiful women and Mutt and said, "They're nervous about the same thing the Gardners were, something that happened last summer. And they're afraid of being linked with Willa Mae and Camilla."

Patricia asked, "Any idea what that could be?"

"Yeah, Opie," Mutt said. "I thought we was lookin' for Willa Mae's killer."

"We are. But I think she was a casualty, collateral damage like Camilla." I asked, "Anything big happen in the city then?"

Darcy said, "Nothing's come up so far. I've got some people on it."

She was my favorite news girl for several reasons, not only because of how good she looked in anything I'd seen her wear. Just like Jo. I saw the wheels turning in her mind. Whatever it was that happened, she'd find it.

The roofie they'd slipped in my drink put me in a coma for the night so I was good to go. But Mutt wanted sleep so I dropped him off at his house. Now, with some free time on my hands, I stopped by Chauncey's to visit Shelby. My dog ran down the drive to greet me, jumping and barking. We wrestled on the driveway until Trish came into view, at which point he gave me one last lick and went to stand by her side. Just like he always did whenever I left him here.

She patted his head, a diamond tennis bracelet sliding down her thin wrist. "He misses you." For a woman twenty years older than me, she carried herself well. I was pretty sure she indulged in little or no extra maintenance work other than personal-trainer appointments.

Brushing myself off, I stood and shook her hand. "Thanks for taking such good care of him."

"We were just about to have some lunch. Would you care to join us?"

"Chauncey home from the office?" I asked.

"No. I was referring to Shelby and me."

Her two labs barked at us through the wrought iron fence that enclosed the backyard. I figured they were jealous. I could relate.

Inside, Trish set another place at the kitchen table and served ham and cheese sandwiches with Dijon mustard, a really nice egg salad, and potato chips. Not the diet I expected her to have, but I suspected that Shelby might have been her taste tester. He munched innocently on Eukanuba while we talked.

"Are you aware of anything that happened last summer?" I asked.

"What are you talking about?"

"Anything involving call girls and the Gardners or other powerful Charlestonians?" I swallowed half a sandwich and washed it down with sweet tea.

Chauncey and Trish were Charleston socialites. They ran in the right circles, went to all the right parties, concerts, and other events, and were regularly photographed for the city magazine. If anyone knew something that might have rocked the boat, Trish would.

She nibbled on a chip. "Nothing comes to mind. I'll have to think about that."

Back in the Audi, I drove to the Pirate's Cove. I hadn't been here in almost a week and it felt even longer. From the deck, Paige watched me pull into my parking spot and get out. She'd last seen me drive a rental. Now my wheels were an Audi. I hoped I wouldn't have to explain the change.

She said, "We need to talk."

This wouldn't be one of our better conversations, I sensed. Without meeting her glare, I walked into the bar and didn't stop until I entered my office. Easing into my uncle's chair, I sighed.

She closed the door. "How long are we going to run this place with no liquor license and no customers?"

"Are we out of money yet?"

Folding her arms across her chest, she said, "That's not the point."

"We're not closing."

"The girls are getting restless."

"Have them clean and paint the place."

She banged the desk with a clenched fist. "Look around! We've already done that."

Her eyes were puffy like she was on the ragged edge.

"We're not closing."

She asked, "What are we supposed to do to keep busy?"

An idea came to mind. A male sexist pig of an idea. It was perfect. "Have them suit up and play some beach volleyball."

"You can't be serious?"

I stood and rested my hands on her shoulders. "I am. With advertising and prizes. The girls'll love it."

"Yeah, right. I'm sure that's what you had in mind." She looked past me as if in thought. Then she said, "What are we going to sell to the customers? We can't serve them anything besides sodas and iced tea."

"Nothing. Call our distributors and see if any of them want to bring a truck and trailer and sell beer by the cup. And find out what kind of permits we need for that."

She gave me a weak slap on the cheek. After a smirk, she said, "That's really not that bad of an idea. We'll still make money on T-shirts and food."

Backing out of the office, I said, "Call Lester Brogan and make sure he doesn't see anything illegal with it."

"Lester Brogan?" she asked. "I thought Chauncey was our lawyer."

"Long story."

I explained the situation to her, which was painful because it made me realize how truly impulsive I'd been. She let me off easy by just listening.

And then we discussed the volleyball match. Paige and the single-mom army would do a bang-up job with the whole thing, which was good because I wouldn't be around for it. When I told her that, she got quiet again.

As long as the beer truck showed, every able-bodied male within fifty miles would come. We'd barely break even on trinkets and hamburgers but the publicity and the town council annoyance would be priceless. If we were going down, it was going to be in a flaming fireball. And it would keep them busy so I could keep looking for Willa Mae's killer without too much disturbance.

Rosalita called, upset that I hadn't informed her of what happened with Caroline and Rafe. She agreed to meet me for dinner, but I could tell she was reluctant. Following a shower and change of clothes, I drove downtown and found a parking spot on Church Street. The restaurant was only a few short blocks away but with the heat, I still broke a sweat. At least the parasitic insects weren't bad downtown. Just the crunch of palmetto bugs underfoot.

I noticed my date waiting for me at the hostess station. She wore a nice blue dress and black heels and looked down when I approached.

We were seated and the hostess had taken our drink orders and left.

I asked, "Everything all right?"

A faint smile. "Not really."

The waitress, a twenty-year-old with big eyeglasses and tattoos on the underside of her wrists, brought our drinks and told us the specials.

"I think we're going to need a few minutes," I said.

She smiled and said she'd come back.

Rosalita said, "Aren't you going to look at your menu?"

"What's the matter?"

Avoiding my eyes, she said, "Why don't we at least order first?"

"I already know what I want." And it probably wasn't what Rosalita was going to tell me.

Our eyes met.

She reached across the table and took my hand. "I don't know how to say what I need to say."

"I ignore authority, put myself in danger, and beat up people."

"That's part of it. The other part—"

The waitress returned to the table. I said we needed a few more minutes.

Rosalita said, "I need some time to think."

There it was.

After a peck on the cheek from Rosalita, I was alone at the corner of Calhoun and King and felt an internal tug for a drink. The vodka Mickey Finn from the night before had reopened that door. And the rooftop bar where Mutt and I had taken Kali seemed like a good place to be since I didn't want to go home or anywhere else at the moment. I found an open stool at the end of the bar.

A tall brunette with easy eyes and a name tag that read "Sheila" took my drink order and left to make it. I really wanted a cigar but decided to save it for a walk on the beach later. Sheila brought me my drink and asked, with a nice smile, if there was anything else I needed. A difficult question at the moment, but I declined. She left to serve her other customers.

A tumbler with ice and Maker's Mark rested on a napkin in front of me. Drinking had never been a friend of mine. More of a crutch and a downfall. Aside from having friends, I'd been alone since Jo's passing. There'd been other women, but they were better forgotten than remembered.

I took a long pull on the whiskey. It burned going down. Before long, I asked for another. And another.

An effeminate male voice broke my downward spiral. "Hi, detective guy. Who you spying on now?"

Despite my numbness, I recognized the spiked-up hair as belonging to the kid from the soap and body lotion shop on King Street.

"Take your pick," I said.

He waved at someone down the bar and said, "Hey, Elizabeth? Look who's here."

The noise of the bar dissipated as the blond beauty from the shop strolled to where my effeminate friend and I sat. Her dress, this one yellow, fit as perfectly as the last one. I tried to hold her gaze, but came up short.

She said, "Come here often?"

"Apparently not often enough."

Her coworker said, "He's smitten. I'll see you later, sweetie."

I stood and offered my seat and she sat.

Sheila returned, smiled at me, and took Elizabeth's drink order. While Sheila poured the glass of white wine for Elizabeth, she asked me if I needed anything.

"No thanks." Not at the moment, anyway.

Elizabeth touched the side of my face and said, "It looks like I'm not the first one to get hold of you tonight."

"Huh?" I wasn't sure if she was referring to the bruises I'd accumulated.

Smiling, she dabbed a napkin in her wine glass, rubbed my cheek, and showed me a white napkin with a shade of color very similar to the lipstick Rosalita wore when she gave me the farewell peck.

Just great.

I opened my mouth to speak but Elizabeth placed a finger on my lips.

"No need to explain. Leon and I saw you come in and go through several drinks by yourself. We debated on leaving you alone but I couldn't help myself." She took a sip from her wine. "So I'm guessing the lipstick on your cheek is the reason I haven't received a call."

"It's complicated."

She giggled. "That was a movie, silly."

"Also an understatement." My drink tasted mostly of whiskey-flavored water.

"I heard you're having problems with your bar."

"You did, huh?"

"Yeah, I asked around. Pretty impressive how much trouble one person can cause in such a short amount of time."

Elizabeth crossed her legs and I tried not to notice.

"I'm just getting started."

"Did you really shoot those men last year?" she asked, a little too loud.

Two guys standing next to us glanced my way.

"Don't believe everything you hear," I said. "What about you?"

"What about me?"

"All I know is your first name and that you look lovely in the dresses you wear."

A pink blush colored her cheeks, then left. She said, "Compliments will get you only so far, mister. You also know where I work."

"Don't dodge the question. How long have you lived in Charleston?"

"All my life."

"A local girl. I thought so. Have you ever been in my bar?"

Another grin. "Have you seen me in your bar?"

"Touché." I could feel my face redden.

"Sorry. That was unfair. I *have* been to your bar but it was a long time ago. An old man ran it then."

"He was my uncle." And the memory of him made me want another drink. I signaled Sheila.

Elizabeth put a hand to her mouth. "I'm sorry. I did read about what happened to him."

Sheila brought me my whiskey and Elizabeth ordered another glass of wine.

"Okay," Elizabeth said, "you want to know about me? I grew up in Mount Pleasant and am in my senior year at College of Charleston."

"What's your major?"

"Psychology."

"Good field. You interested in solving other people's problems or your own?"

Another grin. "Double touché, Mr. Pelton. You're probably referring to my bad choice in men."

"I only know of one so far, maybe a second in the making."

"The night is still young," she said. "I guess that means I have more self-evaluation to do."

My turn to grin.

She set her glass on the bar. "Jon-Jon was rich and I was stupid."

Into my glass, I said, "We all have baggage."

"So what happened between you and the owner of the purple lipstick?"

"I was rich and she was stupid."

That made her laugh. Thc bar seemed to get brighter, or was that just me focusing on her perfect teeth?

She said, "Okay, you've earned yourself a slow dance. What do you say we go find one?"

Chapter Twenty-Seven

The sound of my phone vibrating across a wood surface woke me. Squinting, I had to take in my surroundings, which were pink and unfamiliar.

A mound of blond curls snuggled next to me. "Tell them to call back later."

Picking up the phone, I stared at the caller I.D. It was Darcy. I shut the phone off, and turned to go back to sleep but couldn't.

The apartment was small and tidy. And really pink. My headache informed me I'd once again had too much to drink and that I was getting too old for this.

An hour later, Elizabeth awoke and got ready for an early class. She walked me to the door. Instead of a quick peck on the cheek and a promise to call, she gave me a hug and a kiss. "I had a really good time last night."

"Me, too," I said and meant it. Unlike the rest of my life, there was no drama with this girl. I liked that.

"If you don't patch things up with purple lipstick, give me a call."

Her words reminded me of everything I'd gotten drunk to forget.

I drove my Audi to the Church of Redemption. Brother Thomas was in a counseling session with a couple and I waited in the sanctuary. After an amount of time sufficient for me to take a much-needed nap, he came out and woke me up. In his office, I told him how I'd messed things up with Rosalita and used Elizabeth to nurse the wound I didn't want to deal with. It felt like confession, and I needed to confess. Mutt would have cheered and demanded more detail. Brother Thomas simply listened and then said a prayer for me.

Walking out of the church, I heard *Witchy Woman* buzz from my phone and I answered it. "Hey, Darcy. I was just about to call—"

"Do I have to remind you I've got sources all over this town? You've been in the paper too many times not to be noticed."

I didn't reply.

She said, "I thought we had an understanding."

Not really sure what that meant, or not really wanting to think about the implications, I kept quiet.

"Since you're not talking, I'll tell you what I know. Her name is Elizabeth Powell and she used to date our friend, Jon-Jon."

"No kidding," I said. "Anything else?"

"Meet me at the paper."

Ten minutes later, I parked in front of my aunt's office and got out of my car. Darcy emerged from the *Palmetto Pulse* headquarters.

Pointing to the Audi, she asked, "Didn't you have one of these before?"

With the key fob in my hand, I pressed the unlock button and opened Darcy's door.

Without any tell as to what she was thinking or what kind of mood she was in, she said, "This doesn't get you off the hook."

"Of course not."

She sat and swung her legs in, and I shut her door.

Getting in my side, I buckled up, hit the start button, and asked, "Where to?"

Darcy and I watched Gardner the candidate's office from the front seats of my car while parked in the back of the lot. I tapped the steering wheel and periodically checked the rearview mirror in case we were attacked from behind, like a previous mission when one of the bad guys had shot Darcy.

Two figures exited the Gardner building, Gardner and someone I hadn't seen before.

"Who's the black guy?" I said.

"His name is Ernest Brown and he's who I think killed Willa Mae and Camilla."

This man was far different from the four goons in the Caddy I'd put down. From this distance, Ernest Brown appeared to be about my size. He seemed fit and walked with a military posture. Even in this heat, he wore black jeans and a black T-shirt.

Darcy reclined in her seat and stretched her legs.

I asked, "How long were you going to hold out on me?"

"It's not my fault you're too busy being led around by your penis to do any real investigating."

I locked in on Ernest Brown. As if sensing he was being watched, he turned and looked in our direction. A little unnerved, I asked, "Who is he?"

"Daddy's fix-it man. He used to work for Jack Towler."

"The guy who won the election that everyone said was rigged last year?"

She nodded.

Ernest Brown most likely could not see us. That's what I told myself, anyway, as he shook Gardner's hand, then got in a nineties black Impala SS. It boasted large chrome wheels and twin exhaust pipes sticking out underneath the bumper. He drove away and I pressed the Audi's start button.

Darcy said, "I know where he's going."

We followed the Impala at a distance. The last thing I wanted was to tip off this Ernest fix-it guy that he had company. If he was actually a killer—and Darcy thought he was—then two more names wouldn't matter much to him. Ours.

At the entrance to an upscale nursing-home community, he pulled in.

"Bingo," Darcy said.

"Bingo what?"

"He's a creature of habit. Every day at lunchtime he comes here to visit with his mother."

I passed the entrance and kept going. "You don't expect to sneak in there and hide behind the potted plants to watch him feed her split-pea soup, do you?"

"No, Brack. I expect you to contribute to this investigation."

Shooting around a slow-moving van with ladders tied to the roof, I asked, "Like how?"

"I just gave you his schedule for the next hour. Drop me off at the *Pulse* and come back here. We need to know what he does next."

Sometimes, and this was one of those times, I could be the dumbest man in the world. When I pulled up to the front entrance of the paper, Darcy got out of the car. She turned and ducked her head back in.

"Paige got another job offer," she said. "Get your head out of your pants and figure out how to save your bar before you lose her."

She walked away. I let out a long breath and gripped the steering wheel tight.

"This just gets better and better."

Before heading back to the nursing home, I picked up Mutt at his house. For some reason, I didn't want to be alone. I wanted another drink, not that Mutt would discourage me in that regard. If I left decisions to him, we'd bail on the stakeout and close out the evening at the Treasure Chest. Part of me even thought that might be a good idea.

Rain that an hour earlier was nowhere in sight now pelted

the windshield. Such was the weather in the lowcountry summer. Mutt ran from his front door and jumped in the car.

"Let's git it," he said.

Ten minutes later we pulled into the parking lot of the nursing home.

"Which car's his?" Mutt asked.

As we passed the black Impala, I pointed.

"Now that's a nice ride," he said. "Not as nice as yo' uncle's Caddy could be, but not bad. I'd steal it."

As if on cue, Ernest Brown exited the main building and walked to his car.

"Aw, man," said Mutt.

"Aw, man, what?"

Mutt blew out a long sigh.

"What?" I asked.

"I know that brother."

Frustrated, I asked, "You what? Know him? How?"

"He come in the bar a few times."

Ernest got in his car and pulled out of the parking lot. I gave him a long lead, then followed.

"He came in your bar?"

My friend turned to face me. "Look, Opie. I ain't got hot mammas with no clothes on flashing gold cards at me. I take what I can get. And another brother is always welcome."

I didn't have the heart to remind him his bar was no more. Instead, I asked, "How many times did he come in?"

Scratching his chin as if in thought, he said, "I'd say two or three. All in the same week."

We were catching up to Ernest so I backed off and slid behind a big Toyota SUV. "You remember when that week was?"

"Yeah," he said. "Right before that cracker blew the place up."

Ernest ran a yellow light and we got stuck three cars back.

Cars crossed the intersection in front of us.

Mutt said, “You think he mighta had something to do with it?”

“Yes.”

The light turned green. I revved the engine and dropped the clutch, using the empty turning lane to our left to get us around several slow moving cars. Two red-line shifts later and the traffic was way behind us. The problem was that Ernest and his shiny Impala were nowhere to be seen.

“You lost him?”

Darcy had an uncanny way of pointing out the obvious. With the iPhone to my ear, I nodded at Mutt as if the conversation with my favorite news girl was going great.

“I think he might have spotted us.”

We were parked in the lot of a Piggly Wiggly grocery store. Yes, I was Big on the Pig.

Mutt lowered his window and lit a Kool.

Thrumming the steering wheel, I said, “So, what else do you know about his routine?”

“I thought we agreed you were going to do the tailing and phone me with updates, not the other way around.”

“Yeah, well. It didn’t work out that way.”

“No kidding.” She sighed. “Okay, let me see what else I can do for you.”

She hung up.

I put my phone in my shirt pocket, took out a Dominican cigar, and pressed in the cigarette lighter. As if an omen, this car actually had one. Must have been ordered with the lung cancer package.

Mutt asked, “What she say?”

“She’ll get back to me.”

“You know what I’d do?”

This was going to be good. "Let me guess. Cruise the strip clubs?"

"I was gonna say drive back to his boss man's house and see if he showed up there, but you got a good point."

Pictures of Willa Mae and Camilla took over my mind like internet pop-ups. If Ernest had a taste for women in the business, then maybe that's where we should be looking.

I said, "Okay, Casanova. You win."

A big smile lit Mutt's face. "How!"

Raising a hand, I said, "Easy there. What we're going to do is cruise the parking lots."

As quickly as the smile appeared on his face, it vanished. "You sure a lot of fun, Opie."

"When this is over, you can hit all the clubs you want. Right now, we need to find a killer and this Ernest guy is our target. Are we Ebony and Ivory or what?"

"You had to go and bring that up, huh? All they did was take advantage of a blind brother when they made that one."

I said, "How."

The parking lot of the Treasure Chest was packed. We did a slow roll up one side and down the other. And in the last spot sat our target's Impala. I stopped the Audi behind it.

"Opie, when you right, you right."

Through the windshield, I watched the doorman. He looked our way, then went back to his smartphone. But if we stayed here much longer, he might get interested. I said, "We can't go in there."

Mutt rested an arm on the window ledge. "Why not?"

"He might see us." I unlocked my phone and made a call. When the other end picked up, I said, "Detective Crawford? This is Brack Pelton."

"Hey, um, Brack."

"I've got a source that identified Willa Mae's killer. If it's him, he's the same one who murdered that girl in the alley."

Crawford said, "Well, I appreciate your calling me. Why are you calling me? I thought you were close with Detective Warrez."

"Long story."

"Uh-huh."

I gave him Ernest Brown's name and tag number.

"So what kind of proof do you have this perp's the one?"

"A reliable source."

"That's it? I'm going to need more than that."

"Like what?"

"A little something called evidence. *Anything.* A knife with prints. Her underwear in his car. Video of him committing a crime."

"Gee, that's all?" I said, "How come every time I talk to you guys, I end up having to do your job for you?"

"It's not like that."

"How about this? Since you let Jon-Jon go, do you have any suspects?"

Crawford didn't respond right away. When he did, he said, "The investigation is open and ongoing. The Charleston Police Department is—"

"Yeah, yeah, yeah. Look, I'm hanging up now. I thought you might like to be cut in on solving this case. I guess I was wrong."

"Don't do anything stupid, Pelton."

I'd heard that one before. It didn't stop me then, either.

After I ended the call, I put the phone in my pocket.

Mutt said, "Why'd you have to go and tell the po-lice what we up to?"

"I wanted a record in case they find our bones burned up in some trash barrel."

He shook himself like a dog. "That waren't even funny, Opie."

★ ★ ★ ★ ★

We pulled across the street and waited for Ernest Brown to get in his car and drive away. At least, that was my plan. Mutt wanted to head inside and check out the show. To get him to comply, I had to promise to front him an all-expense-paid night of debauchery when this was over.

Lucky for us, across the street stood a vacant building with no lights over its parking lot. We both lit up smokes, mine another nice Dominican, his a domestic in the cigarette family. *Papa Was a Rolling Stone* played on the old-school station, Mutt's favorite.

He snapped his fingers. "Oh, yeah!"

I blew smoke rings out the window. We'd been in the car only a short time, but it looked as if we lived in it. Drink cups, candy wrappers, and an almost-empty box of doughnuts littered the interior. The front windshield also needed a good cleaning.

Ernest Brown walked out of the Treasure Chest with a girl on each arm, one black and the other Asian.

"Ho boy!" Mutt said.

"That must be costing him a fortune."

"All you white people think about is money."

"What do you think about?" As soon as I asked, I knew the answer would be bad.

"My man Ernest over there is walkin' it to his car. How!"

We watched our target open the rear door to his whip. The girls slid in the back, and he followed.

I said, "I don't believe this."

"Believe it," Mutt said. "My boy got a two-for-one sale and ain't gonna wait."

Before I made up my mind what to do, Ernest got out of the backseat and into the driver's seat. The brake lights lit up and we heard the rumble of the barely muffled V-8. He reversed from the parking spot and pulled out of the lot onto the main drag. I gave him a hundred yards and followed.

"Don't lose him this time, Opie."

"Thanks, Darcy," I said.

Mutt shifted in his seat. "My girl give you a hard time, didn't she?"

As if on queue, the Bluetooth announced her call.

Mutt pressed the phone button and said, "How you doin', you sweet thang you!"

Darcy's voice came out of the car speakers. "Mutt! I didn't know you were with him. He needs all the help he can get."

"You know that's right!" he said.

"Did you find Ernest?" I asked.

"His credit card just recorded a thousand-dollar transaction at the Treasure Chest."

"A thousand dollars?" Mutt punched my arm. "That brother paid a thousand dollars for them strippers, Opie. A thousand dollars!"

"Where are you?" she asked.

Ahead, Ernest turned on to the main four-lane.

"Following Ernest," I said.

"So you found him. You've almost redeemed yourself."

"I guess that's better than nothing."

She said, "Call me when you get something, Opie."

The next sound was the chime of a disconnected line.

The black Impala, now only twenty yards ahead, pulled into the parking lot of a motel.

Actually calling the place a motel was being generous. The place not only rented by the hour, but charged extra for the rooms with the least amount of bedbugs.

Mutt said, "My man ain't got no class, bringin' them fine ladies to a place like this."

That coming from the man whose bar, before it burned, was held together by more termites than wood particles.

I passed the motel and turned into the lot of a run-down restaurant next door.

"What we doin' here?" Mutt asked.

"I got an idea."

Chapter Twenty-Eight

The inside of the restaurant mimicked the outside in that it, too, was grungy and unkempt. We took a booth with ripped seats and a chipped table by the window with a clear view of the exit from the hotel's parking lot. Not wanting to risk the food, I ordered coffee from an overweight woman stretching her tight jeans and boasting a low-cut top. Mutt ordered the same. I wanted to give Ernest enough time to get comfortable with the ladies.

Mutt said, "So what's this crazy idea you got?"

Before I could respond, the waitress brought our coffee.

Mutt watched her depart. "Whoa."

"I think she may be a little too much for you, Shaft."

With his eyes still on the waitress, he said, "Ain't no woman too much for Shaft."

"What do you say you and me go and make sure Ernest doesn't get his money's worth?"

His eyes met mine. "You know, I been thinkin' maybe those girls he wit' could use a break."

I gulped my coffee and stood.

Mutt did the same. I left a five dollar bill on the table and we walked out.

Outside the restaurant, I handed Mutt the keys. "Pull the car around and wait."

"Opie, this ain't no time to be the Lone Ranger. It took me

all night to find you the last time."

"I'm not going to go and kick down the door." I had something better planned.

Mutt gave me a weary look but accepted the keys.

I walked down the sidewalk to the motel but didn't enter its lobby since I didn't want lodging. I continued along the side of the two-story building to where the cars were parked. Doors to all the rooms opened to the outside, including those on the second floor, accessible from a walkway with a flight of stairs at each end. A quick reconnaissance of the parking lot and I found Ernest's car parked in front of room one-fifteen. Of course, I couldn't be sure precisely which room he was in, or on which level. But for what I had planned, it didn't matter. I took the stairs nearest to his car. Close to the ice machine on the second floor, I found what I was looking for—and it offered a great vantage point from which to watch the fun.

After a quick prayer that the fire alarm would actually work, I reached out and yanked the handle. Two long seconds passed before it kicked on, and a loud wail erupted from the aged system.

Happily, I waited for the small crowd of people to emerge from their rooms and move down the stairs to the safety of the parking lot. From where I stood, I could see most of the room doors. A quick tally of the occupants revealed a disproportionate number of older men and younger women, all haphazardly dressed, and all looking thoroughly irritated.

Ernest stumbled out of room two-thirteen, his shirt off but otherwise clothed. The two young ladies with him walked out unabashedly in lace brassieres, leather-looking panties, and heels.

When the threesome and the other en déshabillé occupants had gone down the stairs, I entered Ernest's room, thanks to old-school door locks. Over the winter, Darcy had taught me how to pick them. I found Ernest's wallet on a TV stand, along with his cell phone. The phone had a security lock but his wallet offered up a driver's license and some business cards. I memorized the address on his license and slipped one of his business cards in my pocket. Also in the wallet I found a business card for none other than Gordon Sykes, Esquire. Willa Mae's lawyer. The one selling information. Written on the card was tomorrow's date and ten A.M.

I eased out of the room. After I did a quick wipe of the alarm switch to remove my prints, I scrambled down the farthest flight of stairs and ran around the end of the building to the street.

Mutt passed the motel and stopped at the next intersection. Out of the line of sight of the crowd gathered at the motel, I sauntered to the car, opened the passenger-side door, and slid in. Mutt eased away from the curb.

"Where to now, boss?" he asked.

Chuckling, I said, "You think he's got to return the girls to the Chest?"

"I ain't thought of that. I bet you're right."

Ernest returned his thousand-dollar lady friends to the Treasure Chest an hour later. My guess was he tried to salvage the remainder of the time he'd paid for, but it was fun messing with him. Mutt and I followed him to the address on his driver's license.

After dropping Mutt at his house, I made my way home. Without Shelby, my inherited shack was not a pleasant place to be. Since I hadn't changed the furniture from the time I moved in—because mine had burned up along with my Sullivan's Island house—this place reminded me of my uncle. As I unloaded my pockets, I noticed I had a text message on my phone. It was from Paige telling me the volleyball tournament had been a hit. Nothing about any job offers.

The letter I'd received from Megan was on the table. It reminded me of Camilla's tip about Friday night at the Courtyard Suites. A good thing I'd seen it because that was tomorrow. I called Paige.

She answered the phone, shouting, "You should have been there!"

"I'm sorry I wasn't."

In a calmer voice, she asked, "Is everything all right?"

Not wanting to get into a discussion of her potential resignation, I said, "Listen, I need a favor from you and the staff."

The next morning, I picked up Mutt and his thirty-eights at nine-thirty and drove to the same parking lot from which Brother Thomas, Darcy, and I had staked out Gordon Sykes, Esquire.

With all four windows down, what breeze there was did not relieve the inferno. The engine ticked as it cooled. Mutt fired up a Kool. I sparked a Dominican.

At a quarter to ten Sykes walked to his Grand Prix, got in, and drove away.

"Let's see where Mr. Sykes goes for his ten o'clock appointment," I said.

He turned down several side streets and got on the interstate heading into downtown. When I-26 ended, he got off on King Street and headed to the tourist shopping district. At a side street just past the shop where Elizabeth worked, Sykes turned and parked by an open meter. I found a spot a half block away and pulled in. Scanning the area, I caught the back of the crooked lawyer's bald head as he entered the building where Jon-Jon lived.

Mutt blew a stream of smoke outside the car.

From habit, I stuck the cigar in my mouth and pulled one of the thirty-eights.

"You expectin' trouble?"

Around the ten-dollar stogie, I spoke. "We step out of this car, you better be locked and loaded. This guy is dirt and two girls he knew are dead. If something goes down here I'm shooting first and asking questions later."

"I knew there was a reason I hung out wit' you, Opie."

Twenty minutes, one cigar, and two Kools later, Sykes exited the building. A stupid grin crossed his lizard face.

I snapped a few pictures with my iPhone. "Jon-Jon must have given him something extra."

Mutt chuckled.

"At least we now know Willa Mae's attorney is in bed with the enemy."

Sykes got in his car and pulled away from the curb, heading down the street.

We banged over the ancient brick street decorated with rough-patched sinkholes. Sykes's piece of junk on four wheels lumbered along at the speed limit a block ahead. It took a lot of finesse to keep cars between us because no one except for him seemed to want to drive that slow.

After a few miles, I said, "A pack of Kools says I know where he's going." It was not a bet I really wanted to win because winning meant we were wasting our time.

"If he got a pocket full of cash, he goin' to the Chest."

I didn't reply. Instead, I made sure we were right. The strip club seemed a central feature in this whole tale. Sykes pulled in and parked. We idled at the curb, giving him a few minutes to go inside. It was eleven A.M.

A rap on my door made both of us jump.

Detective Warrez smiled and said, "You guys planning on going inside or what?"

Mutt said, "I am if you are. Opie can wait in the car."

I asked, "What are you doing here?"

"Police business," she said. "What are you doing here?"

"Mutt was showing me where he wanted his birthday party held."

"Mm-hmm," she said. "Well, now that you've seen it, I suggest you head on out."

"You're on a stakeout, aren't you?" I asked.

She slapped the roof twice. "You boys have a nice day. Now, head out."

Mutt and I walked into Patricia's office. Her staff had stumbled onto something from last year. When she told me, I knew why we'd missed it. It happened at the same time Patricia and I had been closing in on another killer—my uncle's.

Apparently the police force didn't like being questioned as to why they'd let the city's sex trade run for so long without so much as a single arrest. They set up a major sting operation and caught a lot of people off guard. While the other papers did their best to keep up with the story, Patricia's and probably the city's best reporters were focused on my uncle and the web of corruption we'd discovered.

Patricia's staff found a plethora of information on the arresting officers and most of the pimps. More elusive were the names of the johns who'd gotten caught. Patricia made two well-placed phone calls and came up with a partial list. It was enough.

I stared at the ten names she'd written on a pad. But I needed only two of them. At the top were senior and junior Jonathan Langston Gardners.

My aunt had her staff comb public records and see if the Gardners showed up. Somehow, the father and son delinquents had managed to escape prosecution and there were no records. It was as if it never happened.

A large contribution had been made to an influential city official's election within twenty-four hours of the supposed arrest.

The same city official that Ernest Brown had worked for. The donating entity turned out to be Estelle Gardner.

"Estelle Gardner?" I asked.

"The wife of treasurer candidate Jonathan Langston Gardner the third and mother of Jon-Jon."

The woman I'd seen at the Gardner party I crashed.

I held the copy of the letter Megan had given me that she'd received from Camilla in my hand and reread the line that could change everything: *Tell him to check out the Courtyard Suites, room 113, on Friday night.*

Well, today was Friday and the parking lot of the Courtyard Suites was full. The tip Camilla put in the letter to Megan had already paid off. After my phone call with Paige the night before, members of the single-mother army had been recruited for stakeout duty. An hour ago, they'd informed me that Camilla's tip had been good. After they'd told me the name of one of the individuals in the room, I knew who I needed to share my new-found information with.

Estelle Gardner, the mother of Jon-Jon and, more importantly for this exercise, the wife of treasurer of South Carolina candidate, fidgeted in the passenger seat of my Audi. "We've been here for ten minutes now," she said. "When I agreed to this, I half-expected you to make a move on me."

Patricia had come up with a location on Estelle, a charitable event at the library. I intercepted her on the way to her car and told her I had something she needed to see. After a cursory dismissal, I told her if she wasn't interested in what I had that she could read about it in the paper in the morning. Curiosity must have gotten the better of her because she relented.

I took my eyes off the white door to suite one-thirteen, the one mentioned in Camilla's letter. "I didn't think you were into peasant bar-owners."

She leaned back against the door. "Don't worry. I most definitely am not. And I'm getting out of this car if you don't tell me what's going on."

I looked at my watch. "Just be patient."

She sighed. "This better be worth my time."

The door to the suite finally opened. Estelle and I watched a tall man with his back to us pull a naked black girl toward him, kiss her, and run his hands down her back. Estelle made a sound, like a bird chirping, then reached for the door handle. She was out of the car before I could hit the lock button, leaving her door wide open.

"I guess it's plan B," I said to the empty seat beside me.

Estelle stopped in front of my car and stood with arms folded across her chest. I think I saw one of her feet tapping the cracked concrete sidewalk. Gardner the candidate was still preoccupied. I got out and slammed my door, catching his attention.

His mouth opened when he saw his wife. The girl behind him put her arms around his chest, but he pushed her off and took a step away. I found it amusing to see him quickly try to distance himself from who he was, as if attempting to pull off his own skin. I put my hand on the fender of my car but didn't get too comfortable. Estelle struck me as being unpredictable and that kept me uneasy. If she pulled out a gun and started shooting, chances were her husband would be dead before I could stop it.

"Don't bother trying to explain yourself," Estelle said to her husband. She motioned to me. "We now have another problem."

Gardner transformed before my eyes from tyrant to scared rabbit. I had set up this ambush, and now I almost felt sorry for him.

Estelle spun on her heels and walked back to the car. "Let's go."

Gardner raised a hand as if trying to stop the future from smacking him across the face, then let it drop. I got in the car and pressed the start button. The engine lit and I pulled away from the curb.

When we reached East Bay, Estelle said, "Care to have a drink with me, Mr. Pelton?"

We sat at a table on the roof-top bar where I'd run into Elizabeth. Mrs. Estelle Gardner ordered a double vodka tonic. I got a sweet tea.

"You really are a piece of work," she said.

"I get that a lot."

The silence that followed was interrupted only by the waitress bringing our drinks.

Estelle lifted the glass and used the cocktail straw to taste hers and said, "So what do you want?"

I squeezed a lemon wedge into mine. "Did you really have to do it?"

"Do what?"

"Have them killed?" I said.

Her eyes opened wide and her cheeks got red. It looked like she clenched her jaw for a second. "I'm sure I don't know what you're talking about."

"Willa Mae was going to give you a mixed grandbaby and you couldn't have that."

"If you're talking about that dead hooker, who knows if she was pregnant or not. And surely the father could have been a whole bunch of men. After all, she was a hooker."

I smiled and said, "But you couldn't take a chance, could you? No room in the Gardner legacy for a black baby. Not with your husband in the running for the treasurer for the state of South Carolina." Bringing my drink to my mouth, I said, "I guess we'll have to wait for the paternity test to come back."

"There was no paternity test."

As soon as the words came out of her mouth, I could tell

Estelle wanted to take them back.

She recovered by opening her purse and checking her face with a compact.

"Besides," she continued, still focused on herself, "I can assure you my son has nothing to do with any prostitutes."

"Is that why you fixed the arrest records from last summer?"

Her head jerked up like I'd just slapped her.

"Hiring Ernest was really not the best idea," I said. "What you did was let a rabid dog into the kennel with your so-called purebred pedigree. And I think you know I'm right. I mean, he dumped the body right in your son's backyard. I'll bet that wasn't part of the plan. One thing, though. Before Ernest killed her, Willa Mae had lost the baby. You had her killed and created this mess for no reason."

She opened her mouth to say something but stopped.

"That's right," I said. "The reason Willa Mae had been on that street was because she was visiting the local midwife. She'll testify that she'd given Willa an examination and confirmed she'd lost the baby."

She stood, threw her drink in my face, and said, "I'm taking a cab."

I guess she forgot all about her husband.

Satisfied that we'd caught Willa Mae's killer, Darcy swung by my house and got me and we picked up Shelby. In celebration of cornering Estelle, we spent the rest of the night at the news office working on the story that would expose her and Ernest Brown.

The next morning, on the way back to my house, Darcy crossed onto Sullivan's Island. She missed the turn onto Jasper that would take us across the bridge and onto the Isle of Palms where my shack of a house was.

"We taking a detour?" I asked.

She didn't say anything. Instead, she turned right onto Middle Street and headed toward my old house before it had been burned to the ground. Now the empty land belonged to my old neighbor.

At the beach access I'd used when I lived here, she pulled into the sand lot and turned the engine off. "How about you, me, and Mr. Shelby take a walk on the beach?"

Without waiting for an answer, she got out and moved her seat forward so Shelby could jump out, which he did without hesitation.

I got out, closed the door, and followed them. At the surf, we turned left and headed up the beach. Shelby walked with his tongue out and his tail up, a spring in his step. I didn't have his leash but he stuck close by. Today, no one else had ventured out this far down the island. Most preferred the wider stretches of beach.

The ocean breeze felt good and the air tasted salty and clean.

After a few minutes of silence, she said, "I'm going to miss this."

Not sure how to reply, I kept quiet.

She put her hand to her face and slowed to a stop.

Shelby sensed the change and nudged against her.

Having never seen her cry before, it took me by surprise. Something had been gnawing at me for some time from deep within. I decided now was as good a time as any to give it voice.

"Then, don't go."

Her shoulders shook and she dropped to a knee. Shelby licked her face and she let out a laugh in the midst of her tears.

I knelt alongside her and put a hand on her shoulder, the one that had taken the bullet. "I don't want you to go."

Darcy looked at me as if for the first time. "What do you mean?"

"I mean, I don't want you to go."

She shook her head from side to side. "No. Why are you telling me this now?" Her eyes explored mine.

It was time to come clean, regardless of how many mistakes I'd made. "Because it's how I feel."

Wiping her nose with the back of her hand, she said, "This isn't fair, Brack."

I leaned in closer, not sure why.

She touched my face and laughed. "Romeo."

Shelby nudged his way in between us.

She laughed again and said, "I love your dog."

"Me, too," I said.

She scratched around his neck.

"Don't go," I said.

Her eyes met mine. "I have to."

"Why?"

She took a deep breath and exhaled. "It's just something I have to do."

My heart sank into the sand. "Is it because of me?"

Using her hand to lift my chin she said, "Let's just say, I had planned on leaving a while ago. I got distracted."

"So that's what this is?" I asked. "A distraction?"

"Neither of us is ready, yet," she said. "At least, I know I'm not."

Almost ten years my junior and she just gave me insight into myself that I hadn't wanted to deal with. I thought about all the women since Jo. I thought about Detective Warrez. And I thought about Elizabeth. What had I done?

Darcy stood and offered to help me up. I took her hand and stood, facing her. We remained that way for a long time, me holding her hand and her letting me. I wanted to tell her not to leave again. Not to marry that peckerwood. But I realized she was right. I wasn't ready. Yet.

★ ★ ★ ★ ★

I sat at the corner of the bar on my uncle's favorite stool and contemplated my lot in life. There were no customers in the place because there was no liquor being poured. There was no liquor being poured because the Gardners had found a way to run me out of business. Paige had found another job and didn't have the stones to tell me. Rosalita needed time. Elizabeth could be just using me to get back at Jon-Jon. And Darcy was leaving.

I took a long pull on a Dominican cigar, blew three rings toward the silent cash register, and exhaled the rest away from Bonnie's cage.

"I love you, Brack. *Squawk!*"

"I love you, too, pretty girl."

"Squawk!"

Shelby nudged my leg.

"I love you too, pretty boy."

He lifted a paw to me.

Who could resist that? I put the cigar in an ash tray and got down on all fours in front of him. With a playful growl, he hunched low on his front paws, his butt high in the air, tail wagging. I reached a hand for him and he growled more and gave a light nip at my fingers. The game was on. While he focused on my right hand, I scratched his ear with my left. He jerked his head when he felt it and soon we were busy wrestling on the floor, him winning two out of three rounds.

In the middle of our fourth, Bonnie gave a loud *squawk*. Shelby jumped off me and growled, his attention on the front door.

Detective Crawford cleared his throat.

Shelby eased to the detective, his ears low and back, the fur between his shoulders sticking straight up.

From the floor, I said, "Let him smell your hand."

"You sure it's safe?"

"Yeah." I stood and dusted myself off. "In his mind you snuck up on us and he doesn't like that." Shelby's read on a person's character was spot on so if he did bite Crawford, then I'd know not to trust him.

The detective stooped and held out a hand. Shelby moved in closer, a low grumble coming from deep within his belly, and took a quick sniff. Then a second. His ears perked up and he licked the offered appendage.

I walked behind the bar. "So, what can I get you to drink?"

He petted Shelby. "I thought you couldn't serve drinks?"

"I can't. But I've been known to give a few away."

"In that case, I'll take a shot of Jack and a beer."

I poured a shot from the bottle of Jack Daniels and the beer from the Yuengling tap. "So, to what do I owe this honor?"

He said, "Warrez is missing."

Chapter Twenty-Nine

Crawford downed his shot and took a long pull on the beer.

"You want to run that by me again?" I asked.

"She called me to say she was taking a few days off. I haven't heard from her since."

I said, "I saw her yesterday in the parking lot of this shady strip club called the Treasure Chest. Mutt and I were following someone and ran into her. She told us to leave so we did."

"We better check it out, then," he said.

"You're sure she isn't spending time with her daughter?"

Crawford set his now half-empty mug on the bar. "I checked there. They haven't heard from her either."

"She could just want to be alone." Though I said it, I didn't believe it.

"There is something wrong and it isn't because of you. I've been her partner for five years. I know her."

"What does your boss say?"

He sat on a stool and rolled the mug between his hands. "What can he say? She's on vacation and he doesn't want to know anything else."

"What do you want from me?"

The glass stopped moving. "I want to find my partner."

"I'm the last person she wants to see."

"Wilson said you'd say that. He also said tough situations are exactly what you're good at."

I had forgotten that Detective Wilson would have worked

with Crawford since he'd also known Warrez.

Leaning back against the liquor shelf, I said, "Yeah, well tell that to the next person who gets murdered because all I managed to do was get a story in the paper." In fact, the only tangible thing out of that was wrecking Gardner's chances at election. The killer and his master were still at large.

Crawford said, "The next one could be Warrez."

We dropped off Shelby at Trish's. I tried to let her know it was just for another day or so. Of course she was more than willing to take him back.

Afterwards, as Crawford drove I told him what I knew about Ernest Brown, including his connection to the Gardners. When he'd gotten an earful about Mr. Fix-it, he picked up his handset and ran the name and car. Something he should have done when I first gave it to him over the phone.

He asked, "And is that who you were following?"

"No," I said. "We were tailing Willa Mae's lawyer."

"Gordon Sykes?"

"Yeah."

"Oh, no."

"Oh, no, what?" I asked.

"His body was found an hour ago in his car four blocks from the Treasure Chest. Strangled. The press doesn't even know that yet."

My mind did a simple calculation. Detective Warrez was staking out the Treasure Chest. She must have followed Sykes and witnessed his murder. And now she's missing.

"This isn't good," I said.

Crawford said, "You really think this Ernest Brown killed the two women?"

"Yes but I don't have any proof. If you can get DNA off him, maybe you can match it to the sample you took that night from the roof of the car I shoved his face into."

Crawford nodded. "That's not a bad idea."

The handset beeped and Crawford answered and received the background on Ernest Brown. After a stretch in prison for assault and battery, Ernest operated under the radar.

My guess was he'd gotten smarter.

I said, "We're going to stick out if we roll up in this unmarked car."

"You got any suggestions?"

"Yes." I called Mutt, put him on the speaker, and explained where we were.

"You mean Ernest got that smokin' detective hostage?"

"Something's not right about it all," I said, not wanting to admit that she could already be dead.

Mutt said, "Well, pick me up and let's go get him."

After convincing Detective Crawford to swap his unmarked for my Audi, which he didn't want to do because he could lose his connection with headquarters, we swung by and picked up Mutt.

From the backseat, Mutt said, "I didn't know you was bringing the cub scout, Opie."

Crawford, portable radio in his lap, kept quiet.

I said, "Warrez's his partner. He deserves to be here."

"He know how we roll?"

Crawford asked, "How do you roll?"

Mutt spun the barrel of his thirty-eight special and snapped it shut. "All the way."

"You guys think you're going to shoot someone?"

"You're the one who brought me in on this," I said. "Mutt and the heaters come with the package."

"Yeah," Mutt said, "and we get results. How!"

How was right. Of course, we also acquired casualties along

the way. But we weren't about to let Crawford in on that little detail.

Twenty minutes later we rode through the North Charleston community known more for drug busts than tourist attractions.

At Ernest's rundown apartment complex, we pulled in and parked at a building down from his.

Mutt got out, walked around to the driver's side. "You keep your eyes open, Opie. You see anything look out of place, shoot first like we talked about before."

My friend walked away from the car and up the stairs to Ernest's second-floor apartment.

Crawford said, "Why does he call you Opie?"

Mutt cleared the top of the stairs.

I said, "He's my brother. He can call me anything he wants."

With the window down, I pulled a stogie out and pressed in the lighter.

Crawford said, "Cigars are out of style, you know."

The lighter popped, letting me know it was ready. I pulled it and lit my cigar. "So is dressing like a metrosexual but that doesn't seem to stop you."

Coughing, he said, "Very funny."

As I replaced the lighter, a loud blast refocused our attention. Immediately I saw Mutt dive down the stairs.

I threw the cigar into the gutter and jumped out of the car. A tall black man the size of a Sub-Zero refrigerator racked a shotgun. The gorilla was halfway down the stairs aiming at Mutt and my hands were still patting my pockets for a handgun that wasn't there. Mutt ducked behind a car and pulled his thirty-eight.

Crawford looked like a deer in the headlights. He froze in the front seat of the car.

I yelled, "Get out of there!" and met the gorilla in three long strides. I grabbed the barrel of the shogun and aimed it away from Mutt. The blast came a second later. I hit the monster with everything I had. He backed up half a step and I locked my hands on the Remington. I kneed him in the crotch and his legs buckled. Wrenching the shotgun from his hands, I slammed the butt across his face hard. He didn't go down.

Mutt joined me and smashed the guy's head with his thirty-eight. That move tamed the savage beast. Or at least knocked him out cold.

Catching his breath, Mutt said, "Where's the cub scout?"

I turned and didn't see him. "Crawford?"

No answer.

Mutt and I looked at each other. I held the monster's shotgun by the barrel and followed Mutt to my car. The windshield had taken the errant blast. So had Crawford, now lying on the asphalt beside the car. His face was a mess. I checked for a pulse—present but faint.

On the opposite side of the parking lot a V-8 engine barked to life through glass-pack mufflers. I'd heard that sound before. Memories flashed for an instant. Willa Mae being shot. Running with Aphisha in my arms. Without thinking I ran toward the noise, the shotgun in my hands. Ernest's black Impala roared away. Instinctively, I racked the shotgun and trained it on the escaping car. But Warrez might be in there. I didn't pull the trigger. Instead, I did what I should have done first. I went to Crawford. Used my shirt to apply pressure and stop the bleeding. Told Mutt to call an ambulance.

As soon as he hung up, my phone vibrated. "You got a call comin', Opie."

The caller I.D. said Detective Warrez.

I said, "Swap places with me," and picked up.

The same growl I'd heard when Willa Mae died said, "You

better back off or your girlfriend here dies."

So she *had* been in Ernest's Impala.

I said, "Your boy with the shotgun already shot a cop. Killing one won't win you any friends on the police force."

"I said, back off. If you try to follow me, you won't see her again."

I said, "Remember the night we met? How romantic it was?"

"What you talking about?"

"You know," I said, "that hot and steamy night. The full moon. Me slamming your butt-ugly face onto the roof of that car."

"I remember you running away like a girl."

I chuckled. "Yeah, it must make you feel like a real man shooting innocent women and children."

"That ho warn't innocent."

"You're still going to pay for chopping her up and burning her with the garbage."

Ernest Brown didn't speak right away. I hoped I was getting to him, winding him up. Maybe distracting him enough to make a mistake.

"After I finish with your girlfriend here," he snarled, "you next."

I asked, "Hey, Ernest?"

"What?"

"You're going to lose."

His laugh was deep and sinister, like a vampire. He said, "You gonna wish you never got in the way." He ended the call.

Rosalita Warrez did not deserve any of this. I couldn't fix what had already been done, but I could stop Ernest. Mutt was right. Impossible situations were what I was good at.

Mutt said, "What we gonna do?"

The sound of police sirens wailed in the distance.

I said, "Walk away."

My friend said, "Huh?"

"You heard me." I handed him all the cash we'd retrieved from the madam that had been in my car. "Get a cab back to the city. Call my lawyer. His name is Lester Brogan."

The police were real sweethearts. At least, compared to usual. Crawford was sent to the emergency room and Ernest's gorilla was charged with attempted murder. They weren't sure what to do with me.

Lester Brogan gave the district attorney a hard time for not being able to see me. With Lester's relentlessness, and a fortuitous ten-year-old who videoed the whole incident with his smart phone, I became a free man. Again. But I had no idea where Ernest or Warrez were. The cops seemed unconcerned about her when I tried to explain that was why Crawford and I went to the apartment complex in the first place. All they cared about was retribution for Crawford being shot. Which almost made me feel sorry for the stupid ape with the shotgun.

They'd impounded my Audi, which was okay because the dealer said my truck was fixed. The police had sent it to the garage when they were done with it. I had the dealer deliver it to my house.

Darcy was waiting for me in front of the police station in her convertible Infiniti.

I said, "I thought you were on your way out of here?"

She said, "Ernest has vanished."

I got in her car. "No kidding."

She handed me something wrapped in a paper bag. "Compliments of Mutt."

I opened the bag, pulled out a thirty-eight revolver, and opened the chamber. It was loaded. I asked, "Have you a plan for finding Detective Warrez?"

My favorite news reporter said, "The first question should

be, 'Why did Ernest kidnap her?' "

Shoving the gun into a pocket, I said, "I think she might have witnessed him killing Sykes."

"Yeah, but why not just kill her?"

I thought about it. "I'm not sure. That's been nagging me a little, too. Maybe for leverage?"

Fifteen minutes later, the convertible pulled into the deserted parking lot of my bar.

"Where is everyone?" she asked.

"Spending their money in places allowed to serve drinks, obviously."

Inside, I went behind the bar. Darcy sat at one of the stools.

Bonny landed on my shoulder. "Hi, Brack. *Squawk!*"

I stroked her feathers. "Hi, pretty girl. Where's Paige?"

A voice coming out of my office said, "I'm here."

And so she was. At least she hadn't left yet. But I almost didn't recognize her when she came into the room.

I said, "What's with that get-up?"

Darcy said, "I love your shoes."

In place of her usual T-shirt that barely covered anything, she wore a cream-colored blouse, and in place of what tried to pass for shorts was a cotton skirt. The shoes were, well, what did I know about women's shoes? They matched the skirt with three-inch heels. That was as far as I could go.

"Whose wedding did you just come from?" I asked, hoping it hadn't been a job interview.

"Cute, boss," she said. "Real cute."

I scanned the bottles on the top shelf. "Can I get either of you ladies something to drink?"

"If you'll shut up and listen," the manager of my bar said, "I'd like to tell you where I've been while you were busy getting arrested. Again." Emphasis on the word *again.*

I said, "Detective Warrez got kidnapped. And her partner,

Crawford, got shot."

Paige opened her mouth but no sound came out. The color drained out of her face.

Darcy stood and hugged Paige. Something wasn't clicking with me. Paige wouldn't be reacting this way because of Warrez. And she only knew Crawford from the times he came to the bar. Like when he remained with the single-mom staff while Warrez and I drove downtown.

Then it hit me. "I'm sorry, Paige. I didn't know. He's in critical condition."

Paige leaned back against a table. "I don't know why I'm so upset. It's . . . it's—"

"It's okay," Darcy said.

"You want to go see him at the hospital?" I asked.

She shook her head and slumped into a chair. "I can't go like this."

I poured an inch of Absolut Limon into two tumblers and slid the glasses across the bar to the women.

Paige reached for hers and took a sip. "What happened?"

To buy time, I felt the outside of my cargo shorts pockets for my cigar and lighter.

"Really, Brack," she said, "I want to know."

"No, you don't."

Darcy said, "Tell her."

Using the cutter, I clipped off the end of the cigar. It took a few seconds to light. I blew a stream toward the ceiling. "We found the kidnapper and someone with a shotgun wounded Crawford." After the kid froze up, I thought, but didn't say.

Chapter Thirty

Even with Darcy's extensive network, we had no line on Ernest. The police did not like the fact that Crawford was with me when he was shot. They would not be a source of information on anything relevant. My Myrtle Beach friend, Wilson, didn't have anything new to offer, either.

So far, the only bright spot had come from Paige. Before she left for the hospital to see Crawford, her apparently-new boyfriend, she told us she'd had a meeting with Lester Brogan and we had a very good chance of appealing our license suspension.

Darcy went to tape her evening news clip so she dropped me off at my house. As the sun set, I thought about my next move and received a text.

After reading it, I said, "No way."

I started my recently returned and fixed pickup and used every ounce of horsepower it had to get me moving.

Once in North Charleston, I turned into a run-down apartment complex and pulled to a stop in front of the address I'd been to before. I stuck Mutt's thirty-eight down the waistband of my shorts, went to the door, and knocked.

Kali, the cocktail waitress from the Treasure Chest, opened the door and said, "You miss me, baby?"

"I got your text."

She took my arm and tugged me to her. "You wanna come in or what?"

Face to face with a fragrance of vanilla and a slight whiff of reefer, I looked into her dilated pupils and said, "I want Ernest."

She giggled. "What if he don't want you, baby?"

"He's got a friend of mine, and not because she likes his company."

"We all need rescuin', baby."

I stepped inside and took in the surroundings. The small apartment held a decent green cloth couch that faced a medium-sized flatscreen. A toy dump truck, a football, and some action figures cluttered up one corner. "Where's your son?"

Her eyebrows raised. "With his grandmother. We got the place all to ourselves, baby."

"The longer we play this game, the worse off my friend could be."

Kali shut the door. "How you know someone's in trouble, anyway?"

"Ernest is an evil man. Didn't you see the news article on him? I'm pretty sure he killed three people I knew, Willa Mae, a white girl named Camilla, and Willa Mae's lawyer."

"What are you talking about?"

I said, "The message you sent me said you knew where the man I've been looking for is. I'm here for that reason. Do you know where Ernest is or not?"

Turning her head slowly from side to side, she sighed.

"Is that a no?" I asked. "Who is Ernest to you, anyway?"

"My brother."

I hadn't expected that one.

She said, "He got a message for you."

"What's that?"

"Kiss me first."

"Kali—"

Before I could finish, she put her index finger to my lips.

"Ain't I good enough for you, baby? You liked what you saw at that fancy bar we was at. Why don't you like me now?"

I put my arms around her. "I do like what I see. I like it a lot."

"Then kiss me."

I did.

Her lips were big and soft and inviting. She locked her arms around me tight. I ran my hands down her back and she moaned. The craziness of the moment was not lost on me. My goal was finding Ernest, and if this is what it took, well . . .

She pushed me back with a hand. "After you done with what you gotta do, I want you to come back and rescue me."

Nodding, my only thought was Warrez.

Kali said, "Ernest say he at the house Mary Ellen turned tricks at. He say you know where it is 'cause you been there before. You and Brother Thomas."

Before I realized it, I was out the door and running to my truck.

This was a trap and I knew it. On the way, I called Mutt and explained the situation. He was locked and loaded and ready for Ernest when I picked him up.

The target house was dark. In fact, the whole street was. We left the truck two blocks away and walked so Ernest wouldn't see the headlights. Not that it mattered. Kali had probably called and tipped him off that I was coming. I prayed he didn't expect both of us, pulled the thirty-eight, and scanned the area. Mutt circled the block and was coming from the other side.

No streetlights meant he couldn't see me and I couldn't see him. Unless he had night vision.

Instead of knocking on the door, which I was sure he knew I wouldn't do, I walked the perimeter of the house. Two windows were open and only the screen door stood between anyone on the front porch and inside.

A misplaced step and my foot crunched on dry vegetation or trash. I stopped and listened.

A voice behind me growled, “I see you got my message.”

In the darkness, I said, “Where’s Detective Warrez?”

Ernest snorted. “She might be Detective Warrez to you, but she one nice piece to me. You need to try some of that. Mm-mm good.”

The sound of his familiar snarl put him to my left. I turned around, hoping Mutt knew I was now in the crosshairs.

“Don’t you be gettin’ any ideas, white boy. You juss keep facin’ the house like you supposed to.”

“What if I don’t want to?”

The next sound I heard was a shotgun being racked. I closed my eyes and cussed. One pull of the trigger and I’d be splattered all over the side of this dump. *Now would be a good time, Mutt.*

Ernest jammed the barrel into my back. “I already took care of your partner with the thirty-eight. Drop your pistol and get in the house.”

I did as he asked, shell-shocked that Mutt could be dead. Ernest was right behind me, and my training came into focus. As we entered the house, a new plan formed. If he turned on a light, we’d both be blind while our eyes adjusted. The Marines had taught me to use every advantage.

He flipped on the light switch. Immediately I dropped to all fours and kicked back with my foot. It caught Ernest squarely in the crotch. He grunted and I sprang off the floor like a cat. Grabbing the shotgun with both hands, I fought him for control. The weapon went off with a loud boom. Buckshot peppered the ceiling. His two-inch height advantage and twenty pounds over me made him more than a formidable opponent. He did not let go of the shotgun.

I pushed him against a wall. He slammed the stock into my abdomen and I gasped for breath and dropped to the ground.

"I told you not to get any ideas, boy," he said, standing over me.

I spit blood. Movement in the doorway caught my attention. I looked over and saw Trevor, Willa Mae's ex-boyfriend, peeking in.

Motioning with the shotgun, Ernest said, "Get up."

He hadn't seen Trevor.

"I understand why you felt you had to get rid of Willa Mae," I said, struggling to get to my feet and move away from the doorway. "You had to get rid of the evidence of the baby. The one thing I can't figure out is why you cut her up and burned her on Gardner's property?"

Ernest chuckled. "I needed leverage on those crackers."

When Ernest's back was to the door, Trevor jumped inside, screamed "Killer!" and grabbed for the shotgun. Ernest hit him with the stock. Trevor fell backwards and Ernest spun around and shot him, coating the wall with his blood.

Ernest rotated back around to cover me. I threw a punch. His nose exploded against my fist. The gun slipped out of his hands and I tagged him again. He shoved me backward with all his weight. I fell and he landed on me.

We struggled and I forced my way on top of him. Seeing nothing but red, I grabbed the fallen shotgun and slammed the stock into Ernest's face three times. As I raised the gun for a fourth hit, I noticed that his face was a mess—broken nose, busted lips, bleeding forehead.

Ernest stayed still when I rolled off him and went to Trevor. He didn't have a pulse.

A quick search of the house and I found Warrez. She'd been stripped to her underwear, beaten, and tied up and God only knew what else. I untied her, grabbed the shotgun again, and headed back to Ernest. One pull of the trigger and his face would be wall art. For killing Mutt. For killing Willa Mae and Camilla. For everything.

Just one pull.

I racked the slide.

Warrez staggered into the room. "Don't."

My finger on the trigger. The barrel in Ernest's mouth.

I looked at her. "This is your one chance. No one else has to know."

"Leave him to the police."

Mutt stumbled in from the front porch, pistol drawn, his head bleeding. He looked at me with the gun in Ernest's mouth, then at Warrez, then at Trevor, then back to me. "Don't do it, Opie. He ain't worth it."

Brother Thomas's words came to mind. *"Man cannot afford to lose his own soul while he trying to do right."*

The paramedics took Detective Warrez away in an ambulance. While I was thankful to hear her say she hadn't been raped, she did suffer from dehydration and bruising. Ernest didn't fare as well. Especially after the police confirmed his connection with the gorilla that shot Crawford. Without benefit of immediate medical treatment for a broken nose and jaw, Ernest was handcuffed and thrown into the back of a patrol car by another set of detectives who arrived on the scene along with the uniforms.

I hoped they didn't end up killing Ernest by their negligence. We needed him alive to convict the Gardners.

Trevor was taken to the morgue. Brother Thomas, who'd shown up when we called, volunteered to notify his family.

Epilogue

With Ernest in custody and cutting every deal he could to avoid the needle, Estelle Gardner realized the evidence was stacked against her and pled guilty to a whole slew of charges. She was sentenced to ten years for conspiracy to commit murder. Gardner lost the primary but managed to avoid indictment. He stood by his wife's side through the whole thing, and now could keep all his money and his affection for young prostitutes while she was away. Personally, I think she was still covering for his sins.

As if living up to the nickname copped from another man who'd died too young, Jon-Jon, on another DUI run, wrapped his Ferrari and a friend around a live oak. Neither walked away. I felt sorry for his friend.

A bright side to this story was Rosalita Warrez's daughter. The news of Jon-Jon's demise gave her a peace she would never have been able to experience if he were still walking around. Rosalita resigned from the Charleston police department, collected her daughter from the institution, and moved them both to California to start over.

After a few rounds of plastic surgery, Crawford recovered. The blast had taken out his right eye, but otherwise he would be okay. From what I could gather, he'd never carry a badge again, which seemed to suit Paige just fine. Love was in the air for those two.

Sister Mary Ellen overdosed and was found collapsed on the

floor in the women's restroom of the Treasure Chest. I sat with Mr. Porter, her uncle, at the funeral, another one Brother Thomas officiated, and thought about the way crazy choices she'd made determined her destiny. At one time, I thought she was in danger by being associated with Willa Mae. She really knew nothing.

Mutt broke the news to me that since he no longer had his bar, this seemed a good time to move closer to his daughter in Atlanta. He'd actually managed to insure that termite-infested dive and received a small check, though he wouldn't say for how much. I couldn't blame him for wanting to leave Charleston. His daughter was all he really had now. As a reward for helping me solve the murder of Willa Mae, I finished my uncle's Cadillac and gave it to him. After all, a man needed a set of wheels and Mutt would love that car more than I ever could. He rode off to Atlanta in style.

I didn't think I'd ever understand how Trevor knew to show up that night. But at his funeral, the plump Treasure Chest stripper who'd been working the pole when I'd walked in for the first time with Mutt was in attendance. Mutt introduced me to her. She'd been a friend of Kali's and told me, amidst a lot of crying, that she'd given Trevor Ernest's location.

Before D-Go could finish what he started with me, Shamiqua got her revenge for the gang-raping. When he and an accomplice, out on bail, tried to mess with her and her baby, she took an errant shovel and killed them. After I finished laughing at the story as Brother Thomas told it, we financed Shamiqua's relocation from Charleston. D-Go's fellow gang members would surely try to settle the score, especially for such an embarrassing death as being nearly decapitated by a workman's spade.

The Pirate's Cove received an envelope from the state of South Carolina. In it was our replacement license to sell alcohol. I could only guess that the Gardners had lost their clout and whoever had been doing them a favor holding up our paperwork had severed all ties. Regardless of what really happened, Paige, who had turned down a very lucrative job offer to manage a chain of restaurants, and I were back in business. And I owed her big.

Elizabeth must have gotten tired of waiting on me, if in fact she had been. I ran into her spikey-haired assistant at my bar and he'd informed me that she went on a two-month tour of Europe for the summer.

Some things were better left unsaid. And right now my dog wanted a wrestling rematch.

ABOUT THE AUTHOR

Burning Heat is the second in **David Burnsworth**'s series featuring Brack Pelton. David graduated from the University of Tennessee with a degree in Mechanical Engineering. After fifteen years in manufacturing, he made the decision to write a novel. *Southern Heat* was his first mystery. Having lived in Charleston for five years, the setting was a foregone conclusion. He and his wife live in South Carolina.